PRETTY DEAD THINGS

Also by Kelsey Cox

Party of Liars

PRETTY DEAD THINGS

A Novel

KELSEY COX

MINOTAUR BOOKS
NEW YORK

This is a work of fiction. All of the names, characters, organizations, places, and events portrayed in this work are either products of the author's imagination or used fictitiously.

First published in the United States by Minotaur Books, an imprint of St. Martin's Publishing Group

EU Representative: Macmillan Publishers Ireland Ltd, 1st Floor, The Liffey Trust Centre, 117–126 Sheriff Street Upper, Dublin 1, D01 YC43

Designed by Meryl Sussman Levavi

ISBN 978-1-250-37884-2

For Resa, my fairy godmother

The beauty is an illusion, and also a warning: there's a dark side to beauty, as with poisonous butterflies.

—Margaret Atwood, "Alphinland"

PRETTY DEAD THINGS

CHAPTER ONE

THE NIGHT OF THE LONE STAR PRINCESS PAGEANT

2025

Hail taps the windows, and the roof creaks from the weight of heavy snow. The contestants are trapped by the storm's bitter cold. Frozen in shut.

The auditorium is a murmur of voices overlapping and dresses rustling, of chairs shifting and mothers shouting for their daughters. The generator hums, and the speaker plays a steady, frantic drumroll. Down a hallway, the sound fades, the world narrows, lit only by the glow of the exit sign. And at the end, there is a door.

Within the room, a standing mirror reflects the wall of glittering gowns, each rhinestone and crystal appliqué catching the light in sharp, splintered glints, like the watchful eyes of creatures lurking in shadow. Under a single dim bulb, sequins and stones pulse, glimmering alive.

A multifeathered headpiece, once pristine white, is splattered with red ribbons of blood. Cans of hair spray and jars of body shimmer are misted in crimson. A large clump of brain matter, still warm, clings to the tulle layers of an emerald-colored gown.

It is still, but for the overhead fixture swaying, its light twinkling off the beading on dresses and the sparkles on high heels. Still, but for the blood trails snaking slowly down the mirror, pooling on the vanity around tubes of lipstick and pots of blush.

From beyond the door come the sounds of screaming young girls. One's high-pitched shriek of terror cuts sharper than the rest, pierces through the echoes of pounding feet across the hollow stage floor. A killer is among them, and panic spreads, stretches its fingers like the fractal shards of ice chilling their bones.

The storm persists, battering the walls as wind continues to howl and scrape and claw.

But the night is far from over.

CHAPTER TWO

SARAH LYNN

Six Days Before the Pageant

"Thank you for stopping by Smoothie Palace, and have a delicious day." I smile with all my teeth as I hand Mr. Mackey back his loyal customer punch card, the kind of smile that is like a gun, making whoever it's aimed at feel super special. *Smile like you mean it, Sarah Lynn*, is one of my mother's mantras. It works for pageants and for sketchy old men like Mr. Mackey, who Hannah swears eyes my ass every time I turn around to blend his chocolate bananarama. But Mr. Mackey's wife is a member of the board of Miss Lone Star Princess and has been selected as one of the judges this year.

Beauty is a weapon. That's another thing Mom says.

But so is kindness. "Oh, and Mr. Mackey, I got an extra punch on there for you."

"Well, aren't you a sweetheart?" He gives me a wink, which he never does when his wife is in the passenger seat. I've been on the stage enough that I bet I could maintain my smile through a plane crash if I needed to.

Suddenly Hannah is beside me, wet rag wiping along the counter. Our manager is always telling her to tie her hair back, and she does, winding it into an unkempt ball that wobbles on her head as she talks animatedly with her hands. She has the kind of hair that needs a seriously time-consuming curl routine. Frizzy tendrils pop out around her face at random, and despite the colorful butterfly clips haphazardly shoved in, you can't be sure she isn't cosplaying as a tumbleweed.

"Yeah, Mr. Mackey," she says, mocking my cheery tone. "Have the day you deserve."

His wiry caterpillar eyebrows twitch together. The squeaky wheels of his brain are working overtime as he tries to figure out if he's being insulted, but Hannah has handed him a verbal Escher staircase where the steps loop back on themselves. It's only an insult if he deserves one.

He looks back to me, and my smile sets his world back on its axis.

Just as the automatic drive-through window soft-closes on him, Hannah adds, "You old pervert."

Olivia, who's been waiting to Windex the glass, shushes Hannah. She tries staring disapproving daggers at us, but it's no use. We're laughing so hard that Hannah snorts, which has me clutching at my stomach for relief.

"We're gonna get in trouble," Olivia whines, peering over her shoulder to check if Mr. Mackey has pulled away yet.

"Relax," Hannah says, once she catches her breath. "He couldn't hear us past all that hair in his ears even if he wanted to."

Olivia catches her giggle in a cupped palm. She is so quiet, it's like she doesn't even want her laugh to make a sound. She puts the spray bottle away, and turns to start refilling the fruit containers.

While the shop is empty, I go to the break room to grab my purse. "I have a surprise for y'all," I say, pulling out two gold folders and handing one to each of them.

Hannah opens hers and flips through the pages, then looks up at me blankly. "Miss Lone Star? Sarah Lynn, what the hell is this?"

"Surprise!" I throw my hands up and wiggle my fingers for full effect. "You two are going to be princesses."

"Very funny," she deadpans, trying to hand the forms right back to me, but I don't take them.

"This"—I tap the application on top—"is exactly what you need to get over your stage fright."

A few weeks back, when it was just Hannah and me working the last shift together, I heard the faint sound of music coming through the door of the walk-in freezer. I pressed my ear up against the cold steel and listened. It was Hannah, singing. And it sounded beautiful. Her voice made my ribs tingle, made emotions I couldn't name fill my throat with sandpaper grit. After closing, I had her covering all my favorite songs. She only ever sings for me when the shop is empty, never in front of people she doesn't know well. It feels wrong, her hiding her talent away, like she's stealing something from the world.

Last week, she let it slip she once dreamt of being on Broadway, but when she tried out for choir freshman year, things didn't go so well. *I froze up like I was on bad Wi-Fi. Just stood with my brain buffering right there in the auditorium.*

"You want me to overcome my stage fright by getting up on a stage?" Hannah asks now.

"It's just walking." I shove the papers back to her chest, then hand her a pen. "Walking in a dress and smiling. Anyone can do that."

"I'll do it with you, Han," Olivia says, sucking in her lips to hide her smile. Olivia is like one of those flowers that only grows in the shade. She's pretty, actually, if you ever take the time to look at her. But she styles herself like she's trying to vanish—her dark-blond hair a veil she never quite lifts, wearing baggy T-shirts and opting for stiff black slacks at work instead of the second-skin leggings the other girls and I wear.

"Well, look at that," I say, hand on my hip, clicking my tongue behind my teeth. "Olivia has the balls. Do you?"

Hannah sighs in a way that makes Olivia and me know we've won her over.

Olivia squeals, fingers steepled under her nose. "This'll be so fun." She twirls around and grabs three one-ounce measuring cups, the ones we use for energy boosters in the smoothies. She fills them with pineapple juice and passes them out. "To the Lone Star Princess Pageant," she says, raising her makeshift shot glass.

Hannah rolls her eyes. "What the hell." She clinks her glass to ours and downs it like she knows what she's doing. "I mean, what's the worst that can happen?"

CHAPTER THREE

CAT

The robot vacuum follows me, dutiful as a cocker spaniel, into the kitchen, sweeping up a stray muffin crumb, a dried leaf that must have tracked in on somebody's shoe. It hums along the baseboard, nosing every corner like it's looking for trouble. The white granite countertops gleam to a shine that reflects the pendant lights mounted to the high ceilings.

It's nearly 6 PM. I have a few minutes. I spin the carousel of coffee pods, choose a pecan blend, and start up the Keurig. Then, I scan the fridge. The glass shelves are clean, lined with a variety of flavored sparkling waters, coffee creamers, fresh-pressed juices, plastic packages of blueberries and blackberries and pre-cut strawberries. In the door, there is only a half-bottle of champagne from an event earlier today, resealed with an airtight stopper. While the Keurig groans and spits the last of the coffee, I open the champagne, my heart skipping a second at the delightful pop, the nose-tickling scent. I pour it down the sink, then toss the bottle in the hidden pull-out trash.

Just as I'm stirring vanilla soy creamer into my coffee, I hear the beep-beep-beep-whir of the front door pad.

Mark comes in first. He's wearing a button-up that at first glance fits him just right, shows off the broadness of his shoulders, but the bottom few buttons cling to his belly. I like the way he's filled out over the years, as if the generous waistline better suits his generous nature. He flashes me a half-tipped smile, carrying a cream-colored canvas bag. Something about the tie matching his blue eyes makes me think, absurdly, of our wedding. Mark's a contractor. He usually wears a polo and jeans on the job. He must have been meeting with investors today. But maybe it isn't the tie that's transported me. Maybe it's that tilted grin, the look that lets me know I have an ally, that we are in this together.

Shuffling in behind him is our seventeen-year-old daughter, Olivia. She's still wearing her Smoothie Palace uniform, and her dark-blond sheet of hair covers her face, which is bent over her phone as she types furiously. A pink duffel bag hangs from her shoulder—her old dance bag, with her name embroidered in glittering gold thread, the letters frayed from wear and tear.

Tonight is the first night Olivia is staying over with me. Mark and I agreed to take it slow this time. For six months we've only met up for lunch or dinner, working our way up to this.

"Hey, baby," I say. "You ready for tonight?"

Olivia doesn't respond.

Mark elbows her gently in the side and points to his ear. She pulls back her long hair to remove the AirPods.

"Hey, Mom," she says quietly, averting her eyes. It makes me think of when she was little, when she used to hide behind my legs whenever I introduced her to someone new. Only, now I'm the stranger.

"I ordered Thai," I say. "Green curry with tofu. That's your favorite, right?"

Her eyes flick to her father and back to me. "Did Dad tell you that?"

"Olivia," Mark says, warning.

There was a time when I was the one who knew all her preferences—dino nuggets and french fries, but only the crinkle-cut kind, the red plate, but the blue spoon. *It's fine*, I mouth to Mark. She has every right to be difficult.

I push past it, keeping the brightness in my voice. "I thought after dinner, we could put on a movie, pop some popcorn. What do you think?"

From behind her hair, Olivia's eyes scan slowly around the room. "What's with the apples?"

We all look to the heavy marble bowl atop the oak dining table, filled with glistening Granny Smiths. "I thought they looked nice."

"Are they fake?"

"Well, yes," I say.

Olivia hikes the bag higher onto her shoulder. "Is there anywhere I'm allowed to put my things?"

"Upstairs. Second door on the right." I start to walk her there, but she scurries ahead.

As she disappears upstairs, Mark reaches into the canvas bag he carried in. "I picked these up for y'all."

"Fashion magazines?"

"She and Hannah are entering Miss Lone Star. I just found out myself. Tell her you picked them up. Y'all can look through them tonight."

"Hannah is doing Miss Lone Star?" I ask, taking the stack from him. Hannah is my best friend's daughter, which means the girls have been besties since birth. I've known Hannah her whole life, and she's about the furthest thing I can imagine from a pageant girl.

Mark shrugs and checks his watch. "I better get going. I promised Em I'd grill up some steaks tonight."

"Don't want to keep the wife waiting," I say.

He breathes a laugh through his nose.

I place the magazines in a drawer, shutting it before Olivia returns. At the foot of the stairs, Mark pulls her into a hug. "Have fun," he says into her hair. Then low, probably so I won't hear, he adds, "She's trying."

Olivia pulls away and starts up the steps again, but as she does, she turns her face to me and gives me a tight smile. She's trying too, in her own teenage way.

* * *

The dining table is set for four—four china plates, four cloth napkins with silverware, four crystal glasses. When the Thai food arrives, I pick up the place settings and put them aside. I set out the curry in the Styrofoam containers, then call Olivia down, and we eat with plastic spoons.

"I was thinking we could watch *The Princess Bride*," I say, because Olivia was obsessed with that movie when she was little. I can't remember how many times we watched it. Mark worried the giant rats would give her nightmares. *For the love of God,* he'd say, *turn that off*. Even then, his instinct was to shield her. But the rats were her favorite part. She'd sit up on her knees, eyes wide as poker chips.

"I haven't seen that movie since I was, like, five. Isn't it kind of cheesy?"

"It's a classic," I say.

"Whatever you want," she says, and it's just another reminder of how long it has been since I've truly known her. I should be up to date on which actor she has a crush on or which Netflix series she quotes nonstop with her friends. We both push rice around in our containers, and Olivia eats a single green bean.

I switch tactics, getting up and making my way over to the kitchen drawer. "Your father told me you're entering Miss Lone Star Princess this year." I pull the magazines out. "He picked these up and wanted me to tell you that I did."

Olivia cuts her eyes up from her plate, and I'm hoping my honesty will create even the smallest crack in her walls.

"I've already looked at dresses online," she says flatly.

I turn back to the drawer before she can see my eyes, before she can see that all this trying is starting to break me. I think of when she was little, when I'd hear her stirring from her naps, when I'd crack open the door and find her lying in her crib, babbling at her toes. When she'd finally see me peering over the railing. The look on her face, that smile, like I was the sun and she was so happy to see it rising again in her sky.

Then, while my back is still turned, Olivia says, "There's this one dress." I look over to see her pulling her phone from her lap onto the table. "It's really expensive, but Dad said maybe."

I hold my breath as she swipes through her phone.

"Want to check it out?" She doesn't look up at me when she asks.

I return to the table, drop into the seat beside her, and she tilts the phone toward me. I catch a glimpse of a sequined dress that looks like liquid silver. My pulse quickens. I feel like I'm on a date with someone out of my league. I'd do just about anything to make her like me. "How about we pick a time this week to go try it on?"

Her face lights up. "Yeah?" There's an eagerness in her eyes, and it's the most beautiful thing I've ever seen.

Then, there is a sudden knock on the front door. I know before I answer that it will be Sheriff Ryan, and there he stands, white mustache combed neatly, shirt tucked into Wrangler jeans, cowboy hat in his hands. Behind him, the Texas Hill Country stretches out, hills rising into the horizon, with cedars and live oaks. The evening is quiet, just the sound of the flag snapping in the wind, the metal clasp hooks clanking against the pole. And in the distance, the flowing water of the river where we all used to float as kids.

"Like clockwork," I say.

"Picked this up for you, Cat. Comes in handy, what with all the construction." Sheriff Ryan hands me a can of Fix-a-Flat. "Just shake it, screw that doohickey on there, and press the button on top. It'll take care of the rest."

He doesn't come by every day, but he finds his reasons to pop in. The sheriff doesn't like me staying here alone.

He catches sight of Olivia over my shoulder. "Well, hello, darling."

"Hi, Sheriff."

"I'll get out of your hair. Don't want to be interrupting your dinner."

I move aside, let the door open wider. "We got plenty. Want to come in?"

I have known Sheriff Ryan all my life, and the man has never changed. He's one of those men, like Steve Martin, whose hair went white early and then he didn't age another day over the next forty years. Same horseshoe mustache, same dusty boots, same need to protect everyone. When I first moved in here a few weeks ago, he showed up with an armful of wooden dowels, started measuring my windows, cutting the dowels to size, and sliding them into the frame, so the windows couldn't be slid open from the outside.

The house has a security system, I told him.

He just nodded and went about his work.

"Can't," he says now. "I'm on duty."

"When are you ever off duty?"

He laughs.

Model homes are dangerous places to be at night, the sheriff has told me. Construction sites are a common target for thieves—all the tools and equipment, the brand-new appliances in this house, and the fancy furniture. No one expects anyone to be here after hours.

The truth is, I don't want to be here either, but I have no choice.

Mark was the one who got me this position, a job showing the model off to prospective buyers, giving them a tour of the luxury Amenity Center, selling the idea of an enviable life. He talked the developer into letting me stay at the model, so long as I promised to keep things tidy, which I do. Every morning, I pack my things, even my toiletries, into a suitcase and slide it under the bed.

All Mark has ever wanted was for me to get back on my feet, and this is the fastest way to get there. The free rent means I can save up for a place of my own, a real place, one Olivia can visit without fake apples, where I can hang my own pictures on the wall, where she can throw her shoes and her bags on the ground, and maybe, just maybe Olivia will believe that I've laid anchor. Maybe she'll believe I'm here to stay.

"You give me a call," he says, "if you need anything at all. You know I won't be far." He puts his hat back on his head, tips it to Olivia, and heads back to his truck.

I lean against the doorframe to watch him leave.

The site is so loud during the day, the beep of the vehicles, the workers playing music and laughing, and all that banging. But at night, it's dark and dead silent.

When I was a kid, this was all ranchland owned by the Shermans, acres and acres of scrubby grass, cows, and trees. Now the woods are being cleared, the earth overturned, releasing scorpions and displacing the animals. Coyotes and armadillos and deer make their way to the highway. It's the talk of the town—accidents have been on the rise—just one in a long list of complaints.

The sheriff has started his truck, but he hasn't left yet, and I realize he's waiting for me to close the door, to lock myself and Olivia safely inside.

I take one last look down the street before I do just that. The place can be creepy at night. Despite acting like I don't need his protection, it does give me peace of mind that the sheriff checks up on me. There are no lights but the moon, which elongates every shadow, the bulldozers and the backhoes like sleeping beasts, the bones of half-finished houses. From the milky darkness come the odd sounds of animals searching for a home that's no longer there.

CHAPTER FOUR

INGRID

Five Days Before the Pageant

Show up for the big things. That's what my husband, Joel, always says. And it says a lot about where things stand with us that he isn't here with me now.

You can forget to text people back, cancel on happy hour, even blow off a birthday party every once in a while. But you show up for the big things—weddings, funerals, the births of babies. Because these are linchpin moments in a person's life, moments when their identity shifts, when they become a new version of themselves, forever changed. And when you love someone, you show up to witness the change, to meet the new version so you can keep moving forward with them.

So that's what I'm doing. I'm showing up. I'm coming back home to Anhalt, Texas.

When my plane landed, I had another text from Dad, asking one last time if I needed him to pick me up at the airport. But I'd already reserved a rental car, the exact same make and model that I own back in Colorado, because I don't like driving a car I don't know.

The drive from the Austin airport to Anhalt—about an hour west, along the Blanco River where the hills start to rise—is almost unrecognizable from the one I used to make years ago, after I first left home. Back then, the city fell away right after the airport—no Tesla factory, no Amazon facility, no cookie-cutter subdivisions yet. Just fields, mesquite, and sky. But every time I visit, the city has expanded, bleeding into the nearby towns—Buda, Kyle, even Dripping Springs—encroaching closer to our little rural community. As I pull into town, I pass under a banner for the FIFTIETH ANNUAL LONE STAR PRINCESS PAGEANT, strung between Herman Smith's boot shop and a new Aveda hair salon where Timeless Treasures used to be. Back then, Mom dragged us there every Saturday, always on the hunt for something pretty to clutter up her already cluttered display cabinets. That's where, on a whim, she bought me my first film camera, a 35mm Canon AE-1, which I used all through high school to snap photos of Izzy and me and all our friends.

The Dairy Queen is gone now too, where in the parking lot out back, Jimmy Marino tried to get to second base. *Y'all might look the same, but you're cuter than your sister*, he had said as his hand slid up my shirt. It was exactly what I wanted him to think, but not what I wanted him to say. It's a drive-through smoothie place now, touting acai bowls and fresh-pressed juices. They've repurposed the old DQ sign—the shape of something that once was, with something new plastered on top.

I hate coming back home. I hate seeing the things that have changed. And, probably even more, I hate the things that have stayed the same. Everything's a trigger, memories come like buckshot, little pellets of remembering that burrow deep beneath my skin.

So I've found excuses to avoid it these last few years, and before that, my trips have always been short. A few days for Christmas or a cousin's wedding. In and out.

And up until now, I've always had Joel by my side, a layer of protection, a separation between the person I was when I lived here and the person I am now.

Mom has kept me up to date on the town's changes. But it's still odd to see. The woods have been dug up away from the narrow roads, streets widened, construction cones warning of the town's hollowing.

And, of course, there's the new housing development.

They sold the Sherman land, Mom had said one day on the phone.

Oh? I'd said.

They're going to put a bunch of new houses there. They started digging. And before either of us could express what exactly that might mean, she told me about the newly painted benches at the library, and we didn't say anything more about the Sherman land. We didn't say Izzy's name. But she was there anyway, like she always is, the oxidized layers of an antique mirror splotching the surface of our lives.

I pass the developer's signpost, announcing, SHERMAN RANCH. BUILD ON YOUR OWN LOT! RIVERFRONT PROPERTY AVAILABLE. I can't help but look over as I nudge through traffic that didn't used to be here when I was a kid. Trees have been swept away, wild earth leveled into neat, flat parcels. A few houses stand in various stages of completion.

The construction vehicles tear the earth apart just outside my window, beeping, rolling, digging, tracks grinding over dry dirt. I watch as an excavator jerks, like an animal being shoved forward against its will, before its metal teeth muscle down, audibly straining as the ground breaks and gives way. Its neck lifts, its mouth full. The long yellow arm spins and releases a bucketful of soil and chunks of limestone, white as bone. It gnaws into the earth again. And again. And it groans. It gnaws at me—the sound—all those gears crunching, all that unearthing.

I jump at the sound of a horn. I've missed the light turning green, and the rusty pickup behind me is annoyed. I look in the rearview to wave an apology and lock eyes with the driver.

It's him. It's been twenty-five years, he's let his hair get long and scraggly, he's grown a beard, but I would recognize Ben Sherman anywhere.

And he recognizes me.

I know that for sure, because he's looking at me now like he's seeing a ghost.

I stare back, certain I'm looking at a killer.

CHAPTER FIVE

MELANIE

I hurry past the break room door, hoping my coworker, Tom, won't notice me, but the swish of my scrub pants gives me away.

"Melanie Jane Campbell," he says with the cadence of a headmaster calling out the truant student, "you are not skipping your lunch again."

I turn to him, holding up two decks of cards like the guilty evidence they are.

Tom crosses his arms. "You can't keep giving up your breaks. You are running yourself ragged."

Just this last weekend, I stayed up late to bake Tom's husband my famous turtle cheesecake for his birthday. And Tom never minds asking me for a lift home when he's had one too many margaritas at happy hour. People love to tell people pleasers how to stand up for themselves, but don't mind leaning on us when they need it. I don't hold it against them though. It's just how people are. And besides, I love people fawning over my cheesecakes.

"We stopped yesterday when Mrs. Whitmore was up by seven hundred points, and I can't have that old biddy thinking she can clean the floor with me."

Tom chews his lip, considering this. Tom is tall, with thick dark hair and thick dark eyebrows over chocolatey dark eyes. The old ladies here go gaga for him. Earlier today, I heard Doris telling Lenore about how good his tight rear end looked in his navy scrubs. "Canasta again?" he asks. He already knows it's a lost cause.

I smile. "Canasta."

"You better not let her win."

"It's all I can do to keep up."

I spin on my heel and make my way to room 301, picking up Mrs. Whitmore's chart before I enter. My stomach dropped the first time I saw her name on my patient list. Tom isn't from Anhalt—he doesn't know the Whitmore name, doesn't know the way people in this town still lower their voices when it comes up.

I take extra care with all my patients, but with Mrs. Whitmore it feels different, like a kind of duty. Playing cards with her is the least I can do.

I was in the same grade as her twins, Ingrid and Isabelle. Of course I remember the day Izzy went missing—everybody my age does. At the time, I only saw it through the lens of a teenage girl, whispers at lockers and candlelight vigils. Now, with a seventeen-year-old daughter of my own, I can't stop myself from imagining what it must have been like for her mother.

Mrs. Whitmore is sitting up in bed, pillows propped behind her back, watching HGTV on a volume so low I don't even know that she can hear it. It happens a lot here. Too much time to think. So much time to worry.

When she turns to me, I hold up the cards. "Mind if we finish our game?"

Her face brightens. I love that, love when people look at me like I've made their whole day, their whole week.

"Honey, you bring that chair over here." She straightens the hand-knit blanket that's been laid over her hospital sheets. She is wearing a soft, pink terry cloth robe her husband brought from home. Her hair is smoothed, a rich dark shade like black coffee, though faint threads of gray glint at the roots. Mrs. Whitmore has always been a portrait. Even after surgery, she still finds the energy to put on makeup, to put in gold hoop earrings.

She pulls out a folded piece of notebook paper from between the pages of a paperback book, holds it at a distance to read our score from yesterday. "I believe," she says, as I deal out the cards, "that I was in the lead."

"Tides are about to turn, Mrs. Whitmore."

She chuckles.

Two days ago, she told me that she'd be missing her weekly canasta night with "the girls."

When people receive a cancer diagnosis, the fear comes from the unknown. Will the treatments work? Will I die? As a nurse, I don't have the answers to those questions.

But canasta? I can learn to play canasta. That's why I always tell families to maintain every bit of normalcy they can. Because the day-to-day anxieties arise from the disruption of the known. Bring a favorite blanket, a familiar terry cloth robe. Keep your routines.

Mrs. Whitmore discards a four. I draw two and discard a four of my own. She picks up the deck, showing me the two hidden fours in her hand. The smallest of pleased smiles turns her lips.

I raise an eyebrow at her. "Oh, you are clever."

"I've just been playing too long." She uses her little pencil and scrap paper, tallying up her canastas from the spoils of the deck. There will be no comeback.

"That's a lovely bouquet," I say of the flowers on her bedside table.

"Isn't it? It's from the ladies on the pageant board. They're trying to butter me up." She laughs.

Mrs. Whitmore has been a member of that board for as long as I can remember. She was the very first to win the title of Miss Lone Star Princess fifty years ago.

"Well, who wouldn't want to stay on your good side?" I rearrange the cards in my hand. "My oldest is entering this year."

Hannah blindsided me with the news last night. I love my daughter to pieces, and I think she's beautiful, inside and out, but Hannah is not your typical pageant girl.

When she was little, we called Hannah "The Ham." A wild mass of curls, a Jack Nicholson brow, and a smile that spread her chipmunk cheeks wide. She'd go to church in July, wearing Christmas pajamas with a pink tutu, Peppa Pig rain boots, and seven plastic bracelets.

For heaven's sake, my mother would sigh. *What happened to all those cute dresses I bought her?* Mama was always pushing the pinks and sparkles, the patent Mary Janes. I'd shrug and say, *She dresses herself*, feeling a secret bloom of pride. It was the one time I'd allow myself to disappoint my mother, to disappoint anyone, because I was preserving Hannah.

When Hannah started kindergarten, she became best friends with a boy named Samuel. They were inseparable, holding hands on the playground and sharing snacks. One morning, Hannah tried on a frilly pink dress from Mama. Waylon whistled when she walked in, told her Samuel would *have hearts in his eyes*. I know my husband meant well, but in that moment, I could have killed him. Hannah wore the dress to school, and everyone—Waylon, Mama, the teachers—told her how pretty she was.

After that, she refused to wear any of her old favorites. I'd hold up her blue *T. rex* shirt, reminding her how much she loved dinosaurs, but she'd stamp her foot. *I don't want to be cute. I want to be pretty.*

Waylon yelled from the couch. *Since when do you care what she wears?*

I didn't care what she wore. I cared about the why. I didn't like that she looked at her closet, looked at her reflection, and thought about what someone else might think.

So I don't like the idea now of her getting up on a stage to be picked at and judged. And, to be honest, I don't like that she's getting dragged into this whole thing by the likes of Sarah Lynn Preston. Hannah insists the two of them are friends, but I can't help my suspicions. I know from experience the way pretty, popular girls can find a target in a chubby girl who doesn't fit their mold.

"They want me to do the crowning," Mrs. Whitmore says. "I'll have to get my hair done." She touches the top of her head gently with the tips of her fingers. "That'll be nice, I suppose. Getting my hair done. While I still have it."

My eyes go to hers, and she looks away. She blinks, and I see the glitter of tears on her lashes.

"You must think I'm so silly," she says, pressing her fingertips into the corners of her eyes. "Crying over hair."

I pull a tissue from the packet I keep in my pocket, hand it to her. "Mrs. Whitmore, you get to feel however you feel."

She dabs at her eyes and nose. "I don't want people to look at me and just see a sick person. I'm still me. I don't want to remind people of death."

I pick up my cards just as the door opens behind me, and we both turn.

The blood drains from my face, leaving me lightheaded and cold. The cards slip from my grip, fall to the tile floor like a tumble of leaves.

I don't bend to pick them up. I can't take my eyes off the woman in the doorway, Mrs. Whitmore's daughter, the one who didn't disappear.

If there is anyone who makes people think of death, it is Ingrid Whitmore.

CHAPTER SIX

SARAH LYNN

Mom has me doing standing squats in her pageant room upstairs as she thumbs through the Miss Lone Star Princess applications. To Mom, everything is training for the pageant. And the pageant is training for life.

She gets chipper when calling out familiar names—girls I've known since kindergarten, daughters of her friends from church. *So-and-so is so cute*, she'll say, like she's rooting for them. But I know what she's really doing. This is reconnaissance. A threat assessment disguised as chitchat.

Each contestant gets an index card, a color-coded dot, and then a pushpin onto the corkboard mounted above her desk. The board looks like something out of a war room, all neat rows and shifting ranks.

The way I see it, there is no competition.

In Anhalt, Miss Lone Star Princess isn't just a pageant. It's a religion. The board of directors is made up of the same women who've run it since before I was born—the mayor's wife, the head of the First Baptist Women's Missionary Union, a few former queens who still wear their sashes to town events. They worship tradition, legacy, and perfect posture.

And since Mom won the title twenty-five years ago, everyone already knows whose turn it is next.

But my mother is nothing if she isn't thorough. *Complacency breeds failure*. Another of her maxims. Probably something she picked up from one of those white-teethed, "unleash-your-power" seminars she swears are "life-changing" every time.

I've won crowns before—plenty of them, enough that the shelf in my bedroom sags under the weight of rhinestones. But those were practice runs. Every step, every sash, every stage-ready smile has been training for Miss Lone Star Princess.

This is the pageant Mom cares about. Because, for her, it was the beginning of everything.

"Hold and squeeze at the bottom, Sarah Lynn, and go slower on your way up," she says, nipping at me. It's like being in the room with a shark circling, only instead of biting off chunks, she nibbles off the pieces of me she doesn't like.

I glance up at the life-sized photo of her Miss Texas 2006 crowning, anchored in a large frame in the center of the room. The roses in her arms are lush, velvety red. Her hand covers her mouth, eyes glistening with tears. She wears a smile so genuine and giant, it's like she could swallow the whole of the world. She is at her most beautiful and, I know, it's the happiest moment of her life. I love this picture, even if it's kind of sad that Mom's pinnacle came before my brother, Kayden, and me.

I fix my eyes to the portrait and squat low. My thighs burn, and a bead of sweat slips down my spine. I force myself to stay steady, to look composed, to make it look easy. That's part of the training too—never let her see you struggle.

"Hannah Campbell?" Mom says, "is that Melanie's daughter?"

Slowly and with control, I push myself back up to standing. "Yeah, she works with me up at Smoothie Palace. She's brand-new to pageants. Actually, do you think she could train with us today? She's going to need it," I say, hoping to soften any of her predatory inclinations. I told the girls that the pageant will be fun. And, for them, it will be. They have no stake in this game.

"Sure thing," Mom says, jotting a quick note on Hannah's index card before pinning it up in the yellow—"unknown"—section. Then she pauses at the next name, tapping her pen on the paper. "Hmm," she says. "Sabrina Doyle signed up." She presses a red dot onto the card and pins it high on the board, in the "watch list."

I roll my eyes. Sabrina Doyle is pretty, sure. A cheerleader with a mama that will buy her the best dresses money can buy. But she's never set foot on a stage. Sabrina Doyle is not a threat. None of the girls on that corkboard are.

No one has trained like I have—early mornings and late nights, countless coaches, wardrobe fittings, mock interviews. Mom's been raising me for this stage since I could walk in heels. Some cheerleader in a brand-new gown is not taking this crown from us.

No one is.

CHAPTER SEVEN

CAT

I cross the bridge, the river threading beneath it, and turn in to Sherman Ranch, heading back to the model home. My groceries slide sideways in the trunk, and I try to remember if the kid at H-E-B double-bagged the champagne. That's just what I'd need—a car reeking of alcohol. My sponsor would love that.

At the development's entrance, bouquets slump in the sun, petals browned and curling in on themselves. A few teddy bears sag against the post, rain warped and matted. One fading poster board sign asks: WHERE IS IZZY?

All this construction has dug up more than dirt. It's brought the story of Izzy Whitmore back to the forefront of everyone's minds. Twenty-five years ago, Izzy disappeared without a trace. Everyone in town believes she's buried somewhere right here, on the Sherman land. And now they're all just holding their breath, waiting for one of these backhoes to dig her up.

I wonder if that's partly why her sister, Iggy, is back in town. Though I know from Melanie that her mom is sick. I passed Iggy on the road a few minutes ago, and the sight of her nearly gave me a heart attack. I wonder if she gets that a lot—if she's used to people looking at her and seeing Izzy instead—and if that's why she moved so far away.

I pull up and park in front of the model home. On the porch, beside the rocking chairs, the plaid throw, and the vase of sunflowers, stand

Kennedy Claire Preston and her copy-paste daughter. Oh, Lord, I haven't seen Kennedy Claire since high school, and, annoyingly, she looks just as good as she did back then. I have the momentary urge to shift the car back into drive and escape.

But she's already spotted me, throwing up her hand and waggling her lilac-painted fingers at me. I take a breath and open the door.

"Cat?" she says, lifting her sunglasses to the top of her blond extensions so she can squint across the yard. "Cat Dennis? I heard you were working here, honey. Good for you."

I ignore the subtle dig. Back in high school, Kennedy Claire was the master of the backhanded compliment. I go around to open the trunk, loading my arms up with groceries.

"What a surprise," I say, walking toward her. "You look amazing."

She looks down at her dress, smoothing the skirt and smiling like she agrees. "This is my daughter, Sarah Lynn."

"Hi, ma'am," Sarah Lynn says, holding out her hand. I notice that her fingernails are painted the exact same shade of lilac. Even without the matching nails and matching hair, the resemblance is uncanny.

I punch the code into the keypad on the door and let them into the model home. They follow me into the kitchen, where I set the groceries on the counter. "How can I help you, Kennedy Claire? Are you thinking about buying a Sherman Ranch home?"

As far as I know, these days, Kennedy Claire owns an enormous home on the old money side of town. After she won Miss Texas, she married into one of the most established families in town: the Prestons. Oil money. Generational wealth. The kind that gets a high school named after them—Preston High, which we all attended. In Anhalt, if you beat all the levels in the game of keeping up with the Joneses, you'll find that the final boss is a Preston.

"Oh, no," Kennedy Claire chuckles like the idea is ridiculous. "We're here to scope out the Events Hall."

"That's right," I say, "the pageant."

"Our golden jubilee. Can you believe it? After forty-nine years in that little high school auditorium." She holds her hands up like she's praising Jesus. "This is the start of something bigger."

"Let me get these squared away, and I'll grab the keys." I see her eyeing the champagne as I store it away in the pantry, and I try my best to keep my head high, my shoulders back. I owe a lot of people an explanation, an apology, but Kennedy Claire isn't one of them.

We walk out together. One strip of sidewalk gleams pristine, wide enough for golf carts, but beyond it the roads break off into dirt, piles of gravel heaped up like anthills.

"Do you think we can get rid of that display by the entrance before orientation tomorrow?" Kennedy Claire asks as we walk. "The flowers and the teddy bears? It just kind of brings down the mood, don't you think?"

"I'll talk to Mark," I say, though I think it's unlikely that anyone from Anhalt will be able to step foot on the Sherman land without thinking of Izzy.

We pass along the river and between the trees, we can see The Hollow, a local spot where we all used to gather on sun-filled days to jump from the cliffs into water that stayed cool even in the hottest Texas summer heat. A natural spring flows from the riverbed, feeding a deep blue-green well that glimmers like an open eye. Limestone shelves curve around it, worn smooth by decades of bare feet and river water. And beside it looms the cave, dark, damp, and echoey.

I pick up the pace, and the Amenity Center rises in front of us, an immense building of glass and stone, the one finished jewel of the development.

Inside, the air is cool, smelling faintly of chlorine. Floor-to-ceiling windows open to the pool—cabanas, a lazy river curling through manicured gardens, even a swim-up bar. Kennedy Claire clasps her hands under her chin, delighted. "Can you imagine the photo ops?"

We move on. The gym gleams with untouched machines, Peloton spin bikes and treadmills, a rock wall. Hallways stretch off toward conference rooms, lined with polished oak doors. And then the

Events Hall, where the pageant will actually take place. Vaulted ceilings, crystal chandeliers, walls of glass looking out over the Hill Country. Opulent enough for a wedding.

"There's even a bridal suite," I say, pointing back toward the hallway. "It'll make a perfect dressing room for the pageant."

Kennedy Claire spins in the middle of the room, her heels clicking like applause. "Mark had sent me photos, of course, but this is truly to die for." She snaps her fingers at her daughter. "Sarah Lynn, take notes."

Sarah Lynn pulls a notebook from her purse, clicks her pen.

"You don't mind if we spend some time here, do you, Cat? I'm going to jot down some instructions, and then my volunteer committee will be here later today to set up for orientation."

"That's fine. I'll leave a key with you." I spin one off my key ring and hand it to her. I'm about to leave them to it, when I have a sudden stroke of genius.

Last night, Olivia and I didn't end up watching a movie. Instead, we pulled up YouTube videos about pageant prep, and in between, we talked more than we have in years. I collected tidbits—names of her friends and places they'd been and songs she likes—folding each away like pressed flowers between the pages of a book.

The pageant is my *in* with Olivia, my way to spend time with her. She has opened a door, just this little crack, and I'll be damned if I pass it up.

"Do you need more volunteers?" I ask. "I'd love to help."

I register the slight tick of surprise on Kennedy Claire's face. "Well," she breathes the word out, like she is genuinely shocked. Then she smiles from ear to ear. "Honey, I'll put you on my list. No one understands how much work it is to run a pageant of this magnitude." She pulls her phone from her purse, unlocks it, and hands it to me.

"My daughter is competing this year," I say as I type my number in.

"Is she now?"

"Olivia." I hand the phone back to her.

Kennedy Claire turns to Sarah Lynn. "Do I know Olivia?"

Sarah Lynn shakes her head. "It's her first pageant. She's super sweet," she adds to me.

"Aw, newbies are so cute," Kennedy Claire says, and I ignore the way she has just flippantly dismissed my daughter. She types something out on her phone, and I hear my own ding in my back pocket. "There. Sent you a text. So now you have my number too." She puts her hand to her hip and scans me from head to toe. "You have no idea how excited I am to have an extra set of hands. Actually, you know what, I have something for you." She digs around in her bag and pulls out a small stack of ivory-colored cards with loopy gold lettering. "Invitations to the pageant. Hand them out to whoever you like. We're aiming to get the whole town in attendance this year."

I take the invitations, run the pad of my thumb slowly over the shiny embossed letters, feeling like I've just been handed a Willy Wonka Golden Ticket to win back my daughter.

"She's really excited about it. We were practicing poses last night." And I can't help but gush, thinking about the way Olivia transformed before my eyes, no longer a shy teenager hiding behind her hair, but all long neck and poised grace, the posture of a ballerina. "She's a natural—so much stage presence. She's been doing competitive dance since she was three, you know?"

Kennedy Claire's smile freezes. "Has she?" she says, but the honey has slid from her voice. She turns to her daughter. "Did you know that?"

Sarah Lynn shakes her head, and something silent passes between them—an exchange I can't quite read, but one that has me wondering if I've said too much. One that sends a wriggle of warning inching up my spine.

CHAPTER EIGHT

INGRID

Back in Colorado, I had called Joel to tell him about my mother's cancer diagnosis.

Oh, Iggy. I could picture him sitting down wherever he was, the way he'd run a hand through his hair, knew the expression on his face, even though I couldn't see him. *I'm sorry to hear that.* And I knew he meant it.

I have to go down there. She's having surgery, and I want to be able to help out once she's home. Dad can't do it all by himself, not at his age.

I figured Joel would come with me. I guess that's why I was calling, really, though I didn't say it.

Instead, at the end of the conversation, he asked, *Have you told them about us yet?*

Joel moved out two months ago. When Mom asks about him now, I just say, *Oh, Joel's fine.* Because I don't want to burden her. Not now. But also because I didn't think it was permanent. Joel was going through some kind of midlife crisis, and a few months from now, he'd be crawling back with his tail between his legs. I didn't want to taint everyone's opinion of him, of our relationship, of my life.

But then Joel didn't offer to come with me on this trip. Not even as a friend. Didn't bother to give me an excuse as to why he couldn't.

Like the thought hadn't even occurred to him. Because you show up for the big things when you love someone.

Mom is sitting up in the hospital bed, and bars of sunlight spill through the blinds and wrap around the knitted blanket on her lap. She has her makeup on, her gold hoop earrings in, but she looks frail—the hospital gown, the large purple bruises at her wrists. If I try to say anything meaningful, tears will choke my words.

The nurse drops playing cards across the floor. I go to help pick them up, thankful for the distraction. Putting things back in order settles me.

"Well, hello, honey." Mom peers down at me.

"Hi, Mom." I look up and lock eyes with her. She looks tired, older, but somehow exactly the same. I rise up and give her a kiss on her dry cheek. Her White Diamonds perfume almost masks the smell of hospital.

"Where's Joel?" she says, looking to the open doorway behind me.

"He couldn't get away."

She tsks. "That's too bad. Did you see my flowers?" She points to a bright bouquet in a vase on her bedside table, three miniature sunflowers like happy faces. "Kennedy Claire brought them by for me earlier. Isn't that sweet? She was wanting to know when you'd be coming into town. She sure is eager to see you."

I think of all those bouquets piled up along the construction site at Sherman Ranch. I've always hated flowers. The ratio of sentiments is all wrong, like an equation that doesn't balance: *Hey, I know you're devastated right now, so here's some pointless, pretty dead things.*

"I'll give her a call," I say, reaching past the flowers to grab the oversized Styrofoam cup from the table. "Are you drinking enough water? You need to stay hydrated."

"Iggy," Mom admonishes.

"Is she eating the food?" I ask the nurse, who is up from her hands and knees, having gathered the rest of the playing cards. I pull a binder from my purse, organized into tabbed sections, and flip to a research paper I'd found on diet in preparation for chemo. "You need lots of protein, Mom. Now, before you lose your appetite."

"Iggy, for heaven's sake," Mom says. "Sit down. Can't we just visit?"

Six weeks ago, the doctors found a lump in Mom's right breast. Cancerous cells had spread to nearby lymph nodes. A few days ago, she underwent surgery to have the mass removed.

I check my watch. "I'm meeting with your doctor in ten minutes. Then I'm going to the house to start setting things up."

Mom tugs a wrinkle out of her blanket.

You cannot prevent bad things from happening, Sheryl, my therapist, has told me time and time again. *No matter how prepared you are.* Sheryl owns a cardigan sweater in every color and speaks in a voice so measured it's as if her cadence were calibrated down to being paid by the minute. Which it is.

I, of all people, understand that bad things cannot be avoided in life. But risks can be mitigated.

I'm the one who kept a reminder on my calendar for Mom's routine mammogram, who called to nag her to make the appointment. When they found the cancer, it was still regional. It hadn't yet spread to the distant parts of her body—her bones, her blood, her brain. Her chance of survival is better because I'm a nag. The risk, hopefully, mitigated.

When I brought this up to Sheryl, I felt it was a strong piece of evidence in my favor. But she was more interested in whether Mom's cancer diagnosis had stirred up old grief.

Stirred up.

As though my grief were a layer of silt that had settled at the bottom of my life, just waiting to be kicked back up.

* * *

When Izzy didn't come home the night before the pageant, Mom and Dad assumed she'd stayed over at the Sherman house. She spent the night with Ben all the time—they'd been dating since middle school. Our families had always been intertwined: rodeos, carpools, dinners. If Mrs. Sherman brought McDonald's up to the elementary school for Ben, she bought Happy Meals for us too. If Mom made T-shirts for Spirit Week, she made extras for Ben and his little sister, Laurie. I'd spent just as much time roaming the river and the woods of the Sherman land as I had spent in my own house. They were basically family.

The next morning was a whirlwind. Kennedy Claire and I were getting ready for the pageant. Mom was on the committee, driving around all day, picking up floral arrangements, meeting with vendors, and chauffeuring around the guest judges. It wasn't like now, everyone glued to their cell phones every second of the day, everyone always checking in. And in small towns like Anhalt, bad things simply didn't happen.

I wasn't worried. I knew Izzy would show up. Earlier that week, I'd tweaked my ankle, just enough that I had to ditch my gymnastics routine. Izzy had come up with a magic trick we could do instead.

But when the talent acts started without her, I panicked and tried to tumble anyway. I hit the mat wrong on my first landing, pain shooting white-hot up my leg, and I went down hard. I ended up in the wings with a bag of ice while the show kept going.

That's when the worry started. Izzy would never have let me down like that. I knew something wasn't right, and so did my parents.

I watched Mom fidget in her seat, check over her shoulder. I watched Dad lean in to whisper, then get up, disappearing into the dark shadow that held the rest of the audience in their seats.

After Kennedy Claire's crowning, I limped through contestants hugging and moms packing away makeup and dresses.

You can't go yet, Kennedy Claire said. She was wearing her evening gown, the Miss Lone Star crown pinned to her head, a big bouquet in her arms and a pout on her face. *We're supposed to celebrate.*

I threw my things in a bag, gave Kennedy Claire a hug. *We'll celebrate tomorrow*, I said, annoyed at the way she always had to make everything about her, when I just wanted to be with my parents, just wanted to be looking for my sister.

In the car, Mom kept wiping her palms on her skirt. Dad had already talked to Sheriff Ryan, told him that they hadn't heard from Izzy all day.

Dad dropped Mom and me off at the house, then headed out to the Shermans' himself. *Look*, he said, standing outside the car before he left, arms around Mom. *She's probably there, okay? But if she isn't, I'll get Abel, and we'll find her, and we'll bring her home.*

His words had soothed me. Because Dad, Abel, and the sheriff—the three best men I knew—would be out there looking for Izzy. There was no doubt in my mind in that moment that she would be coming home safe and sound.

But nearly two hours ticked by, the frozen bag of peas on my ankle going lukewarm and mushy, Mom pacing around the living room, peeking out the blinds, calling the Sherman house to no answer. Finally, Dad came home. He didn't have Izzy with him. But he did have the sheriff. They came into the living room, where Mom was perched on the edge of the recliner, back straight and hands knotted in her lap, and I lay on the sofa, my hurt leg elevated on a pillow.

We found Isabelle's car parked out by the river entrance on Ranch Road 20, the sheriff said.

No, she wasn't going to the river, I said, sitting up on the sofa, my ankle screaming at the shift. *She was going out with Ben.* I remembered her packing her little black date night purse.

Where's Abel? Mom said.

That's when I noticed Dad's face, dark and hard like I'd never seen it. *They're not talking.*

Mom's head jerked back slightly, and a quiet scoff escaped her. *What do you mean they're not talking? Did you go up to the house?*

Abel barely opened the door, Barb. Said they hadn't seen Izzy, said they didn't know anything.

Didn't know anything? Mom asked, her voice incredulous. She stood up from her chair then. *Did you talk to Ben?*

Dad shook his head. *Abel wouldn't let me.*

I'm going over there, Mom said, walking to the entryway so she could step into her tennis shoes. *Carol will talk to me. This is ridiculous.*

I've already been up there, Barbara, Sheriff Ryan said, gently reaching for her shoulder. *Abel told me to get off his property. Said if I wanted to poke around, I'd need a warrant.*

Mom's breathing sharpened and her eyes turned steely. *Then get one*, she spat.

I stood in the doorway, holding the frame for balance.

I will, the sheriff said, putting a hand to her shoulder. *But we need evidence.*

Evidence of what? I said.

Then Mom started to cry.

And, like her, I realized what it meant that Abel didn't want us to come onto his property, what it meant that he wouldn't let Ben talk to the police, that they hadn't answered their phone when Mom called. Izzy was missing. And Ben had something to do with it.

* * *

"Are you her nurse?" I say to the woman in scrubs. She's picked up the cards, swept the rest from my mother's lap.

"Honey, don't you recognize Melanie?" Mom says. "My goodness. You two went to school together."

I look at the woman properly. She's short, plump, her mousey-brown hair tied back in a limp ponytail. My mind shuffles memories like the decks of cards.

"Sheriff Ryan's daughter," Mom prompts.

And, oh God, Melanie.

Melon-ball Melanie. That's what we'd called her. Kids can be so casually cruel. Melanie had tripped during gym class, going for a soccer ball, tangled up by her own clumsy feet. She had actually rolled. Dry dirt kicked up behind her. *Like a big ball*, Kennedy Claire said, drawing out the words *big* and *ball* so they bounced out and into my ears. *Melon-ball Melanie.* I'd snorted a laugh. Izzy had snapped disapproving eyes at me and gone to help Melanie up. I'd felt a slither of shame. But other girls had heard. Other girls laughed too. *Good try, Mel*, Kennedy Claire had said, loud enough this time for even the teacher to hear. Melanie was tugging her shirt down, grass stains on the wide butt of her gym shorts, her knee skinned, and still she smiled, her cheeks burning red. *Sorry*, she said. *Sorry, everyone.*

"Melanie," I say now. "Oh my God, it's been forever. I wasn't paying attention." Now I'm the one with burning cheeks.

Melanie puts a hand to my upper arm. "It's so good to see you." Her whole face is pure reassurance. She cuts her eyes over to my mother. "Now, Mrs. Whitmore. I have the next few days off, but I expect my rematch when I get back. That is, if you're not too tired of counting all those points you're racking up against me."

Mom laughs a pretty, tinkling laugh.

Melanie pats my arm before letting go, smiling at me with that sweet smile of hers. She was always so sweet. And that sense of old shame tightens. Even though it's in the past, a lifetime ago, and we were just kids, I remember what we did to Melanie.

I remember what cruel really means.

CHAPTER NINE

ABEL SHERMAN

2000

Abel Sherman walks along the river on his property, a black trash bag in one hand and a mesquite branch in the other, using it like a makeshift trash grabber, picking up cans and potato chip bags the careless kids leave behind when they float the river. His daughter, Laurie, skips ahead, collecting twigs and flower buds and whatever else catches her eye.

It's an unseasonably hot spring, and the Blanco River runs low. Abel likes to put on that he's glad about it, that at least it means fewer kids swarming the banks, leaving their trash, nearly killing themselves swinging from half-assed tied rope swings. But, the truth of it is, Abel doesn't much mind the kids. Sure, he chews out the ones he catches throwing out their beer cans or tossing rocks at the turtles.

But he likes watching them. Likes the way his land is a vital piece of the town, of everyone's childhood. Their memories like the roots of mesquite trees searching for water, boring deep and vast, until they're anchored solid to the ground.

He spots a scrap of bright blue fabric caught on a rock, lapping gently with the current. He stoops to pick it up, and watches it unfurl like a dead snake. He knows that it is Izzy Whitmore's. Can see it in his mind, the fabric pulling back her long, dark hair.

Izzy, who was over at their house all the time, just as comfortable as a spoon in the sugar bowl, lounging around their living room in her pj's, teasing Abel by snatching the hat off his head, helping Carol set the table.

Every Friday morning, Abel meets with Jim Whitmore and Sheriff Ryan for coffee to talk out the week's problems and share their solutions, keeping their homes together and their houses in order. They'd been meeting one way or another their whole lives. Abel remembers lying belly down in Jim's room, arguing over the stats on the backs of baseball cards. The three of them losing Preston High's first state championship, but Anhalt still coming together and throwing the team a parade anyhow. Getting drunk the night Ryan got deputized, using his new status in the eyes of the law as a free pass to go hog wild one last time.

When Jim found out Barbara was having twins, he called Abel, wondering how he'd make ends meet. Abel showed up with two boxes of IT'S A GIRL cigars and told him what his daddy told him—that it'll all work out, one way or the other. It always did.

The women were close too. They didn't talk current affairs or fixing things. Instead, Carol and Barbara would sit by the fire pit for hours, glasses of chardonnay glowing orange from the flames, and talk circles around the past, spin out imaginations for the future. Sometimes they'd let themselves imagine Ben and Izzy getting married, having babies. He'd seen Carol's and Barbara's eyes well with happy tears just thinking about sitting in that hospital together, waiting for the baby that would make them both a grandma. How uniquely lucky they'd be to watch their grandbabies grow up side by side.

There is a stain on the blue fabric that could be mistaken for rust-colored clay. But Abel knows better. He smears it, rubbing the blood between his fingers. He turns his head and listens upstream, listens for the sounds of kids coming on inner tubes. But he only hears the water flowing and a pair of mockingbirds scolding each other in the trees.

Then his youngest, Laurie, is suddenly beside him, and Abel is quick to shove the headband into his pocket.

"Time to head back," he says. "Your mama'll have supper ready soon."

Ben was supposed to be out on a date with Izzy last night. Instead, he came home early and went straight to bed. This morning, while Carol cooked breakfast, Barbara Whitmore called the house, asking to speak to her daughter. He'd heard Carol say, *Oh, the kids are out, but I'll have her call if she shows up.*

As Abel walks back to the house, he thinks about the words of his father, who never much liked churches. *Life is church*, he'd say. *The only person you ever have to look in the mirror is yourself. If you can still do that, you're good in God's book.*

He watches Laurie run ahead, skipping through the last of the shade, toward the home he built with his own two hands. Out in the open pasture, away from the umbrella of cypress trees that line the river, the sun needles the back of his neck. Dry blades of grass crack under his boots.

The wood creaks as Abel steps up onto his porch. He looks at Laurie's rocking horse and the chair where he likes to sit and watch the sun go to sleep behind the rolling Texas hills. Just outside the screen door, he sees Ben's socks and boots, covered in dried mud.

He finds his son at the kitchen table. The phone rings, and Ben jumps like a hunting dog who'd heard a stick snap, like he'd been waiting for that phone to ring all day.

Abel walks over and pulls the cord from the wall.

Later that night, when Jim Whitmore and the sheriff come to his door, Abel stands between them and his family, keeping his house in order the only way he knows how. "You need to get off my property," he says to the men he's known since he was a little boy.

He suspects the entryway mirror must be watching him as he shuts, then deadbolts the door. But, as he walks past it, Abel doesn't bother looking its way. He doubts he'll ever be able to look himself in the mirror again.

By midnight, the bottle of whiskey is already half empty. He lights the fire pit. The flames welcome Izzy Whitmore's headband, dancing around it in bright cursive letters, until the fire ticks and pops, until the cedar it lies on is all but consumed. Abel smokes his pipe as the fabric begins to singe, then scorch, then burn.

CHAPTER TEN

SARAH LYNN

"Son of a bitch," Hannah says beside me, her ankle wobbling on the cobblestone. I've forced her out of her usual Chuck Taylors and into some kitten heels, and I'm quick to loop an arm through hers before she tumbles.

"The stones are small, but evenly spaced. Aim the point of your heel in the dead center. Then listen to the click of your heels to keep a steady pace."

"Like a fucking show pony," she says.

"Language, Hannah Leigh," I say, mimicking her mother's country-twanged accent, and it's a good thing we're already holding on to each other, because we stumble in a fit of giggles.

That gets Mom's head snapping back toward us. I watch her eyes flick from Hannah's fuzzy hair down to her rounded shoulder posture and plus-sized jeans, and I know exactly what she'll say once we're alone again: *If you lie down with dogs, Sarah Lynn, you get up with fleas.* I guess a part of me knew she wouldn't approve, which is why I've never brought Hannah around to meet Mom before. Why, up until this moment, our friendship has been confined to our Smoothie Palace shifts.

As soon as we get home, Mom will drop Hannah down to the bottom of that corkboard, summing her up by her superficial parts and assigning her a score: No competition. Zero threat. And it kind of pisses me off. Because there's so much Mom isn't factoring in, like the way Hannah's singing voice makes me want to cry or how laughing with her is a better ab workout than any three-minute plank Mom forces me to do.

But am I really any better? The truth is, I never would have invited Hannah to compete in Miss Lone Star Princess if I'd thought she had any chance of beating me. The realization makes me queasy, like that one time I did a cayenne lemon water cleanse and ended up questioning all my life choices.

"If you can walk on cobblestone, ladies, you can walk on the stage," Mom says, before turning back around, her hair swishing over her shoulder as she does.

"Your mom is such a bad bitch," Hannah whispers, completely oblivious.

"Yeah," I agree. She's not wrong. By anyone's standards, Mom is impressive. Just look at her now, striding ahead in six-inch heels. It may only be a quarter-mile stretch of dinky shops in the middle of nowhere, but with every step, every flip of her hair, she simply owns it. Owns who she is.

People in town see the big house, the perfect smile, and they assume she was born that way—that life's been easy as silk. Sure, they might know she was raised by her Aunt Birdie, might even know that her mother lost custody of her when Mom was nine. But they don't know the details. They don't know what she's been through. Or what she's done to build the life she has now.

But I do. So, yeah, I get why she's so hard on people. She's a pull-yourself-up-by-your-bootstraps kind of woman. In her eyes, you're either the best you can possibly be, or you're weak. And Mom hates weakness.

Hannah missteps again, nearly takes me down with her, but I don't falter. I'm able to self-correct.

"You said walking was the easy part," Hannah says.

"No, I said walking was the only thing you had to do. Now giddyup."

We're halfway down the block when Mom suddenly lets out a

squeal that makes both of us jump. "Oh my God!" Mom breaks into a sprint—an elbows-tucked-tight shuffle that is nothing short of miraculous in those heels. I realize she's running toward Ingrid Whitmore, who's walking into Leake Family Pharmacy. Iggy is technically my godmother, but I think the last time I saw her was at some wedding when I was fourteen. She always sends Kayden and me gift cards on our birthdays though, gushes in the comments on my socials in that over-the-top *I can't believe how grown up you are, beautiful girl!* way that older people always seem to.

I let go of Hannah's arm to catch up with Mom.

"Iggy, you little sneak, you promised me you'd tell me the minute you landed," Mom says as she throws her arms around her. Mom's been low-key stressing about whether or not Iggy will show up. She's been trying to convince Iggy's mother, Barbara Whitmore—the very first Miss Lone Star Princess—to crown the winner this year. For Mom, it's all about pomp and circumstance. She's already envisioned the photographs, the local newspaper headlines, the way it'll all play on social media. And she knows if anyone has sway over Barbara Whitmore, it's Iggy.

"I pulled into town not two hours ago, I swear," Iggy says, laughing as she returns the hug. "I went straight to the hospital."

"Drinks tonight," Mom says. "Don't even try to tell me no."

"I promised my dad we'd do dinner. How about after?"

"Perfect." Mom turns sharply and points to the ground beside her, marking my spot. "Sarah Lynn."

I take my place, and Iggy's jaw drops open. "Oh my gosh. Sarah Lynn, you look even more like your mother than you do in the pictures. Seriously, you could have stepped right out of the pages of our yearbook."

It's meant to be the highest compliment. I get it a lot. Just last week, we walked by a crusty old man sitting in a rocking chair outside Herman Smith's boot shop. He watched us pass by, head turning to follow his eyes.

It's like she spit you out right on the ground, he said, before spitting a dark stream of tobacco juice onto the concrete. It was pretty gross, but I smiled at him anyway. Like I meant it. And, if I'm being honest, that's how I feel about it sometimes. Being Mom's mini-me. It's cool, I guess. But it's also kind of disgusting.

I lean over to Hannah, who's finally caught up with us. "You are coming over to my house tonight. I'm going to find you something killer to wear to orientation."

Because, fine, I don't believe Hannah can win the pageant. And, I don't want her to either. That crown is basically mine by birthright. But Mom isn't right about everything, and maybe helping Hannah is how I prove it.

CHAPTER ELEVEN

CAT

I have a showing scheduled. So I twist open all the blinds, letting warm afternoon light illuminate every architectural detail of the model home. Then I erase any hint that an actual human being lives here. No stray hairs, no water droplets by the sink, no sandwich crumbs on the counter. There needs to be only the impression of a perfect family that could be, a little girl who loves pink flamingos, a boy into baseball, blemish-free apples in a bowl. I pull the chocolate chip cookies out of the oven—my mother's recipe, a sprinkle of salt on top—and the house smells like someone's perfect future.

The high-pitched door chime alerts me to the opening front door. I pull the wrinkles from my blouse before pasting on my most professional smile.

But when I turn the corner, I stop dead in my tracks.

Abel Sherman stands in the entryway, half turned from me, studying the enormous painting of a massive longhorn steer, horns stretching nearly wall to wall. He rakes his fingers deep into the underside of his beard, scratching the skin beneath. Swimming in his oversized camouflage jacket, he looks like a husk of the man he used to be. Like maybe when he closed up the river, he severed an artery to his own beating heart, then spent the last two decades drying up into dust.

Mark told me they had to drag Abel away when construction

began, call the cops to haul him off in handcuffs, that he spit in Sheriff Ryan's face. Now he's living out in the trailer park on the edge of town with his son. He's been a recluse since what happened to Izzy, since his wife left him and took their daughter with her. But losing his land has him rutted out like a feral hog.

"Sherman Ranch, huh?" he says, his words coming out like he has a handful of marbles in his mouth. He turns his deep-set hazel eyes on me. I watch his lip curl. "That's mighty respectful of y'all to keep the name. Truly do 'ppreciate it."

I maintain eye contact. The muscles of my face hold my smile. So much of being a woman is composing yourself. Presenting opposite from how you feel deep down inside. "Mr. Sherman—" I start, but he cuts me off.

He takes a step forward. "Didn't keep the house though, did you?" His boot leaves a muddy imprint on the spotless white tile. "Cleared it away." He swats a hand out aggressively. "Trees too. Some of them were hundreds of years old. You ever think about that?" He jabs a finger hard to his temple.

I can remember Abel the way he was. Gruff and stoop shouldered, sure, like he was hunkered down to the earth, like it would be no easier to knock him over than it would be to knock over a tree stump. But as grumpy as he liked to pretend to be, every time I served him at the Coffee Haus, he offered me a soft *Thank you, darling*, and left a generous tip, folded neatly and hidden beneath the empty plate where his bear claw had been.

Now, I can smell the whiskey sweating through his skin. And I know, better than most, the way alcohol can make a person mean. Make him dangerous.

He must have seen my eyes flick down to the mud. He looks at his feet, lifting the toe of his boot, turning it on his heel to inspect the mud underneath. He snuffs a breath like a laugh through his nose and continues walking toward me, and more clumps of dirt fall like jagged puzzle pieces.

I feel a shiver of something up my spine. I am alone in this house. With this man. My cell phone is tucked away in my purse inside my suitcase. Hidden beneath the bed. All the way upstairs. The security pad is by the front door, currently disarmed. There is a landline in the office, but he is between that door and me now, and he's closing the distance between us.

I want to tell him that I am not the developer, that I am not the person who took his land away from him, but my throat refuses to form the words.

I think of the movie *Body Double*, an erotic thriller from the '80s. How Craig Wasson watches helplessly while Deborah Shelton has a curly telephone cord wrapped around her neck—the leathery-skinned intruder pulling the cord tightly, so it digs into her soft skin, her fingers clawing at her throat. I think of her beautiful eyes lighting bright with fear, before the scene cuts to her high heels lifting off the floor.

"Well, why don't you show me around?" He says it while shaking his hands in his pockets, making the loose coins jingle with a nervous clatter, like a kettle rattling just before it starts screeching. He walks past me, tracking his dirt through the great room, head on a slow swivel, as he takes in the space. He stops at the plate of cookies, fishes a hand from his pocket to pick one up. There are fine lines of dirt beneath his fingernails.

He takes a bite of the cookie. I watch his tongue lift the broken chunks like he's tasting it with the roof of his mouth. Then he makes an ugly face and acts like it's difficult to swallow. "Delicious," he says flatly.

The entryway door chimes and a spill of relief floods me.

"Hello?" a voice calls from the foyer.

"Enjoy the refreshments," I say and hurry away from him. As I head toward the front door, I try to compose myself, and somehow I'm smiling again by the time I reach the couple. They look to be in their early thirties. He is wearing slim-cut khakis and suspenders over a polka-dotted button-up. She has on a floral dress, a wide-brimmed hat, and big sunglasses. She holds her husband's hand while cupping the underside of her belly, as they gape at the skylight.

"This is gorgeous," she says.

"John Delaney," the man says, stepping up from the sunken foyer to shake my hand. "This is my wife, Faith."

The couple is from Austin, they tell me.

"But who can afford to live there anymore?" Faith says. "It's so serene out here. The views. Wasn't I saying that John? The views. And so quaint. We drove through your town square. That old-fashioned ice cream shop? That banner for Lone Star Princess over the main street? I can't believe they still have those little pageants out here."

"It's a great place to start a family," I agree.

They both look down to Faith's belly.

"Can I offer you tea? Lemonade? A cookie?" I lead them toward the kitchen.

"Faith's current craving," John says.

Faith laughs. "Guilty."

As we round the corner, I see that the kitchen is empty. My eyes dart around the expansive room, and I notice the back door wide open. Abel must have let himself out. Thank God. I go to close it and lock it behind me.

"The crime rate out here is low, isn't it?" John is saying. "That's another concern we have in Austin."

"Anhalt is a very safe community," I say, walking back from the door. "Nothing bad ever happens here."

Faith looks up at her husband, smiling like she's already made up her mind.

"Now about that cookie," I say. "I hope you like chocolate chip, it's an old family recipe."

John puts a protective arm around Faith's shoulder, squeezes her in tight.

Then I see the tray of cookies and can't help the small gasp that escapes my lips.

They've all been smashed, as though fists have been pressed down purposefully into each one. Nothing but crumbs scattered across the platter, spilling over onto the once-gleaming countertop.

CHAPTER TWELVE

INGRID

I pull up to the house, the house Mom and Dad never sold, the house Izzy never came back to. The pecan tree out front is taller, the shade of it shielding the entire front porch. When we were little, Dad hung a swing from the strong lower branch. He made it himself, sanding the wooden seat smooth as silk, so we wouldn't get splinters.

The swing isn't there anymore. Eventually the wood warped from rain, the rope frayed and broke. Dad cut it down, so it wouldn't choke the branch.

But I can still see it. One of those quick pop bursts of memory. Izzy lying on the grass, counting dandelion petals. *He loves me, he loves me not.* While Ben pushed me higher and higher until the toes of my sneakers brushed the yellow leaves.

Even my good memories—maybe especially the good ones—taste sour on my tongue.

Sheriff Ryan never did get that warrant. Because there was never any evidence to find. Izzy's car was parked near the Sherman land, but not on it, abandoned at the river entrance that everyone in town used. In Texas, the waterways are public, even if the land is private. The sheriff and a few deputies floated the Blanco on kayaks, calling Izzy's name down every bend, while Abel looked on from his front porch, a shotgun across his lap, making sure no one set so much as a toe onto the bank. The missing posters plastered around town slowly weathered and faded. The tip lines stopped ringing. Life kept going, and we were never given any answers. Izzy had simply vanished.

As soon as I park in the driveway, the garage door begins to rise and Dad emerges, like he'd been looking out the window for me.

Mom has given me constant updates on the state of Dad's knee, which has been giving him trouble lately, but seeing him now, he has an easy stride about him. Dad has always made things seem easy. He's shrunk just a little in that way older men seem to deflate.

"How you doing, kiddo?" he asks.

"I picked up new air filters, cleaning supplies, and we need to assemble the shower chair."

He follows me to the trunk and proceeds to tuck the box of air filters under his arm, load all the bags onto his forearms, and hold my luggage waist high in his hands.

"Dad, stop it. Let me help. And the luggage has wheels."

"Those are for regular humans. Strongest daddy in the world, remember?"

Dad's entire parenting method was displaying—at least from a child's perspective—impossible feats of strength. Lifting our toddler bed with one arm and hoisting it above his head. Swinging the hammer on the strongman game at Anhalt's Oktoberfest and winning us the biggest teddy bear.

Once, when he tucked us in, I asked him to leave the door cracked. *What if there's a monster?*

He sat on the edge of my bed. *I'll rip that monster apart. Strongest daddy in the world, remember?*

It was more reassuring than if he'd said monsters didn't exist. Because if Daddy was strong, we were safe.

Now, he grunts under the weight of the luggage and the groceries.

"I'm going to end up taking care of both of you while I'm down here," I say, following with empty arms.

"Oh, me and your mother manage, more than you give us credit for," he says, trying to hide the strain in his breath.

We enter through the garage, where everything is neat and orderly, tools cascaded and evenly aligned above his tool bench, stacked and labeled camping supplies. I rush ahead to open the door to the kitchen, and make sure Dad has enough counter space to finish his grand demonstration of power.

He heaves the bags, luggage, and air filters all in one thrust onto the kitchen island. Then casually places his hands on his hips, gazing at the sprawl of his accomplishment as we stand shoulder to shoulder.

"She called earlier, you know? After you visited. You have no idea what that meant to her." He leans over slightly so that we bump shoulders. "What it means for us to have you home." He puts his arm around me and gives me a squeeze. "Three years is too long between hugs."

"I noticed your crepe myrtle has tripled in size. Well done."

Dad pats my arm and releases the hug. I have this tic, changing the subject when a moment feels too emotional. When we were first dating, Joel teased me about being *playfully aloof*. He thought it was cute. By the end, he just called me *cold*. When I told Sheryl in a session, she asked me, *What are you afraid will happen if you sit too long in the emotion?* It annoyed me. I was paying her to agree that Joel was an asshole.

"Want me to put your suitcase upstairs?" Dad asks.

"No," I say, and I'm quick to grab it off the counter before he can even reach for it. "You go work on the air filters." I head off, and he seems to have gotten the hint, because he doesn't follow me.

Whenever I come to visit, I stay in the downstairs guest room, but we don't want Mom going up and down the stairs after her surgery. I wonder if this temporary situation—Mom staying in the downstairs bedroom—will become permanent for both of them. I guess this is how it happens. Your parents get old so slowly, you don't notice, and then it seems to happen all at once.

I stand for a moment at the bottom. It's been so long since I've gone up these stairs. I lift the suitcase and take the first step.

The wall along the staircase is a timeline in reverse. My wedding photos. High school graduation. And then it's Izzy and Iggy all the way up. The two of us as teenagers, sitting in front of the cave of The Hollow, our legs dangling down into the well. By then, we were trying to separate ourselves. Izzy always wore her long hair down, pulled back with the same blue scarf she used as a headband, face barely kissed with makeup, while I wore a sleek high ponytail and a swipe of red lipstick.

But in earlier pictures, it's hard for even me to tell who is who. An eighth-grade dance with matching dresses. A trip to the zoo, us drinking from a metal rhinoceros's mouth.

At the top is a portrait of us as newborns, two babies swaddled in the same blanket, faces pressed together, still mostly one entity, still accustomed to being together inside one body. Mom told us that she used to paint our toenails to tell us apart. Yellow for me. Green for Izzy.

Maybe you're the real Isabelle, Izzy had whispered one quiet night when we were eight. We had separate beds, pushed up against opposite walls, but often Izzy climbed into mine, buried her freezing-cold feet into the bends of my knees.

I had thought about it then. If Mom had made the decision at some point to use nail polish to tell who was who, that meant there was a very real possibility that we had been switched at some point. It would be so easy, wouldn't it? *It doesn't matter*, I said, my voice heavy with sleep. Because it didn't matter. Not really. It only meant that our names were switched. Izzy had curled up tighter against my back, nuzzled the sharp point of her chin into my shoulder blade. *Good night, Izzy*, she teased.

I stand outside the door to our old bedroom. There are still two construction paper butterflies taped to the wood, our names spelled out in curly, glittering script.

I open it. The two twin beds. The vanity, makeup still scattered on the surface. Izzy's snow globe collection on a set of shelves. My posters. Sashes and crowns from back when we participated in pageants.

Unlike the town, unlike the pecan tree out front or Dad's creaking knees, the room is entirely unchanged.

It's too much to look at. I close my eyes and picture silt at the bottom of a lake. The water clear and calm and blue as the sky, if you stay near the surface. But if you go deep, if you kick your feet, you might stir up the dirt, it might swirl and churn, and then your whole world goes dark.

One of Izzy's snow globes plays a few slow, tinny notes, like an old carousel winding down, like the ghost of something that was once sweet. I don't know if I'm hearing it now or hearing it then. I open my eyes, and I see her, standing just across the room, her long, dark hair parted down the middle, tucked behind her ears and falling in front of her shoulders.

I walk slowly toward her, and as my feet cross the moaning wooden floor, the snow globe lets out one last metallic note.

I reach her, lift my fingers to her face. Her skin is cold as glass.

When she first disappeared, I used to catch glimpses of her all the time, in windows and mirrors and reflective pools of water. Once, in Denver, I saw her on the light rail in a train car opposite. I was so sure it was her, I left my bags behind as I hurried off the train. My heart raced as I pushed my way through the platform, past startled pedestrians. I just barely made it before the doors closed. But when I looked around at all the faces, she wasn't there. She was gone, and I was going the wrong direction.

I study that reflection now. Normally, when someone dies or goes missing, they become frozen in time. They never age beyond the day they were lost. Not Isabelle. I get to watch what she should have become, to see the fine lines develop around her mouth and the corners of her eyes. It's like she's still here, trapped behind the glass of the mirror.

"Knock, knock," Dad says as he steps through the open doorway to stand behind me.

"I drove by Sherman Ranch," I say. "Saw them digging it up."

"Yeah." He puts a hand to my shoulder.

"They're going to find her, aren't they?"

I turn to Dad, and he wraps his arms around me, both arms this time, a real hug.

I think sometimes of when Izzy was heady in love, climbing through our bedroom window in the dead of night, smelling of campfire and giggling to me about Ben. *He's totally obsessed with me*, she said.

At the time, I was jealous. Envious that he loved her that much.

I break the hug. I turn away from Dad.

What are you afraid will happen if you sit too long in the emotion? Sheryl asked.

I'll die. Again and again, imagining all the things he might have done to her.

I lift my luggage onto the bed and start unpacking.

"I'm going to throw some burgers on the grill for us," Dad says. "I just wanted to bring this up." He sets an envelope on the nightstand. "It's been a while since we got mail here addressed to you."

When he leaves, I pick up the letter, turn it over to see my name handwritten on the front. There is no return address. No stamp. I slide my nail beneath the sealed edge and tear it open. Inside, I find a creamy linen card with raised gold curly font, inviting me to the fiftieth annual Miss Lone Star Princess Pageant. I'm sure these are being handed out all over town, but it's strange that this one would be addressed to me. Not many people even know I'm back in town.

I turn the card over, and immediately all the air is sucked from my lungs. I have to sit down, barely catching the edge of my old bed.

Scrawled heavy on the back, hard enough that the pen has torn into the paper—BEN DIDN'T KILL IZZY. I KNOW WHAT REALLY HAPPENED TO YOUR SISTER.

CHAPTER THIRTEEN

MELANIE

I'm sitting at the table in the model home with Cat—I like to check in on her regularly, even if I have a to-do list a mile long when I get home. And I'm glad I do, because she's just finished telling me about how Abel Sherman came by and smashed up all her cookies.

"He looks awful," she says. "Have you seen him? Just awful." Her eyes are fixed somewhere else, like she's replaying the whole horrible thing in her mind. She has a tendency to do that, to fixate. Cat's biggest fault is that she likes pressing on a bruise. I can't count the number of times I've told her, just like my Oma Greta used to tell me, to let sleeping dogs lie. "He kind of scared me, Mel." I watch the way her hand moves slowly to the side of her neck to scratch just beneath her ear.

An old habit.

When you love someone with an addiction, you're always looking for little signs that they might be slipping up.

Cat started drinking hard in high school. Little spritzers and fruity things we could stomach at first, but it wasn't long until she graduated to the harder stuff without me. It got so bad that I would follow her to parties just so I could make sure she made it home safe. But luckily she met Mark, and he made her laugh, made her feel like she deserved to be happy. We had a few good years there, the four of us—Mark and Cat, Waylon and me—barbecuing in each other's backyards, Hannah and Olivia toddling through sprinklers in the grass. She still had her moods about her, when fun party Cat would veer into sad, self-pitying Cat. But I was always there to steer her back on course.

Then she got her wisdom teeth pulled. And whatever comfort I was bringing her by being her best friend was no match for hydrocodone. She told me the pills brought her a kind of quiet she'd never known.

After that, she'd disappear on us. We'd go months not knowing where she was, whether she was dead or alive. Then, out of the blue, I'd get a call from the Austin Police Department—Cat asking if I'd bring her some clean clothes or if I could help her out with some money for bail.

Waylon didn't understand why I stuck by her.

But he didn't know what we'd been through together, didn't know the way our souls were intertwined. *Blood sisters*, Cat used to say. A little inside joke.

* * *

Sophomore year, I'd sat alone in the cafeteria.

Oh my God. What is that? Kennedy Claire leaned over my shoulder, pointing at the sandwich my mom had packed for me. I'd just bitten into it and my mouth was full. Mama got my favorite bread from the bakery, a hard baguette, soft on the inside, and loaded it with salami, relish, mayonnaise, and provolone cheese. When she'd handed me my lunch that morning, she lowered her face to mine and told me she wanted me to have a really good day.

I wasn't having a good day. The hard crust of the baguette must have scraped my gums, because the faintest bit of red blood dragged onto the soft white bread. Of course, Kennedy Claire had smelled it. I was about to be eaten alive. Yet again.

So I just kept chewing, staring down at the flower-printed shirt stretched over my belly, the one my Oma gave me the Christmas prior.

It's blood, Kennedy Claire said, tone dripping with disgust, in that booming, stage-presence voice of hers. I could feel people turning our way, feel them turning to see what kind of freak bleeds on her sandwich, my ears growing hot.

Ingrid plopped down on the bench beside me and tugged the corner of my brown paper bag. The Little Debbie that Mama had packed slid out, followed by the extra one, the one to make sure I had a really good day. Ingrid looked from the cakes to Kennedy Claire, a mean little smirk pulling at her lips.

Maybe it's better if she bleeds out, Kennedy Claire said. *Before her blood sugar kills her.*

The girls around her sniggered.

I didn't have the courage to look up. I didn't even have the courage to swallow. The mouthful of sandwich was gluey on my tongue. My Oma Greta told me that God answers every prayer. Sometimes at night, I prayed He'd send me an angel.

I didn't see her at first. I smelled her. The cigarettes off her black leather jacket as she reached over me, barging through Kennedy Claire's school of piranhas, and grabbed the sandwich from my hands. By the time I turned around, she was already face-to-face with Kennedy Claire. Everyone was watching now, watching as Cat Dennis took a big old bite out of my sandwich, out of the spot that still had my teeth marks, my blood. She chewed with her mouth open, inches from Kennedy Claire's face, close enough that I knew she could smell the salami. Kennedy Claire recoiled, a hand to her chest.

Damn, Cat said. *That's a good-ass sandwich.* She handed it back to me without breaking eyes with Kennedy Claire. *Fuck with her again, and I'll turn your nose sideways.*

She didn't look like an angel, not like one of the porcelain figurines Mama collected, all pastel colors, serene egg-shaped faces, and feathered wings. But I swear, the fluorescent cafeteria lights glowed ethereally through the choppy ends of Cat's shaggy bob.

For the first time in the recorded history of man, Kennedy Claire was not in command. Her eyes flicked from Cat to Ingrid and back. *Come on, Iggy, let's go.*

Then Cat sat down and ate her lunch beside me. That afternoon, and the next and the next and the next. Like an alley cat that won't stop showing up on your porch once it's fed. She had claimed me as her own.

****

"I'll stay the night with you," I say to Cat now. Waylon won't be happy about it. He's probably already expecting me home, and the kids will be wanting supper. But I can't take my chances with Cat.

Her hand drops from her neck and she shakes her head, refocusing on me. "I'm fine," she says. "It just shook me up is all. Seeing Abel Sherman like that."

"I'm not taking no for an answer."

"I'm fine, Mel. Really. I can't have you staying over and Mark and everyone else starting to worry. Seriously. I'm fine."

I don't like leaving her upset, but I can see that her eyes are clear, and I don't smell any alcohol as I bring her in for a hug. "Okay, okay. You call me, you hear? If things are getting to be too much. Anytime. Don't you do something stupid."

"I promise," she says, and I have to believe her.

"I'm proud of you," I tell her when we say goodbye on the porch.

The sun is just beginning to set as I drive away, along the winding road that traces the river, past the skeletons of homes-to-be. I don't realize how tightly I'm squeezing the wheel until I release the tension from my fingers, and they ache for the shape they once were. As I turn around the bend, the trees are cleared now. The river opens, and I see it. The well where we used to gather as kids. And the cave. I keep my eyes forward, refusing to look into the mouth of The Hollow.

CHAPTER FOURTEEN

SARAH LYNN

Hannah's flopped on my bed, head dangling off the edge. Olivia's curled in my pink velvet armchair, knees tucked up under her giant T-shirt like she's hiding out in a tent. And I'm on the floor, blow-drying Hannah's curls with a diffuser after an hour of washing, detangling, and loading her up with every curl product I could find in the shops on the square.

"I'm never going to do this myself," Hannah yells over the blow-dryer. "It takes for-fucking-ever. I already got a job. I'm not looking to add hairstylist to the resume."

I snap off the dryer, so she's basically screaming the last of her sentence at us into dead air. With oil on my hands, I scrunch her curls to loosen them.

"Take a look," I say, sitting back on my heels.

She hauls herself up and Olivia gasps so loud it makes Hannah whip around to her. "Does it look that bad?"

Olivia is covering her mouth with both hands. She shakes her head.

Hannah goes to my floor-length mirror. "Are you shitting me?" She turns her head, lets the waterfall of soft, bouncy ringlets fall over her shoulder. "You're telling me I could have looked like this my whole life? I'm quitting Smoothie Palace. Fuck school too. I'm going full-time into hair care."

I'm laughing, watching Hannah smelling herself, turning her

head this way and that, fluffing up her hair and adjusting one curl and then another around her face.

I lean forward to stand. "Time to talk outfits." Orientation might seem like no big deal. But it's your first chance to make an impression on the board members, the judges, the competition. "Show me what you brought."

Hannah hands me a sweet-looking red floral dress, white flowers scattered across the cherry fabric. "It's my church dress, but it's the only one I have," she says. "Besides my homecoming dress."

I hold it up in front of her. "It might work. Put it on."

Olivia gets up and starts to study the clothes in my closet, giving Hannah privacy with her turned back.

Hannah wriggles her pants off, then pulls her shirt over her head. Instinctively, she wraps her arms around her belly.

Hannah, who lets her mouth run miles ahead of her brain, who is always saying something just for the sake of making herself laugh, not really caring whether or not anyone else even finds it funny, who is completely comfortable with who she is. Seeing her now, shoulders rolled forward like maybe she can shrink herself into nothing—it sends a bolt of anger through me.

"If there's one lesson you both need to know about pageants—it's what's underneath that counts."

"You mean what's on the inside?" Olivia asks.

The dressing room of a pageant is a stage before the stage, a psychological battlefield. Girls get modest. They get shy. Putting on gowns beneath robes, changing behind their travel clothing racks. But I don't turn. I don't hide. I enjoy maintaining eye contact with my competitors, keeping small talk going while I strip in front of them, I enjoy letting my body reflect every one of their hidden insecurities. But it isn't just my body that's doing the work. "It's all about confidence," I say. "I win that crown before the other girls ever put on their thousand-dollar dresses. Before I ever take one step onto that stage." I pull Hannah's hands away. "Never hide," I tell her, looking right into her dark brown eyes.

I guide the dress over her, running my hands down her rib cage, sliding them to the hem and farther down the curve of her thighs. She's already tied the front in a bow at her neck before I pop up. We're face-to-face, and her cheeks are flushed. I'm close enough to smell the sweetness of the pineapple on her breath from the smoothies we picked up earlier. And I know she can smell it on mine.

"Curves are in," I say. "So we use them." I begin to untie the bow. I loop one end of the tie up through her bra and slide the other under, my fingers gliding between her breasts, along her sternum. I tie the ends together tight, pushing her neckline into a deep V, giving her a little more support, a little more exposure, so that her breasts swell up between the girly white flowers on either side. Perfect.

I turn her to face the mirror again. "You have cleavage we'd kill for," I whisper in her ear, my chin resting on her shoulder. "So kill us with it." The corner of her mouth lifts with a mischievous smile. She can't help it. Beauty is power.

"Can I try this on?" Olivia asks, and I turn to see she's holding up a sky-blue minidress.

"Of course, babes."

Mom got all paranoid after Cat told us about Olivia's dance experience, but I'm not worried. Olivia is basically like a tiny little church mouse.

Hannah claims the chair, I perch on the bed, and Olivia positions herself in front of the mirror. She pulls off her leggings, then grabs the hem of her baggy T-shirt and lifts it over her head.

And, holy shit.

I didn't realize that's what Olivia was working with under all that fabric. She's a closet stunner.

She pulls the dress up and reaches back a long, lithe arm to zip it herself. It fits her like a glove.

Hannah lets out a wolf whistle, but I'm struck dumb for the moment.

Then the door opens, and Mom pops her head in. "I'm home," she says. "Just wanted to see if you've had dinner yet. Oh, Hannah, dear. Don't you look just lovely? I really like . . ." But she stops mid-sentence when she catches sight of Olivia. She pushes the door open fully and steps into the room. "And who's this?"

My spine pulls taut as a piano wire, because I swear Mom's eyes just dilated like a cat who's spotted that tiny little church mouse from across the room.

Helplessly, I watch Olivia go to Mom. "Hi, Mrs. Preston. I'm Olivia."

Mom's eyes skate to me and back. "Cat's girl?" She shakes Olivia's hand. "It's so wonderful to have you in Miss Lone Star this year. Is that one of Sarah Lynn's dresses?"

Olivia glances over to me, smiling, blissfully unaware that the room has turned electric, every surface humming like a live wire. "She's letting me borrow it for orientation tomorrow." She smooths it over her flat stomach.

"This color is just divine on that creamy complexion of yours." Mom circles Olivia. "Oh, you know what, though"—she reaches out to grab hold of the skirt's hem—"Sarah Lynn, isn't this the one with that stain, the pen mark? Yes, here it is." She tsks. Olivia tries to twist her head to see the back of the dress, where Mom is rubbing a thumb at the fabric. "Here," Mom says, sliding down the zipper. "I'm actually going out tonight anyway. Let me drop this off at the dry cleaner. I'll pick it up first thing and bring it over to your mama. How does that sound?"

Olivia lifts the dress over her head and Mom snaps it up quickly, folding it into the crook of her elbow.

"Are you sure?" Olivia says, reaching for her clothes. "That's so nice."

Mom waves it away, all Miss Congeniality. "I need to make a trip to the dry cleaner anyway, sweetheart. Don't you worry about it."

Hannah and Olivia get dressed and gather their things, waving goodbye as they leave together. Mom and I are quiet while they take the spiral steps down. But as soon as we hear the front door close behind them, Mom says what I already know she's thinking.

"Be careful of that one, Sarah Lynn." She tosses the blue dress into the corner like it's a dirty hand towel.

Final verdict on Olivia? Red-dot-level threat.

Beauty is power. But it also puts a target on your back.

CHAPTER FIFTEEN

INGRID

One day when we were all thirteen, Izzy, Ben, and I played in the woods on the Sherman land, like we'd done a thousand times before. But that summer, things were shifting like a kaleidoscope, colors brighter and everything sharp and tangy as a penny on the tongue.

My foot slipped on a wet rock as we climbed down the riverbank toward The Hollow, and Ben caught me round the waist. His fingers on my sun-warmed skin. I was hyperaware of his body. Of the maleness of him. He wasn't just Ben, the kid we'd always known. He was a boy, close enough to me that I could count his eyelashes.

But it was Izzy who was bold enough to kiss him that day, while we swam together in the river—one quick whim that had her giggling, spinning away from him in the water, that left him blushing, that led to him taking her to the movies later that week, Abel chauffeuring them around in his truck.

It was inevitable that one of us would have kissed Ben Sherman that summer. And it made sense that it was Izzy. She'd always been the carefree one. The leap-and-never-look one.

When Izzy disappeared, the Shermans did as well. They never answered their phone again, not for us anyway. Abel put up barbed wire fences around the property, TRESPASSERS WILL BE SHOT signs along the river, and everyone believed him. Even Carol avoided

Mom in the grocery store, slipping away before Mom could speak to her, leaving her basket stranded in the aisle.

I waited for Ben. Waited for him to reach out behind his parents' backs, throw pebbles at our window again, leave a note in the knot of the pecan tree, something, anything. Waited for him to explain how it couldn't be true. It couldn't have been him who hurt Izzy.

But the pebbles never came. His parents pulled him out of school with just a few months left of senior year, sent him away to West Texas to work the oil fields. By the time he came back, I'd already left town myself.

If Ben was innocent, he would have reached out to me.

But he didn't.

* * *

Now, the invitation—I KNOW WHAT REALLY HAPPENED TO YOUR SISTER—burns a hole through my purse as I pull open the doors to Barrel & Branch. The bar is a dimly lit mix of rustic and glitz—deer heads and crystal chandeliers.

It's not the first time someone has reached out with a theory about Izzy. Every time a new true crime podcast gets ahold of the story—a beauty queen gone missing in the heart of Texas—my inbox floods with strangers sending blurry photos of "Izzy" in California and links to stories about serial killers who were active in Texas at the time. I learned long ago to delete and block.

And now the twenty-fifth anniversary is coming up, which means the interview requests are back—emails, voicemails, random DMs from producers hoping for a quote. But Mom never talked to them. None of us did. After Izzy vanished, the whole town closed ranks. You don't feed the vultures. You don't turn grief into someone else's entertainment.

But this is different. Whoever sent me this invitation isn't some internet sleuth in another state. They are here in Anhalt right now.

Light pours in behind me, and I feel like I'm entering center stage. Heads lift and whispers ripple around the room, like a rumor spreading in real time. For a moment, I wonder if they think I'm her. Like maybe Izzy has just strolled back into town to grab a drink and tell everyone the crazy story of where she's been.

I lift my sunglasses onto my head and scan the room. People I grew up with avert their eyes, and, for each and every one, I can't help but think: *Was it you?*

I make my way to the two-seater high-top table in the dead middle of the room, where Kennedy Claire perches like the featured sculpture in a museum: chin lifted so she has to look down the slope of her face to see the menu, zebra-print dress hugging every curve. In the wild, that pattern is meant to camouflage. Here, it's meant to stand out.

When I reach her, she rises, air-kisses my cheek, whispering, "If you look back at them, honey, they always wilt away."

And she's right. I glance around, and the gawkers snap their attention elsewhere, like nosy neighbors snapping their blinds shut.

"See? It's a superpower." She takes her seat again and slides a glass of rosé toward me. "How's Joel? It's a shame he couldn't be here."

I should tell her the truth. This is where Kennedy Claire would really shine as a best friend, do exactly what I'm always wanting Sheryl to do—trash-talk Joel. She would remind me that he sucks soda through his teeth, leaves his fingernail clippings on the end table. She'd tell me I'm a goddess and will be better off without him. By the end of the night, we'd be planning out my Eat, Pray, Love tour around the world.

But the truth is, I'm ashamed to admit that Joel left me. Because that's exactly what he did. There was no affair. No dramatic argument. He simply woke up one day, after fifteen years together, and decided he didn't want to be married anymore. Didn't want *me* anymore.

Sheryl says I have a *fear of abandonment, stemming from the loss of my sister*. As if I needed to pay someone for that brilliant insight. But, I guess, someone has to fund Sheryl's cardigan addiction.

"Joel's fine. Just slammed at work," I say, taking my first sip of wine so she can't read my face, can't sniff out the lie.

Luckily, Kennedy Claire has her own agenda. "Please tell me you're coming to orientation tomorrow." She flashes me her best smile and nudges me under the table with the pointy toe of her high heel. "It won't be the same without you."

I know what she's really after, though. She has called me no less than a dozen times about the pageant, and every time I've told her the same thing, that Mom would love nothing more than to crown this year's Miss Lone Star Princess, but it all depends on her health. Whether she's discharged in time. How the chemo hits her. You'd think this would be obvious to any reasonable person. But that's Kennedy Claire for you: self-centered almost to the point of narcissism.

We've been friends for nearly three decades, though. At this point, I don't expect her to be anyone other than who she's always been. Isn't that what real friendship is? Knowing a person fully and loving them anyway.

Besides, a part of me will always be that thirteen-year-old girl, grateful and a little in awe that the dazzling, formidable Kennedy Claire chose—of all people—me.

The start of eighth grade had been hard for me. When Ben and Izzy started dating, I felt suddenly invisible in their world. The world that used to belong to the three of us. They spent time without me, sat close, whispered things I couldn't hear, told inside jokes I didn't understand. I missed them, even when I was with them.

Then, at Oktoberfest that year, I found myself alone with my arms full of paper plates sagging with bratwursts and funnel cakes. I'd been sent off to spend our tickets while Izzy and Ben held our spot by the dance hall, but by the time I got back, they were gone, their laughter already disappearing into the polka music inside. I was embarrassed—standing there with all that food and nowhere to put it and no one to share it with—and embarrassment is the worst possible emotion you can feel when you are thirteen.

Then Kennedy Claire called my name. She was in line for the Ferris wheel with the girls everyone wanted to be friends with, her voice bright and carrying. *Ingrid, you're with me.* She plucked a funnel cake right out of my hands and slid me into place beside her as if it had been decided all along. Nobody complained about me cutting, not when Kennedy Claire was in charge. And, just like that, I wasn't invisible anymore. Wasn't alone anymore.

"I got an invitation," I say, tipping my glass again, pulse ticking at the thought of that message.

"Oh, good. I left one for y'all at the hospital." She's talking about one she must have tucked into that bouquet on Mom's bedside table.

"When did those go out?" I ask, hoping the question sounds casual, not like I'm fishing for information.

But she is unbothered. "We put them in the registration packets, so the girls can hand them out to all their friends and family. I'm determined to make this our biggest pageant yet."

So all the contestants. And their mothers. And anyone else they might have invited. It doesn't narrow the pool much.

"Say you'll be there. I need you." She pouts her bottom lip.

I force a smile. "I'll bring my camera. Take all those candid photos you wanted."

Back in high school, I was always snapping pictures with that old film camera—of Kennedy Claire and me, Izzy and Ben, the rest of our friends. I even started developing the photos myself in the makeshift darkroom Dad helped me put together in the storage closet of the garage, falling in love with the way the image would appear slowly, as if by magic.

I haven't picked up a camera in years, but it'll give me the perfect excuse to chat with all those pageant mothers and daughters.

Kennedy Claire squeals with delight, because there is nothing she likes better than getting her own way. "Look at us," she says, shimmying her shoulders. "Reliving the glory days."

We fall into an old rhythm without even trying. Over a bottle of wine, we trade stories that aren't new but still make us laugh, the kind of inside jokes that survived college, marriages, cross-country moves. Time is an accordion compressed, and we are seventeen again.

Then she taps her phone to check the time. "Oh, gosh, I better skedaddle. Lots to do to get ready for tomorrow." She pulls some cash from her crossbody purse, lays it on the table, then stands and gives me another kiss on the cheek. "I'll see you bright and early, girlie. We start at 9 AM, sharp."

"See you then," I say.

And, just like that, she's gone, and I'm left alone, the soft white light of the chandelier now a spotlight. Without Kennedy Claire as my shield, I'm feeling the eyes of the room on me again. Exposed and stripped down to my bare skin, a dead body on an examination table.

I flag the waitress for the check, but instead, she sets down a cocktail, frothy with grapefruit and charred rosemary.

"From the gentleman at the bar," she says.

I follow her glance. A man I don't know is staring right at me. He's handsome, with sandy-colored hair and a strong jaw, and far too young for me. He looks to be in his mid- to late twenties. He smiles, a warm, mischievous grin that dimples one cheek, like we're in on the same joke. I wonder if he's been watching me this whole time, as I laughed with Kennedy Claire, as I swept my long, dark hair over one shoulder. I guess he liked what he saw.

And something about a man that good-looking seeing me, wanting me—it sends a surprise of butterflies through my abdomen.

Then an alarm goes off on my phone, a rising scale of electronic bells. I don't need to look to know it's my spontaneity alert, but I do, YOLO flashing on the screen, a silly phrase for a silly practice.

I want you to practice spontaneity, Sheryl said once at the end of a session. I like that Sheryl gives me homework. So, I started scheduling in a spot for spontaneity on my calendar. "Scheduled spontaneity" is ludicrous, I know. But there is something intoxicating about the practice. About asking myself: What do you want? Right now, in this moment, what do you want, Ingrid?

I even randomize it, so I don't know the day or time each week when my phone will send an alert, and I have to do something unplanned.

The first time it went off, I took an hour-long bubble bath on a Tuesday night. That's how it started in the beginning, with self-care. But over time, the guardrails came off. I threw out the salad I'd prepped for lunch and got Taco Bell instead. I popped into the corner store, bought a pack of cigarettes, which I hadn't smoked since I was seventeen, took a few drags and tossed the rest. That nicotine buzz kept me floating high all morning long.

I silence the alarm.

When I look back at the bar, the young man is up from his seat. He's taller than I realized, and he's already halfway to my table.

CHAPTER SIXTEEN

MELANIE

Before I've even put the van in park, Waylon is out the front door. His blue work shirt is only half tucked in, his hand large enough to hold both the Igloo cooler with his dinner inside and a large metal thermos of coffee. They swing at his side as he marches down the drive. He looks tired. We're down to one car. The other's still broken down in the driveway.

"Sorry I'm late. I stopped by to say hi to Cat and ended up in traffic." There never used to be any such thing as traffic in Anhalt. You could get clear from one side to the other in ten minutes. When I say I'm sorry, I mean it. I hate being a burden on anyone. I hate that any part of me might make his evening worse.

"Yeah," is all Waylon says, taking the keys from me and turning his back.

Frustration knits tight in my chest, because all I want is a little reassurance.

"Is everything all right?" I ask, touching his shoulder as he's tossing his Igloo onto the passenger seat.

"Just going to work, Mel."

I chew my bottom lip, hating when he gets in these grumpy moods. I want him to turn around and pull me into one of his big bear hugs, kiss the top of my head, and tell me not to worry about anything. Maybe thank me for one of the hundreds of things I've done for him, for this family—washing the work shirt he has on now, picking up Nathan's allergy medicine, tracking down the lunchbox Levi lost again, and reminding everyone about dentist appointments and spirit days and overdue library books. But if I keep pushing it, he'll get frustrated right back at me, saying that I should already know he appreciates me.

Then he'd go off to work and never give the exchange a second thought. Meanwhile, I'd stew on it all night, slamming drawers while I made the kids supper, playing out whole arguments with Waylon in my head. But then the better half of me would be wallowing in guilt—thinking about how he's only grumpy because he's tired, that he's only tired because he works so hard to put a roof over our heads—my stomach sick with the urge to call or text him an apology, to be told the thing I crave the most from every single person in the world: *I'm not upset with you.* That I am a good person.

So I try a different tactic. I slide my hand from his shoulder up to the back of his neck. "How about I sleep in that big T-shirt you like? You can wake me up when you get home."

That gets him turning my way. He grabs me by the waist and pulls me in. "Oh, yeah?" It's funny how quickly people's demeanors change when they get what they want.

I reach up on my tiptoes and give him a kiss, his whiskers rough on my face, and then Waylon is off. I hear Barney at the door barking for me already. They say dogs love you unconditionally, but I went and ruined that too, sneaking him bacon in the mornings before work. Now I'll never know if it's me he loves or what I have to offer.

There's a package at the door from Amazon marked to Hannah. She opened her own account after getting that job up at Smoothie Palace, which I wasn't a fan of. It makes me think she's being sneaky, buying things she doesn't want me knowing about. I reach down to pick it up so I can bring it inside for her, but it rattles when I lift it, and it's like someone has reached into my ribs and wrung my heart out like a dirty sponge. I squeeze the package, my hand gripping round the shape of a pill bottle.

I'm tearing the envelope just as the door swings open. Hannah steps out, looking nothing like herself, her auburn hair twisting into corkscrews that glimmer in the porch light. When she was a kid, Hannah never would sit still long enough for me to fix her hair. She always had better things to be doing, jumping on the trampoline or riding her bike down the street, so I let her, let her be wild and free.

She sees the open envelope, sees the pill bottle in my hand, and her face fills with embarrassment, but she's quick to mask it with anger. "Mom, what the fuck?"

Barney runs out, circling my feet and jumping up to scratch at my calves.

"Honey, what are these?" I ask, but I already know. I'm holding a bottle of Dry XT. Its label is fluorescent blue with metallic silver text: ALL-NATURAL DIURETIC.

This is exactly what I was afraid of. I already know what Miss Lone Star Princess can do to a group of teens. How it can turn them ugly and feral. I already know, because it happened to me.

And I won't let it happen to my little girl. Not over my dead body.

CHAPTER SEVENTEEN

CAT

That interaction with Abel Sherman today has put me on edge.

I keep twisting the locks, checking that the security system is armed, peering between the blinds by the front door. Parked at the curb just outside the model home, a white Chevy Silverado idles in the dark. It's been there twenty minutes now.

The old Cat would march right out there, knock on the window, and ask them what the hell they were doing. Instead, I take out my phone and call Sheriff Ryan.

"Everything all right, darling?" he asks.

I pause, watching the truck, wondering if I was too quick to call him. There are a million innocent reasons that truck might be there. It could be a mom driving her infant around because it's the only way she can get her to sleep. Could be teenagers making out.

"It's probably nothing," I say.

Then the Silverado's headlights come on and it begins to pull away. I watch its taillights fade off into the night.

On the phone, I can hear the sheriff's turn signal. I drop the blinds back into place and make my voice as cheery as possible. "I was just wondering if we were going to see you at the Miss Lone Star orientation tomorrow." I make my way into the living room.

"Is everything all right there at the model home?" he asks.

"Of course. Nothing stirring but the breeze."

The click-click-click of his signal stops, and I drop my shoulders down my back. When I hang up, I let out a long sigh and toss my phone onto the sofa. My pulse is still up. I need to center myself, so I push aside the coffee table in the living room and roll out my yoga mat, pull up a YouTube video and settle into child's pose. I focus on my breath.

During the worst of my addiction, I couldn't trust my senses. I was a seismograph, picking up tremors no one else could feel. Every whisper in public was about me. Every sideways glance held a hidden meaning. A man on the street looking at his phone was actually taking photos of me. The hum of the refrigerator sounded like voices. There was so much noise inside my head. I felt an incessant itch at my neck. Sometimes, I'd scratch it bloody.

Drug-induced psychosis, a doctor diagnosed once when the cops brought me to the hospital after I'd been found wandering an apartment complex, knocking on doors, trying to warn others about the man who was following me.

With sobriety, the mind snaps back. Almost. My mind is something like a Slinky stretched out just a little too far. Sure, it coils back, still looks like a Slinky—if you hold it together. AA meetings, sponsor check-ins, routines, yoga—I'm doing my best to hold it together.

I move through the vinyasa flow, from warrior one to warrior two, paying attention to the minute adjustments of my muscles when I hear a sound from outside. I keep my feet in position as I reach for the remote, pause the TV. The instructor's gentle drone stops. So does the ambient soundtrack beneath. The house is silent, and I listen.

Another sound. A voice, maybe. An animal?

I pick up my phone from the couch and return to the window. The street is empty. The trees shiver in the wind.

I can't call the sheriff again. Not with another false alarm. I'll sound paranoid. Delusional? He'll worry. He'll ask Melanie how I'm doing. He'll tell Mark to keep an eye on me. Everyone, all these people who love me, will be put on alert. And Olivia will feel it, even if no one says anything to her directly. She'll pick up on the vibrations, the collective concern, and whatever guard she dropped, she'll zip right back up, the way you zip a jacket up to your chin to keep out the cold, to protect yourself.

I grab a long cardigan from the office and slide my feet into rubber-soled slippers, unlock the door, and step out into the night. I stop where the walkway meets the sidewalk. The street is scattered with gravel and the cut-off end of a PVC pipe, litter from today's construction. Leaves rustle. A barred owl's hoot reverberates through the trees—a low, stuttering sound like an engine that won't turn over. And beneath it all, I hear the murmur of voices.

I look back to the house, the windows warm with light, and then down the road, the construction site in shadows, a still and silent backhoe-turned-silhouette, the shape of something with claws.

I check my phone. It's not even 10 PM. I shake off the silly edge of fear and start walking toward the sounds, past the single lamppost outside the model home, leaving the safety of its circle of light. Beyond it, the night opens wide, pale with moonlight and thin clouds drifting past. I pull my sweater tight. The paved road devolves into dirt, and as I get closer, I catch words disembodied from their sentences, "over here," "a long time."

But because of the open space, the nooks between clusters of trees, the way echoes bounce off limestone, and the rushing water of the river, I keep stopping, keep turning my head to determine which direction I should be going. The voices sound like they are coming from far away but also somehow just over my shoulder.

The corner lot up ahead has already been sold, and construction started on the grand house that will soon overlook The Hollow. That's where the sounds are coming from, I realize, down by the water, near the mouth of the cave. I pause, scratch absently at that irritated spot on my neck, just under my jawline, where my heartbeat pulses below my ear. The wind opens and closes the thin plastic door of the port-a-potty by the construction trailer with an uneasy clank, clank, clank.

I pick my way onto the property, past a bulldozer, a pallet of wood. The ground is soft, overturned soil mixed with chunks of stone, chewed-up clumps of grass, giving way to woods that slope down to the river.

I can hear them now more clearly as I enter the shadows, and from my vantage on the hill, I spot them through breaks in the trees. Three teenage boys in the water, their inner tubes pulled up on the bank. One, lanky with a mop of loose curls, sits on the rocky ledge, legs dangling in the water. Another, shirtless and leanly muscled, stretches out in his tube, the brim of his ball cap hiding his face. The third, husky and broad shouldered, treads water.

It's been twenty-five years since anyone floated this part of the river. Since Isabelle Whitmore vanished.

The slope down to the river is steep, and dry dirt slides over the rocky earth beneath. I grab hold of the large trunk of a cypress to catch my balance.

The boy with the curls is sitting beside a cooler in its own inner tube. He reaches over to a large speaker and starts up the music, something with thudding bass and a guy singing about hoes.

"I'm telling you, man, she's buried out here somewhere. They're going to find her," the curly-haired boy says.

"Everyone knows her boyfriend did it."

"She was cheating on him," the boy in the ballcap says. "That's what that new podcast said."

"My dad told me that. He used to be friends with Ben Sherman. And, honestly, I get it," the stocky kid in the water says.

"You get it?"

"Yeah, bro, you've seen her picture in that trophy case. She was fucking hot. If I had a piece of ass like that, and she cheated on me? I'd cut her head off."

An eruption of laughter. The kind of dark humor that feels safe in a private group chat, where the goal is to shock each other, push the line, get a reaction. That's what teenage boys do. Still, it doesn't sit well with me. I push off from the tree and march toward them.

"Fuck!"

The word cracks the air before I even register that it came from me. There is a throbbing pain in my foot, and I lift it to see a black drywall screw lodged into the thin sole of my slipper. I peel the shoe off slowly. As the screw backs out, I feel its spiraling ridges tugging at my skin. In the moonlight, I can see blood trickling down the arch of my foot. I look back to the boys, who are quiet now, staring straight at me, and I imagine how I must look to them, a figure in the trees, face drained of color, cardigan rustling in the breeze like a white robe. The ghost of Isabelle Whitmore back from the grave to make them shit their pants. I twist the screw out of my slipper, put it in the pocket of my cardigan, and place my slipper back on my foot.

I'm careful not to put too much weight on it as I continue toward them. The ground changes closer to the water, and I feel the mud begin to suck the slippers away from my feet. "Hey, y'all can't be down here," I call out over the music.

When I clear the trees, the curly-haired kid turns to ask his buddies, still in the water, "Who the fuck is that?"

"I'm the property manager," I call to them again, still making my way over. "I'm—" I hesitate. "I'm staying there." I stop and gesture back up the bank, toward the model home.

"Oh, you're Olivia's mom, right?" The boy in the ball cap replies, pulling himself onto a limestone rock in one swift motion up and out of the water.

"That's me." I give them all a little wave.

"Oh, yeah. Cool to meet you," the boy with the curls says. He sees me eyeing the beer in the cooler and shuts it.

"Listen, you boys know you shouldn't be drinking, you need to chuck that, clean all this mess up, and move along."

"What's going on?" The husky boy has migrated over to the same rock the kid in the ball cap just pulled himself onto.

Curly turns to break the bad news to him. "Party's over, Teddy. We got to bounce." Then he moves to the speaker, still in its float pulled up on the bank, and cuts off the music.

"That's some bullshit." Teddy hoists himself from the water, using a knee as leverage, his wet T-shirt suctioning to his belly. "You can't own the river, man." He turns the music back on. And then twists the volume knob all the way up, obnoxiously.

"I know there's new owners." I reach down to the speaker to kill the music myself. "But this is still private property. Someone has already purchased this lot."

"Lady, my dad paid three hundred bucks for this speaker. Hands off." Teddy bends down, cutting it right back on. He's a stubborn kid, and a sturdy one, that's for sure. Once he's gathered himself, he's a full head taller than me. He's close enough now that the water dripping off him is splashing onto the tops of my feet.

"This is one of them fancy waterproof speakers, right?" I ask. Bending over to turn it back off.

"Yeah," Teddy confirms, hitting the power button back on.

"Well then . . ." I say. Faster than Teddy can react, I grab the plastic speaker by the handle and toss it out into the middle of the river. "Better go fetch it."

Teddy spins around just in time to watch it splash and start to float away. "What the fuck, lady? Are you fucking serious?" He runs his hands through his buzzed hair, sending water misting off it.

"Listen, I don't care how big you are, none of you are old enough to be drinking." I gesture to the cooler. "Chuck the beer." I point to the roll-off dumpster up the bank in the driveway of the unfinished home.

Teddy spins around back to me. "Why? So you can go and dig it out?"

The words sting worse than the pain pulsing through my foot. I wonder if he heard that from his parents or if he heard it from Olivia.

Teddy must sense me diminish, because he leers over me now with a chuckle. "Yeah, we heard you partied quite a bit."

Then, suddenly the boy in the ball cap stops spectating and is behind his friend, slapping a hand on his shoulder. "Teddy, come on, man. It's no big deal. Let's just go. We got to grab the speaker or your dad's going to kill us." I expect Teddy to put up more of a fight, but he deflates, shoulders slumping forward.

"That's some bullshit, man," he says again, then turns away and starts to drag his tube back into the water, the music slowly fading away. The curly-headed kid follows suit, scurrying to clean up what he can as he tugs the cooler with beer and the now-empty tube that held the speaker into the water with them.

"Thanks," I say to the ball cap boy, who's standing with his hand on his hips. I breathe out a sigh of relief, unclench my fists. He smiles. He's the kind of handsome that makes a boy prom king or class president.

"No problem, ma'am," he says and turns to hop effortlessly into his tube.

I watch from the bank as they drift away. When he meets up with the group, there's more grumbling from Teddy. "We're just going to let some drunk tell us what to do?"

"Relax, Teddy, she's not just some drunk," the boy in the ball cap says, then loudly, like he wants to make sure I hear him, wants to make sure his words strike my breastbone: "She's also a cunt!"

They erupt into laughter that's amplified off the limestone wall across the river and back at me before they disappear around the bend. And I am left alone in The Hollow, foot throbbing, neck burning, emotions shredded bare and raw, surrounded by the deep, dark blackness of echoes.

CHAPTER EIGHTEEN

SARAH LYNN

Mom's in a good mood after grabbing drinks with Iggy. She's curled on the sofa, bare feet tucked under her, a glass of chardonnay on the coffee table. We're putting together the welcome bags for orientation, and she's humming Ricky Martin's "Livin' La Vida Loca" as she drops gold pens into each bag.

"That was the song for our opening number. Can you believe that?" she says.

Dad's on yet another business trip. Kayden got home a few minutes ago and went straight to the media room to play *Call of Duty* on the theater screen. The muffled sounds of a war zone come from behind the wall. But, tonight, Mom doesn't seem to mind.

"What did you think of Hannah's makeover?" I ask, taking advantage of her geniality.

She smiles, eyes on the gold ribbon she ties around the neck of a gift bag. "I like seeing you take initiative, sweetheart. That's what separates winners."

My chest loosens, just a little.

Then she says, "Olivia, though . . ." and clicks her tongue. "We'll need to stay ahead of that problem."

"She's not a problem, Mom. Really. She's sweet."

"Yeah, well." She picks up a pair of scissors from the coffee table, uses the open blade to curl the ribbon, then sets the scissors back down. "Some poisons are sweet, Sarah Lynn."

I let out a sigh that I swear is silent, but Mom misses nothing.

She catches my hand. "Look at me," she says, and I obey. "We have worked too hard for this. I'm not about to let some little girl swoop in and steal this from us. Especially the daughter of someone like Cat Dennis, for heaven's sake. Do you understand me?"

"Olivia's never been in a pageant. She literally has no idea what she's doing." I move to slip my hand from hers, but she tightens her grip. Her face is calm, serene, as she tilts her thumb and presses down. The edge of her nail sinks into my skin, a small, perfect puncture of pain. I don't move. I hold her gaze.

"Do you understand me?" she repeats.

"Yes, ma'am," I say.

She releases my hand. The mark stings—just a shallow crescent, already fading. I rub it once, then drop my hand to my lap.

We sit in silence for a heartbeat, and then a knock sounds at the door. Mom hops up to answer it, and I follow behind. Despite the late hour, she is presentable, still in the zebra-print dress she wore to the bar, hair curled and makeup in place from the luxury setting spray she buys for us.

She slips her heels back on and opens the door with a bright smile, and there's good old Sheriff Ryan on our front porch. He takes off that ten-gallon hat of his and holds it in his hands. "Kennedy Claire," he says.

"Sheriff, how nice to see you." Sheriff Ryan, aka Dudley Do-Right, makes it a point to drop by once every few weeks to have coffee with Dad, and checks in on us whenever he's out of town. I used to think Mom was a busybody, but old people are worse. They have the least amount of time left on this earth, but still somehow too much time on their hands.

"Look, Kennedy Claire, this isn't a social visit." He lets out a sigh like he won't be enjoying what he's about to say. "I'm here as a courtesy to you, and to your family. Hi, darling," he says to me. I give him my prettiest smile. Then his attention is back on Mom. "I received a call this evening from Miss Cat Dennis. She's been staying up at the model home at the new Sherman Ranch development. Apparently, Kayden and some of his friends were causing a bit of a disturbance down there at The Hollow."

"Cat Dennis said this?" Mom says, her voice flattening on the name like it leaves a bad taste in her mouth.

"Yes, ma'am. She said the boys were drinking, leaving trash, using some vulgar language. Seems Kayden got into a bit of an altercation with Cat, called her, well . . ." He trails off for a moment, looking to the side, then says it quiet. "The C-word."

Mom clasps her chest and gasps, as if someone spit in her face. "That doesn't sound like my Kayden," she says, shaking her head.

It sounds exactly like Kayden, but Mom is true ride or die, family first, and you've gotta love her for it. Love the acting.

"Besides," she says, "he's been here all night." She tips her head toward the sounds of enemy fire.

Sheriff Ryan nods. No way he buys the lie, but he has to respect it. "I'm only here to say that it might be best if the kids stay away from The Hollow, at least for now. Despite new ownership, it is still private property and an active construction site. Could be dangerous."

"Well, thank you for your concern," she says sweetly—you catch more flies with honey. "Honestly, Sheriff, what would we do without you? You sure you don't want to come in? I'm happy to set out some snacks."

"Not tonight," he says, putting the hat back on his head. "I best be on my way."

Mom shuts the door, gives the sheriff enough time to leave the porch, then she turns and makes a beeline for the media room. She swings the door open, and we are immersed in Kayden's war, the surround sound and subwoofers rat-tat-tatting, machine-gunning bullets.

"Turn that shit off."

The game is loud, but Mom's louder. Kayden jolts, whips his head around. His little commando dude on the screen gets sniped out of existence. He rolls his eyes, pushes a button on the controller to pause the game. That's not good enough. Mom marches to the screen, reaching deep into the entertainment center to pull the cords out of the back of the Xbox. The room goes dark, but there's enough light from the doorway to see her turn and face Kayden, arms crossed. Now there is just the sound of Mom rat-tat-tatting the toe of her high heel on the hardwood floor.

"Sheriff just came by."

Kayden gets up, brushing past her and into the foyer. Mom follows him, and I follow her.

"What in the hell is this business about you getting into it with Cat Dennis? That woman will be telling half the town by morning. What is *wrong* with you?"

Mom's been asking that question since he was a little boy. I'd be all dressed and ready to go, and Mom would tell him to put on his shoes, and it would be like that one instruction flipped a switch in his toddler brain, like *fuck shoes*, you know? And he'd go red-faced, refusing to breathe, kicking Mom's shins. She'd grab him by both arms, shaking him, screaming in his face: *What is wrong with you?*

I used to think her question was fair. What *was* wrong with him? Why couldn't he just behave?

But sometimes, now, when I pass the photo of Kayden at three, wearing cowboy boots and a pull-up, a grin taking up half his face, my heart cracks a little. Because he was so small. And because he *would* put on his shoes, actually, if you gave him the time to get the toe seams on his socks just right. And maybe there hadn't been anything wrong with him at all.

Back then, Kayden couldn't get attention from Mom in the ways that I could. So he found other ways. Now, they are trapped in a well-worn groove. It's like Mom says: *Motivation fades. Habits don't.*

Kayden's fists are clenched at his side. "Billy and Teddy wanted to float the river like you guys used to do back in high school. That's all. She was being a bitch."

Mom levels her eyes at him. If looks could kill, he'd be stone-cold dead.

Then, like pulling the pin from a grenade, he adds, "A bitch just like you."

Mom closes the distance between them. My money's on her merking him right where he stands. She might actually slap him.

"You haven't begun to see what kind of bitch I can be, young man."

Kayden starts climbing the steps. He's halfway to the second floor before Mom says the words she knows will stop him in his tracks.

"Your father is going to hear about this."

She's bullshitting. At least, I think she is. Mom always hides Kayden's shenanigans from Dad, because his constant screwups are a particular kind of thorn in Dad's ass. With his shitty grades and worse behavior, Kayden would already be in military school if Mom hadn't begged Dad not to send him off.

He peers over his shoulder now, down at her, calling her bluff. "Go ahead. Fucking tell him." Then he bolts up the remaining steps, and his bedroom door slams shut.

Mom heads back to the living room, downing the rest of her chardonnay in one swallow. "Calling the sheriff," she says with derision. "Can you believe that?" She moves to the kitchen, pulling champagne bottles from the wine fridge and lining them up on the counter. "She'll regret it," she mutters.

Cat just fed sweet Olivia to the wolves. I don't know what exactly my mother is planning.

But it isn't good.

CHAPTER NINETEEN

INGRID

I'm pressed against the back door of Travis's pickup, the door handle digging into the small of my back. I've learned that much about the handsome young man from the bar—his first name—and that he has a firm grip. His palm cups the back of my head, fingers intertwined in my hair so he can yank it back, tip my face. So he can take my mouth with his.

His other hand is on my skirt, fingertips digging to the bone of my hip. It's not aggression. It's restraint. Like he's afraid of what will happen if our bodies touch. The fact that he wants me this badly drives me wild. I haven't been with anyone since Joel, and it's been a long, long time since Joel wanted me like this. If he ever wanted me like this. I tilt my hips, close the distance between us. He groans against my lips. I get the sudden urge to bite him.

Instead, I reach behind me for the handle, pull open the door. We tumble inside, a confusion of limbs, of teeth bumping against lips. I tug my panties off, kick them onto the floor of his truck, and then I'm on top of him, straddling his lap. I am reaching down for the button of his jeans. He breaks the kiss, asks, between panting breaths, "You sure you want this?"

"I want this," I tell Travis, lifting my hips, sliding my hand between us to guide him. I move my hand and ease myself down slowly until he's deep inside me. Until my thighs shake. And it feels good.

Every nerve exploding with satisfaction. It feels so incredibly good to do something I want. To get what I want.

Once, Izzy and I dared Ben to guess who was who. *Kiss the real Isabelle*, she said, standing shoulder to shoulder with me. I bit the inside corners of my mouth, trying not to smile when he came up close to inspect my face, squinting at my ear, at the hair tucked behind it. He always smelled like the same cologne Izzy bought him every year on his birthday. He searched my eyes then, and suddenly my body was betraying me, abdomen fluttering, breath hitching, heart tripping over its own rhythm. When he leaned forward and pressed his mouth to mine, my lips parted slowly, like a bruise blooming. I was fifteen, and it was my first kiss. Izzy howled with laughter, shoving him in the shoulder, and we all pretended it was fine, that it was nothing but a joke, but my lips burned hot all day like I'd been stung.

CHAPTER TWENTY

KENNEDY CLAIRE

2000

"You look beautiful, darling," Aunt Birdie says, sitting on the edge of her floral-patterned bed. Kennedy Claire is wearing the thrift store dress she's altered herself to be her evening wear for Miss Lone Star Princess. Uncle Richard thinks the pageant is silly. Kennedy Claire knows it isn't. She knows it is a stepping stone. One that comes with scholarships and a walking coach who has trained multiple former Miss Texas winners and even one Miss America.

She combs through Aunt Birdie's best jewelry in a walnut box on her dresser and selects a silver bracelet. The metal is cool as water when it drapes across her wrist, and Kennedy Claire twists her forearm to reach the clasp, seeing the way those two bones—the ulna and the radius—rotate together as she does. She broke her forearm once, when she was seven, raising her arm to block a blow from her stepdad. She can't even remember now what he was angry about. Her mother kicked him out in a flurry of swear words and thrown dishes. But when he came crawling back, a pathetic slur of apologies and promises and kisses, her mother let him back in. A pattern Kennedy Claire could set her watch to.

Her arm healed fine. She has pretty arms, in fact, thin and delicate, her skin unblemished. But she knows from watching *Dateline* episodes with Aunt Birdie that an autopsy can show whether a bone was ever broken, even if it happened years and years and years before. So that even when Kennedy Claire is dead, his marks will still be there on her bones.

She gets the clasp hooked, spins the bracelet on her wrist, and examines herself in the mirror.

Behind her, Aunt Birdie's eyes well with tears. "You're perfect," she says.

And she is. She is absolutely perfect. She has done everything within her capabilities to be perfect.

But perfect won't be enough if the crown is already meant for Ingrid Whitmore. The Whitmore name. The Whitmore smile. The Whitmore mother sitting on the pageant board, the very first Miss Lone Star Princess herself. Iggy has destiny on her side.

Kennedy Claire cares about Iggy—she's her best friend.

But she doesn't care about destiny. She doesn't believe in being powerless against the whims of the universe. Because she is not powerless. Not anymore.

Once upon a time, she was. Powerless, which is just another word for weak. She doesn't think about that time often anymore—she simply won't allow it. But when she does think about that time, she hates that weak little girl she was.

Now, things are different. Now, Kennedy Claire can shape her future however she wants.

As long as she's willing to do whatever it takes.

CHAPTER TWENTY-ONE

MELANIE

Four Days Before the Pageant

"Hey, Melanie, it's so good to see you," Kennedy Claire says, hugging my neck when I first walk into the Sherman Ranch Events Hall. It's a pretty building, vaulted ceilings with exposed wood beams, a massive stone fireplace, and a whole bank of floor-to-ceiling windows. I'm sure once the development is done, the view will be gorgeous. Right now, though, we're looking out on a construction zone, the air filled with chitchat overlapping the background noise of beeps and men yelling and bulldozer blades scraping against stone. I can't imagine that Izzy Whitmore hasn't crossed the mind of every single person in this room at least once.

I hug Kennedy Claire back, giggling nervously and telling her how pretty her decorations look. The two of us don't exactly run in the same circles, but in a town as small as Anhalt, you're bound to bump into each other—at a Preston High football game, or at the Cedar Grove Café, or in the aisles of H-E-B.

The first time I ever ran into Kennedy Claire as an adult, it was at Meet the Teacher, when I was bringing Hannah up for kindergarten and she was doing the same with Sarah Lynn. She gave me a hug then too, and chattered away about their summer trip to Disney World and her plans of joining the PTA, as if we'd been old friends in high school, as if she hadn't made my life a living hell back then. And what was I supposed to do, but chatter right back? That's how it is in small towns, I suppose. Water under the bridge, and all that.

Whenever I see her now, we're friendly, waving down the bleachers at each other. But I always get that momentary puke-in-the-back-of-my-throat feeling when I first lay eyes on her, the same feeling I get anytime I smell artificial watermelon, because the first time I ever got sick drunk was on a bottle of watermelon Boone's Farm that Cat nicked from the Texaco when we were seventeen.

Kennedy Claire hands me a welcome bag and invites me to partake of the snacks table, an elaborate banquet of mini-quiches, pastries, fresh fruit, and a serve-yourself mimosa table.

"Hannah's hair looks so pretty like that," she says. "I didn't realize it was so curly."

Hannah spent the drive over here answering all my questions with grunts and one-word replies, still miffed about me opening her mail last night and confiscating those horrible diet pills. As soon as we walked through the doors, she ditched me, in search of teenage company, like a heat-seeking missile.

"She looks different, that's for sure," I say.

Then Kennedy Claire is off, moving and grooving through the room, handing out her party bags and making connections. I take a front-row seat by myself, the flimsy metal folding chair creaking beneath me, and I flip through the welcome folder, schedules, and recommended vendors. The women beside me are laughing at something I'm not privy to. They're the type who live on Kennedy Claire's side of town, who drive sleek white SUVs and fill their schedules with Pilates classes, manicures every two weeks and highlight retouches every six, and I know it's absurd, but that old feeling that they are laughing about me creeps its way into my mind.

I scan through the prize list.

A fourteen-karat gold crown, custom boots, one year of unlimited spray tans, photo shoot stylings, high-end hair care products.

It all seems nice and fine. Until I see the last one: $3,000 in services from AURA, with their sleek logo stamped at the bottom, listed as the head sponsor of the pageant.

I look it up on my phone. AURA is an acronym for Aesthetic Unification & Rejuvenation Associates, a sly, clinical-sounding veil for what it really is: a boutique plastic surgery clinic.

I imagine Hannah lying back on the crackling paper cover of some quack doctor's exam table. Him injecting her face with all sorts of foreign substances, and her smiling big and bright as he does it, thinking she's about to leave that place somehow prettier than the good God already made her.

I look up to find her. The girls are all gathered by the display table, admiring the Lone Star Princess crown and flipping through albums of past contestants and winners.

Sarah Lynn is touching Hannah's shoulder, leaning in to whisper something. I know how mean girls can be, how they can be like sugar syrup to your face then call you vile things behind your back. How they compliment your sweater while all the other girls snigger and you're left wondering how, exactly, you ended up the butt of the joke.

Hannah looks down at her dress, like Sarah Lynn did in fact comment on it. I see two other girls slide eyes over to look at my daughter.

I feel the urge to spring to my feet and check up on Hannah, to claw at the girls picking at her. Someone like Kennedy Claire could. Cat would. But I don't.

CHAPTER TWENTY-TWO

CAT

I had planned to arrive at the orientation early. I knew it would be rough for Melanie, that she'd need me by her side, but Olivia is in full meltdown mode this morning. She flew into the model home, rambling a mile a minute, high-pitched and on the verge of tears. Something about Sarah Lynn's dress and a dumb dry cleaner. When I asked for details, trying to wrap my head around the drama, she snapped at me, the way an injured dog will bite your hand if you try to help. Every item of clothing she brought over to my place to try on has been strewn across the floor, like a tornado tore through the pink little-girl-decorated bedroom of the model home. She hates her clothes, her hair. She's in one of those moods. We've all been there before.

When she was teeny tiny, she'd sometimes wake in the middle of the night, screaming with growing pains. She'd saw her legs together like a cricket, moan, even break a sweat. Back then, it was only me she wanted. *Mama*, she'd cry, *Mama*. I would have to sit beside her toddler bed and rub her legs, stroke the meaty part of my thumb up and down her calves, whisper soothing words, and kiss her hot, wet forehead until she fell back asleep.

I hadn't seen the beauty of those moments. The moments of being needed.

I'd only been eager to escape, the minutes ticking by like hours. I'd wanted to get back to my drink. To my margarita if Mark and I were hosting one of our regular neighborhood barbecues. Back to my wine if it was just a quiet night in.

When I first met Mark, it was like someone had dimmed the volume in a room with too many sounds blaring all at once. He just had this way of making my mind feel a quiet peace. He made me want to be the person he saw in me.

A backyard wedding out on Sheriff Ryan's land with twinkly lights in mason jars on the table and a speech from Mark's brother that had everyone wiping their eyes with their napkins. Mark and I buying our first house, one of those boxy '60s homes branching off from Main Street. We painted the outside and fixed the sagging porch. We planted Knock Out roses along the front chain-link fence. Melanie and I pressing our pregnant bellies together for a family picture in front of the Christmas tree.

Then, Olivia was born. During those few days we spent in the hospital, Mark and I laughed so much and so hard that I had to keep pressing a pillow to my C-section scar. We were delirious, drunk on the endorphins of becoming parents, of looking at the wonder that was Olivia. And when he held her, I thought my heart would break in two.

It was more than I deserved. And that voice inside my head said: *You can't keep being this person forever.*

Because I knew I was going to let them down, eventually. Knew I couldn't resist the urge to shut off, to numb, to forget about all the mistakes I'd ever made. I just needed that silence sometimes.

At first, it was just a few drinks at night, then just a few nights out with friends, then just a few pills.

Olivia was four when Mark kicked me out after finding me passed out on the patio chair in the backyard, Olivia unattended in the plastic kiddie pool. I'm pretty sure Mark was semibluffing, hoping it would be my wake-up call, the rock bottom that would bring me back to him, to them.

It took him two more years to file for divorce.

Addiction is a self-fulfilling prophecy. You convince yourself that you are the worst version of you. And then you act like it.

Now, Olivia is seventeen. She doesn't cry for Mama in the night anymore. I broke her of that habit a long time ago.

She sits on the floor in the middle of her abandoned clothes, pouting. I sit down behind her. I don't say a word. Instead, I reach gently for the end of her hair, limp and dark blond. She lets me rake my fingers through it, then a brush, closing her eyes as I comb from root to end, careful not to snag her ears. I give her a French braid, then twist it into an updo, like my mom used to do sometimes for school picture day. She looks in the mirror over the little white vanity, and she smiles. Together we pick out one of the outfits. She lets me do her eyeliner.

"Thanks, Mom," she says to the reflection of me over her shoulder in the mirror, and it's like there's a shift in the meaning of the word for her—*Mom*—like maybe I am someone who can have her back.

Because that's what finally got me sober, in the end, not a rock bottom, but a realization. That Olivia would be eighteen soon. That this was my last chance to get to know her as a child.

So I went back to AA, and, this time, I chose to believe that I could be the person I wanted to be, that I could be more than my mistakes.

* * *

When we finally arrive at orientation, we're the last ones here. Olivia bounds off to meet up with Hannah, who stands in a cluster of girls. I watch from across the room for a moment. One of the girls has complimented her hair, I can tell, because she touches the braid gently, and she dips her head to hide her shy smile. Her eyes find mine.

I scan the women by the refreshments table and spot Kennedy Claire, her back to me, her blond hair sculpted into newscaster curls.

She's talking to a few women with mimosas and plates of pastries when I approach her, tap her on the shoulder.

"Oh, Cat," she says, turning to me. She looks to the clipboard in her arms and checks something off her list. "Now we can get started."

"I'm excited to meet up with everyone else on the volunteer committee. If you don't mind pointing some of them out?"

Kennedy Claire scrunches her nose. "Oh, honey, you know I talked to some of the ladies, and I don't think they're going to have much use for you. They've got everything covered. But they did appreciate the offer."

I'm a little taken aback. "Are you sure?" Yesterday, she was chomping at the bit to have an extra set of hands.

Kennedy Claire rests the clipboard on her chest and looks down her nose at me. "Oh, and Cat, next time you have a problem with one of my children, I'd appreciate if you'd just call me. You have my number. I mean, really," she laughs in a way that sends prickles down my scalp, because I don't know what she's talking about. "There's no reason to call the sheriff."

"The sheriff?" I say, but then I realize, blood draining from my face so fast it makes me queasy. The ball cap boy from last night, the one who called me a cunt. "Oh my gosh, I didn't realize he was your son." I put a hand to her elbow. "Otherwise, of course, I would have called you. It's just dangerous. That's all. With all this construction going on, they really shouldn't be out there drinking."

"My Kayden wasn't drinking," she says.

I let out a puff of a laugh, but her face is a steely mask. She looks down at my hand on her elbow, like I've just wiped ketchup on her white dress, and she slides her arm away.

"If you'll excuse me." She turns and walks toward the front of the room. Conversations begin to die down and everyone finds a seat. Melanie is half standing, waving me over to the chair she's saved for me in the front row, and I slink over, like a dog with her tail between her legs.

And all the glimmering potential of this morning has drained from me, and I feel heavy as a wet bag of sand as I drop into the seat beside Melanie.

Because—for Olivia's sake—the last person I wanted to make an enemy of right now was Kennedy Claire Preston.

CHAPTER TWENTY-THREE

INGRID

I'm snapping candid photos of the Miss Lone Star Princess orientation, just like Kennedy Claire wanted. A mother tucking her daughter's hair behind her ear as they wait to talk to one of the judges. Two contestants laughing beside the juice bar. Sheriff Ryan kissing his granddaughter on the cheek.

When I first arrived, I chatted with Melanie, her welcome folder tucked under one arm. Mom's doctors say she's doing well—her weight is up, her incisions are healing—and Melanie promised to walk me through the post-op care tomorrow, to make sure I can handle what comes next.

But for now, I'm behind my camera. Someone in this room sent me that invitation. That's what I keep thinking as I focus each face in my lens. It would make the most sense. Sheriff Ryan interviewed all our friends back then. Everyone but Ben, of course, who refused to speak to police, who lawyered up and then left town.

Had they seen Izzy that day? When had they spoken to her last? Did they know where she might go if she was in trouble? Did they know of anyone who would want to hurt her?

But teenagers lie.

Someone knows something now that they didn't tell the sheriff back then.

Sheriff Ryan interviewed me as well, in our living room, as I sat beside my mother, mugs of tea growing cold on the coffee table. I had never once before seen my mother make hot tea. She brewed sweet tea constantly, always kept a pitcher chilled in the fridge, but she didn't make cups of steaming chamomile. The scent was floral and unfamiliar. I imagined her digging to the back of the pantry to find a forgotten box, dusty and stale. She was on autopilot, and this was what a person did, it seemed, when one daughter was missing and the other was being interviewed by police. To this day, I can't stand chamomile.

Sheriff Ryan didn't bring a notepad or a pen. He didn't take me down to the station or sit formally across from me at our dining room table. He hung his hat by the door then sat on the sofa, in the same spot where he always sat when he came over to watch football with Dad.

Now, Ingrid, sweetheart, can you tell me anything at all about the last time you saw your sister?

Izzy had left the house that afternoon to study at the library for her calculus exam, and then she was supposed to meet Ben for a date. Dinner up on the square.

She was planning to break up with him, I told the sheriff. We were weeks from graduation, about to leave for Texas Tech to share a dorm six hours away. She wanted a clean start. Didn't want to drag a long-distance relationship behind her, didn't want to be tied to who she'd been for all of high school. Plus, and only I knew this, she had a crush on the upperclassman at Tech who had given us our tour, and she had been exchanging emails with him all semester.

She'd been talking about breaking up with Ben for months but dragging her feet. *I don't want to hurt him,* she told me.

And Ben would be hurt. We both knew that. In his mind, they'd get married. They'd build a house on the Sherman land. They'd stay in this town forever. And even though Izzy loved him too, she didn't want that.

In the end, that's the motive everyone gave him. That's the version they believed. The one I eventually believed too: that Izzy broke his heart that night. And Ben killed her for it.

My eyes keep wandering to the windows to watch the excavation. Sherman Ranch is almost eight hundred acres. So much space to hide something you don't want found.

Three men in hard hats stare down into a freshly dug pit, and I hold my breath. I picture a rib cage packed with dirt. Not scattered bones, but neat, the way a chest would fall apart if left long enough. Soft tissue breaking down—skin, fat, muscle, organs—until nothing is left but bone. Soil settling into the hollows.

One of the men waves an arm at the driver, and the digging continues.

Everyone takes their seats, and Kennedy Claire begins her presentation at the front of the room. She is upselling the various vendors, making her spiel complete with a PowerPoint projected onto a portable screen.

"Of course," she says, "contestants are welcome to do their own hair and makeup, but for an additional fee, you can be pampered by the best."

There is a round of subdued applause after every slide. Some girls turn to their mothers, eager for the royal treatment.

"And, to help our young ladies shine onstage, I'm delighted to welcome Preston High's communications teacher, Mr. Magnuson, who specializes in public speaking and presentation. If you check your folders, he was kind enough to include his phone number. Feel free to reach out with any questions you might have about interview prep and stage presence."

This Mr. Magnuson must be the stuff of high school crushes, because a ripple of excitement runs through the girls. They bend toward each other with whispers and giggles. I'm quick to catch the subtle blushes with my camera, the girl who grabs her friend's arm and bites her bottom lip to hold back her grin. I turn to follow all their eyes as he walks onto the stage.

He is smiling politely, waving to his students, eyes scanning quickly over the crowd, but when his eyes finally find me and lock onto mine, I can feel every place where Mr. Magnuson touched me last night light up like pinpoints on a map.

CHAPTER TWENTY-FOUR

SARAH LYNN

We're all sitting beside our mothers in neat rows, listening to Mr. Magnuson run through the numbers and walking patterns we'll need to practice.

"And let's remember, we're all here to support each other, ladies. But don't worry. I won't make you do any trust falls . . . unless you want me to." He winks, and the girls giggle like he's up there doing a Netflix stand-up special. Even the moms lean forward, hanging on every word, and I can't help noticing the dimple that flashes in one cheek when he smiles. Mr. Magnuson is so stupid good-looking that he could read a car manual up there and get the same reaction.

Thirst Trap Travis. That's what the girls call him at school. We even made a game out of it, taking turns flirting with him, seeing who can make him stammer or drop his textbook. Hannah, with her crass mouth and inability to keep a thought inside her head, is leading by two.

Mom takes the mic from him and says, "All right, ladies, come on up. Let's introduce ourselves."

We line up along the stage edge, heels clicking against the wood floor. I slip into a perfect T-stance, smile pointed right at Mrs. Mackey, dead center of the judges in the front row, because everyone knows she's got the most sway. This little round-robin introduction is anything but casual. In a pageant, everything is a move on the chessboard. And this is our first real opportunity to size up the field.

Girls on either side of me tug at hems and smooth their hair. Sabrina Doyle is across the stage, fussing with her curls. I can practically *feel* Mom's eyes on me, even without looking—like a hand on my shoulder, reminding me what needs to be done. Sabrina is one of her red-dot-level concerns, and Mom wants her rattled.

Sabrina and I run in the same circle—cheer squad, homecoming court. I get along with her fine, but she has a tendency to be, well, a bitch. Earlier, while we were all chatting by the table, she sidled up beside Hannah. *You haven't bought your evening gown yet?* she asked. *Oh my gosh, you have to go to Z Couture in Austin.* Then, all sugary sweet: *Don't worry, it's very size-inclusive.*

Hannah didn't miss a beat. *That must be a relief for you*, she said.

I bet Sabrina's still processing that joke.

I catch her eye, smile, and tap my top teeth, like she's got something stuck there. She doesn't, but she doesn't have time to realize it before her name's called. She walks up smiling with her mouth closed, hand half covering her face as she answers the judges. Serves her right, and Mom has the smallest of smiles on her face.

When it's her turn, Hannah manages to get her name out, but freezes up trying to come up with a "fun fact" about herself, and she just shoves the mic back into the stand and rejoins me in line.

Olivia is next, and I shoot her an encouraging smile. She looks pretty today, despite the whole dry cleaner fiasco, in a soft-yellow sundress and a braided updo, but I brace myself for the awkward stumble of someone as shy and quiet as her.

Then she walks across the stage. No. Scratch that. She glides, as though across ice, chin level, shoulders back. She meets the judges' eyes and in the clearest voice I've ever heard from her, she says, "My name is Olivia Blake, and I've studied ballet at Encore Dance Studio since I was three years old. I also volunteer in my free time as a dance instructor for the younger students, and enjoy helping them find confidence onstage."

Mrs. Mackey looks absolutely smitten, like someone just set

down her favorite peach cobbler. She scribbles something down in her notebook, and my stomach knots.

I slide my eyes over to Mom. Her smile is flawless, but I know that vein in her temple, know that beneath that smile, her jaw is clenched tight.

"Where did that come from?" I whisper to Hannah.

"Oh, I know. She's like a completely different person when she's onstage. She's always been that way."

I nod, but my ribs knit in tight, and I can barely breathe. Because Olivia just proved Mom right, proved she's exactly the threat Mom saw from the start.

And Mom never lets a threat go unanswered.

The line of girls keeps moving. I charm the judges, of course—I could do a pageant introduction in my sleep—but Olivia's perfect delivery echoes in my head like a church bell.

When the introductions wrap up, Mom takes the mic back like a queen reclaiming her throne. "A big round of applause for our girls," she says, and polite claps echo across the room. "And thank you to all our wonderful mothers. You're the real foundation of this program. These girls learn poise, generosity, and self-control from watching you. I look around this room and see so many daughters taking after their mothers." The moms are eating it up, puffing up with self-indulgent pride, just like Mom wants. She gestures toward the spread of pastries off to the side of the room. "While your daughters practice the opening number with Mr. Magnuson, please help yourselves to the refreshments."

Everyone is just beginning to shift in their seats, gathering their purses and welcome bags, exchanging soft words with their neighbors, when Mom adds, "Oh," into the mic, like she's just remembered something, and everyone's attention snaps straight back to her.

Mom has this thing planned down to the second. She doesn't just suddenly remember a thing. Her hand drifts over the microphone, but when she speaks, we can all still hear her clearly. "Cat, there are mimosas over there. I didn't even think about you, I'm sorry. Is that going to be too much of a temptation for you?" Her brow is knit with just the perfect amount of empathetic worry. Mom weaponizes concern like a pro.

Cat goes stone-still. The atmosphere in the room is suddenly thick as soup. Women perk up to get a look at Cat, including Mrs. Mackey, pen still poised over her notebook. Everyone knows that, as head of First Baptist Church's Women's Missionary Union, Mrs. Mackey is a staunch teetotaler—the kind of woman who'd side-eye communion wine. A fellow judge leans over and whispers something in Mrs. Mackey's ear. Then they both turn to Olivia, who has gone so red, her ears look hot to the touch.

Mom waits for a response, eyebrows still raised with that sweet concern. She has Cat pinned down, because what can she say? Yes or no, the answer is the same. She's a drunk.

But then she's saved from answering at all, because the heavy glass doors clang open, and everyone turns.

From the stage, I can see the whole Events Hall, polished wood floor, gold balloon arches, sequined tablecloths, women in silk blouses and pearls, their perfumes competing in the air.

So when Abel Sherman shuffles in, wilted ball cap low, dirty hunting jacket swallowing his decrepit frame, an almost-empty whiskey bottle dangling from one hand, he looks like an actor who has stumbled onto the wrong set.

Whispers ripple uneasily, like a breeze stirring the hairs on the backs of our necks.

"Can we help you?" Mom says.

Abel Sherman stops at the end of the center aisle. "Y'all should be ashamed of y'allselves," he says, flat and low. Then he holds out the whiskey bottle, pointing a finger off it and scanning it through the crowd. "Every last fucking one of you."

Sheriff Ryan, who's been posted up by the snacks table, eating up all the Danish, seems hit with a sudden sugar rush, hurrying forward to stand at the other end of the aisle. "Abel," he says, "You don't need to be here."

"This is my land. This is my family's land. *You* shouldn't be here." He jabs that finger directly at the sheriff like it's a knife. "None of y'all should be here." He swings his arm wildly, baptizing those close by in whiskey. "You thieving sons of bitches."

He lifts the whiskey bottle to finish the last of it. When he does, his jacket rises just enough to reveal the handle of a gun. The room stops breathing.

CHAPTER TWENTY-FIVE

CAT

When I see the gun, my heart stops.

Someone gasps. The women around me stiffen, a subtle tightening that ripples down the row.

"Abel," the sheriff says. He's got one hand out, like he's trying to calm a spooked horse, but his other hand lowers to hover just above the revolver at his hip. "Don't do something stupid."

My eyes fly to the stage, to Olivia, just a few feet away, but it feels like miles in this moment. I see the pulse at her neck, see the heartbreaking vulnerability of her.

Then, suddenly, Melanie rises to her feet beside me. "Stop it!" She is using *the* mom voice, the one that shuts up sibling arguments, stops children from doing foolish things, fills you with shame and the fear of retribution.

With her purse tucked tight under her arm, she strides to the center aisle, bumping chairs and brushing past knees.

"Melanie, get back," Sheriff Ryan warns.

But she doesn't flinch. Her fists are clenched, mouth set in a determined line, as she marches straight toward Abel. I've never seen her like this, taking charge without hesitation, without apology.

"Just go, Abel," she says, shooing him out like he's nothing but a nuisance.

He works his jaw, considering, bleary eyes sweeping over the room. But he lets her turn him and steer him out. "Fuck you, Sheriff," he mutters over his shoulder, a last parting shot before Melanie shoves him out.

The door clunks closed behind him.

Melanie turns back toward us, shoulders straight, eyes hard.

"That was reckless, Melanie," the sheriff says, as he pushes past her to follow Abel. "You could have gotten yourself shot."

At first, no one moves. A stunned, uneasy silence lingers. Then Iggy steps forward. "Melanie, that was amazing."

Color rises in Melanie's cheeks. She ducks her head as other mothers start to stand, murmuring gratitude, admiration. Relief blooms through the room, shaking loose with nervous, grateful energy.

But I don't join them.

I'm still staring at the door.

Because I know the truth about Abel Sherman. Know that he is a man with something to protect, and nothing to lose.

And I don't think he's giving up that easy.

CHAPTER TWENTY-SIX

INGRID

The air still thrums with leftover nerves, but Kennedy Claire doesn't miss a beat, clapping her hands, corralling the mothers with her usual pageant-director smile. She reminds them of ticket deadlines, of Thursday's stage setup and Friday's final rehearsal, of all the little details that make the pageant run, as if order can be rebuilt by sheer force of will. As I watch Kennedy Claire beam and flutter, her little jab at Cat still weighs on me. Those two never got along in high school. But calling her out like that in front of her daughter, when Cat is clearly sober and trying to get her life together? That was a low blow, even for Kennedy Claire.

One by one, people gather their things, drifting toward the doors. By the time I step outside, the parking lot is a shimmer of sunlight and movement—car doors slamming, engines coughing awake, teenagers spilling across the asphalt in bursts of chatter.

I spot Travis Magnuson, leaning against his truck, a little island in the sea of teenage girls who've swarmed him. They're all talking at once, asking about stage presence, public speaking tricks, anything that buys them a few extra minutes of his attention. Their laughter follows them as they peel away in twos and threes, still whispering and giggling about him.

When the last of them drifts off, he's left alone next to his truck, jangling his keys. I sidle up, my eyes darting to make sure no one is watching.

"So, *Thirst Trap Travis*, I hear? Nice to meet you. I'm Ingrid."

He smiles slyly. "Mr. Magnuson, actually."

"About last night . . ." I drop my voice, the humor sliding out of it. "I have some complicated things going on. I'd appreciate it if you kept things quiet."

He lifts his hands, like it's none of his business. "Can I get your number?"

I can't help a laugh escaping. I cross my arms and squint at him. The charming ease of his smile tells me he hasn't heard the word *no* many times in his life. "How old are you?"

"Twenty-seven," he says.

"I'm not twenty-seven," I deadpan.

He leans casually against the truck. "Do women your age still eat dinner?" He hands me his phone.

I sigh and lean up against the truck beside him, take the phone and type my number in, against my better judgment. The thing is, when I was in my twenties, I would have run from a man like Travis, would have smelled the heartache coming from a thousand miles away. I chose stability, practicality. If I didn't take risks, I couldn't get hurt. I gave up my dream of being a photographer and opted for an office job with good insurance. I dated Joel because he was solid. He was dependable.

Until he wasn't.

"I'm not saying yes," I say, but a smile still twists my mouth as I hand the phone back to him.

For a moment, we stay there, leaning together and looking out over the Amenity Center parking lot, the construction site, the rolling hills in the distance, and the river.

The sheriff's cruiser is still parked in the lot, and I can see Abel in the back seat, head hung low. The scene inside had been chaotic, but the thing that had shocked me most was Abel himself. Like a man scooped out, replaced with something haunted.

I can't help thinking of him as he used to be. A second father. Or, at least, a grumpy, well-loved uncle. He'd complain nonstop about the kids floating the river and leaving trash along the bank, but he was the one who stocked the inner tubes, driving downriver to collect the strays and hauling them back up to the entrance. He let us ride in his truck, Izzy and me trading off who got the prized spot on the bench seat beside him.

He was the man who tossed us Dr Peppers after long swims, who brought us faded towels, who taught us how to gut a fish, guiding our hands so the knife didn't slip. The man who taped a Polaroid of the three of us to his fridge, Izzy in the middle, smiling like she owned the sun.

I push myself off the truck. "See you around, Mr. Magnuson."

He chuckles, and I head to my own car. Travis has already driven away, and I'm just cranking my engine when I see the rusty pickup pulling up the road. It parks alongside the sheriff's. A knot rises in my throat. My palms are slick with sweat. I know I should leave, but I can't help watching.

The driver's door swings open, and Ben Sherman steps out.

For a second, something in my chest misfires.

I've spent twenty-five years believing that Ben killed my sister. And that belief became the foundation of everything else.

Then that invitation arrived—BEN DIDN'T KILL IZZY—and it is like the ground under my feet has turned to quicksand.

My hands tighten on the wheel as I watch him talk with Sheriff Ryan. The sheriff opens the cruiser door, and Ben helps his father out of the back seat. He holds Abel's elbow with a tenderness that hits me like a punch. A version of Ben I thought I'd buried flickers back to life—the gentle one, the loyal one, the boy who combed the tangles from his sister's hair, who caught me round the waist on the slick river stones before I could fall.

And I hate it. Hate the confusing, chaotic tilt-a-whirl of it all.

When Ben looks over in my direction, something in me breaks.

I floor it, and I don't look back.

CHAPTER TWENTY-SEVEN

MELANIE

It's only Dad, Hannah, and me left in the Amenity Center parking lot, after I got roped in to help Kennedy Claire do all the cleanup from orientation. I don't mind though. I like feeling helpful.

"I shouldn't have gotten between you two," I say to Dad as I stand outside my car. Hannah's already in the passenger seat, air conditioner blowing, two thumbs on her phone.

"No, Mel," he says and sighs. "I'm sorry I snapped. I was just worried, is all. What you did was brave. It was the right thing to do."

When I was little, Daddy used to always tell me that being brave was just doing the hard, right thing. The way he sees it, you do the right thing, no matter what.

He stoops to pick up a stray bottle cap and shakes his head. Under his breath, he mumbles, "Abel's a damn idiot," before tucking the trash into his pocket.

But I know he's not picturing Abel from the orientation today. He's picturing Abel from when they used to meet for coffee every Friday. Thinking of the man who had been his friend. That's why he can't respect Abel, can't forgive him. Because Abel chose to protect his son instead of letting justice run its course. Because he didn't do the hard, right thing.

* * *

In high school, I was a tech theater kid, and we were in charge of the sets and lights for the Miss Lone Star Princess pageant.

By then we were seniors, and Kennedy Claire and Iggy had mostly left me alone. So when we were all together in the auditorium, me painting a backdrop and them pacing the stage for practice, they largely ignored me, as if I were nothing more than furniture.

But then one afternoon, after they'd finished practicing, we found ourselves walking out to the parking lot at the same time—just me, Iggy, and Kennedy Claire.

Us and some of the girls are gonna float the river, Kennedy Claire said. *Want to come?*

Me?

She exchanged a look with Iggy, who climbed into the passenger seat of Kennedy Claire's Jeep. *Yes, you. Who else am I talking to?*

They didn't snicker, like it was all some joke. Iggy didn't make a remark about how I might look in a swimsuit, how I might sink the inner tube.

So I said yes. After going home to change, they picked me up in the Jeep. The top and doors were off, all three of us singing Britney Spears at the top of our voices, wind whipping our hair, and I felt happy, soft around the edges like a sun-drenched photo. And that feeling stayed all the way down the river, the warmth of the air, the heat on the backs of my eyelids, the gentle sway of the water, the light conversation.

When we got to The Hollow, we pulled the inner tubes onto the bank. Kennedy Claire stood on the rock ledge and untied the knots of her bikini top and tossed it aside. Then she wiggled out of her bottoms. I couldn't help noticing her body, so unlike mine, the long legs, the slim waist and the way it folded rather than rolled as she pulled the bottoms down to her feet.

She caught me looking and winked, then leapt into the well with a splash. *Come on, girls. It's tradition.*

In Anhalt, for as long as anyone could remember, kids skinny-dipped in The Hollow, at least once, before graduation. A rite of passage.

Iggy didn't hesitate. She stripped off her bathing suit and jumped in to join Kennedy Claire. And the other girls followed, one by one like a group of penguins jumping into the Arctic, until I was left standing alone.

Come on, Mel, they said. Not Melanie. Not Melon-ball. But Mel. What my friends called me.

I don't know. I hadn't even been brave enough to take off my oversized T-shirt.

We won't look, Kennedy Claire said, spinning in the water. *When else will you get the chance?* she called out, facing away.

Iggy and the other girls turned around as well.

With their backs to me, I took off my clothes in a hurry, sat down, and lowered myself into the water.

You actually did it, Kennedy Claire said, and she sounded kind of impressed, and that happiness bloomed brighter. The water in The Hollow was clear and cool and delicious. As I flapped my arms, kicked my legs to stay afloat, the bubbles tickled up every inch of me. I was weightless. We started taking turns swimming deep down into the well. The first time, I dove under just enough to wet my hair. I don't know why, but I felt sexy for the first time in my life. All of us giggling, the shifting water barely hiding our breasts. As if, somehow, the water itself connected us, our nakedness, and I could borrow some of their beauty. The girls pushed me to go down farther, and I did, letting the silence envelop me, feeling the cold increasing as I slipped away from the sun. I stayed as long as I could, until my ears popped, until I could feel the pulse behind my eyes.

When I burst back up, gasping, everyone was gone.

I spun, disoriented. The ledge was empty. No tubes or bikinis.

On the river, the girls floated off, laughing, some still tugging on their bathing suits. Iggy held up the rope to my tube, dragging it along. In her other hand, high up above her head, she held my dripping clothes like a prize.

All that warm, honeyed happiness drained out of me in an instant, leaving my body raw and cold.

Come on, guys, I called, arms crossing over my chest as I treaded water. My voice cracked into a whimper.

They just laughed harder, paddled faster, putting more distance between us as they floated away.

Please. The word shrank with each repetition, smaller and smaller. *Please, please, please.*

Until they were gone. And I was alone.

* * *

Now I give Dad a squeeze and climb into the driver's seat, and Hannah and I weave our way through the winding roads of Sherman Ranch along the river. Hannah is still immersed in her phone when we come upon the bend, when the river widens into The Hollow, the limestone ledges bleached by sun. The well, an unblinking eye of sapphire blue. I flex my fingers on the wheel, swallow back that feeling of bile rising up my esophagus.

Hannah looks up from her phone. "Everyone is talking about how badass you are, Mom," she says, and I can hear the pride in her voice. "I mean, where did that even come from?"

I have never been a brave person. But I look at Hannah now, at her new shiny, soft curls, at the makeup she's used to cover the freckles that normally scatter her cheeks. Babies aren't born with freckles, you know? I watched each appear on her face, the way you watch the stars appear in a sky sliding from dusk to evening.

Dad says being brave is doing the hard, right thing.

But I know, with absolute clarity, that I would do anything—even the wrong thing—if it meant protecting my daughter.

CHAPTER TWENTY-EIGHT

CAT

I wanted to give Kennedy Claire the benefit of the doubt. After all, I know, better than most, that people can change. But she hasn't. If anything, she's gotten sharper. She didn't pull that little stunt at orientation just to humiliate me. I saw the way she looked at Olivia. She feels threatened by my daughter.

I pull up to Mark's house, a pretty two-story with white siding and blue shutters. Red Knock Out roses grow by the porch. Olivia hops out of the car and I follow her up to the front door. It opens before she even reaches for the knob, and Emily pulls Olivia into a hug. "Oh my goodness. I heard what happened at the orientation. Are you okay?" She leans back to look at her.

Olivia laughs lightly. "I'm okay."

Emily kisses my daughter on the forehead. "Want me to call Smoothie Palace, tell them you can't come in today? They'll understand."

"I'm fine. I promise. I'm gonna go change." Then she turns back to me. "See you tomorrow, Mom."

"Wouldn't miss it," I say, and I watch her disappear into the house.

Emily leans against the doorframe, arms crossed. She's wearing yoga pants and a Cypress Creek Elementary T-shirt. Her shoulder-length auburn hair is clipped back. "You doing all right, Cat?"

"Doing great," I say. It's a loaded question. When Emily asks me if I'm doing all right, what she really means to say is, *Are you staying on the wagon this time?*

Emily has never liked me, never trusted me. To be honest, she has every right to hate me. The night Mark and Emily got married, I called him, drunk, of course, and high on whatever I could find at the time, to tell him that I still loved him, that I hoped he could be happy without me. Then I hung up and refused to answer for weeks, knowing he'd be worried sick. Eventually, Mark had to hire a private eye just to track me down, to make sure I was still alive.

I think of that night sometimes now, and I wonder if Emily was still wearing her white dress while Mark tried his best to talk me off the ledge.

I've apologized to her, for that and the countless other times I was a piece of shit. *I just hope you can keep it together this time. For Olivia's sake*, was all she said in response.

Mark comes up behind her now, puts his arm around her. "I heard about Abel. Came into the orientation waving a gun?"

"He wasn't waving it," I say.

"Well, what do you expect? He's a drunk." Emily burns eyes into me when she says it.

"Want to come in?" Mark says. "I can put on a pot of coffee."

Emily glances up at him, and I can tell she isn't too happy with his offer.

"I better get back," I say.

On the drive back to the model home, I think about the ninth step in recovery: *make direct amends*. With the caveat, of course, *wherever possible*. Because some damage can't be undone.

I'm still turning that over in my mind when I spot the truck in my rearview mirror. A white Chevy Silverado. Just like the one parked outside last night.

I wonder how long it's been following me.

CHAPTER TWENTY-NINE

INGRID

When Izzy and I were little, Dad used to pop a Jim Croce cassette tape in and start singing along, loud and out of key, which meant it was time for us to crawl into his lap on the rocking chair. By the third or fourth song, we'd pretend to fall asleep, so that he'd carry us up the stairs to bed together, one of us in each arm. Mom followed close behind, always afraid he'd drop us. They'd tuck us in, and we'd wait a full minute or two before crawling back out to play Barbies.

Dad told me later that they were never fooled, that they could hear our giggles from under the door, that they would stand together and listen, muffling their own childish laughter. *Kids let you see the world new again*, he said. And in the dark, Izzy and I would strip down the dolls, dress them back up, lost in our own little world.

Pageants were just more of that, a way to play together into our teenage years.

Dad is outside now, working in the yard. The drone of the lawn mower buzzes all the way upstairs and over the surface of my skin.

I drag the heavy rolling chair from the office, its wheels thumping and shuddering across the floorboards. Balancing in the center of the seat, I stand carefully so it doesn't roll out from under me, then reach for the string dangling from the ceiling. The hinges creak, and the attic door yawns open.

When I climb up the thin wooden rungs of the ladder, I'm met by a wall of stagnant heat. Stooped beneath the low ceiling, I navigate through Christmas decorations and the cotton-candy glass of insulation. It doesn't take me long to find the cardboard boxes, Dad's neat labeling and humor still legible on them—PAGEANT STUFF, PAGEANT STUFF MOM WON'T THROW OUT, DEAR GOD MORE PAGEANT STUFF.

I kneel on the splintery, unfinished plywood floor.

A trickle of hot sweat rolls down my forehead and I wipe it away with my forearm, as the storm of questions churns up inside me. I open the first box and begin shuffling through time—ivory sashes, high heels, and tins of photos.

The photos are ones I took. The first time I'd tried developing my own film, Izzy was with me, holding my hand in the dark, as we watched an image appear, seemingly from nowhere and nothing, onto a blank sheet of paper. Izzy's fingers between mine, her body leaned in, her breath on my ear, tickling the tendrils of hair at the nape of my neck as she whispered, *Do you see it, Iggy? Do you see?*

But I don't even know what I'm looking for, digging down through memories, through the days surrounding Izzy's disappearance, hoping to find something, to remember anything that matters.

I flip the pictures, one after the other. Izzy with her arms around her friends in the cafeteria, her long hair pulled back with that blue scarf she always wore. Izzy at a pasture party, sitting on Ben's lap, both their smiling faces vivid in the bonfire's glow. Kennedy Claire in Mom's bedroom, trying on her sash and crown.

All those podcasts that cover Izzy's story focus on the "beauty queen" angle, but the truth is Izzy wasn't even a contestant in Miss Lone Star the year she went missing. She had backed out, her schedule already full with track meets and honors classes, and she was stressed about college in the fall, stressed about Ben.

It's our last chance to do it together, I'd whined.

It'll make it easier for you to win, she said. *With both of us there, I'll just split the votes.* She had a point. It had happened to us before.

But, as Mom's only daughter in the competition, exactly twenty-five years after she won the very first Miss Lone Star Princess crown, I had the hearts of all the judges.

Then, three days before the pageant, Kennedy Claire and I were practicing the opening number routine in the living room when my high heel gave out, snapping clean beneath me, and I came down hard. A bright spark of pain flared up my leg so fast it stole my breath.

Kennedy Claire shrieked and dropped to her knees beside me. *Oh my God, Iggy!* Her hands hovered over me, fluttering like she didn't know where to touch first, before she bolted for the kitchen.

By the time she came back with an ice pack, tears were stinging my eyes. She guided me onto the sofa, propped up my foot, and wrapped my ankle tight, her movements crisp and urgent.

It wasn't enough, though. There was no way I could do my gymnastics routine.

At first, I begged Izzy to do it in my place. *No one will know it's you.* But she hadn't tumbled since sophomore year and didn't have time to learn a whole routine, so we settled on that magic trick instead—Izzy disappearing from one end of the stage and me "magically" reappearing on the other end in an instant. Inherently less impressive, given everyone knew we were twins.

Then Izzy really did vanish, and none of my silly teenage concerns—pageants and boys and final exams and dorm preferences—mattered anymore.

"Honey?" My dad's voice comes from the bottom of the ladder and feels like a splash of cool water down my back.

"Up here," I say. "Don't climb that ladder, Dad. I'm coming down." I shove a stack of photos into the back pocket of my jeans and hurriedly put back the sashes and the empty tins. But then I see the black high heel, the one that snapped beneath me. Mom never did throw anything out. Dad was right.

I hear the creak of the bottom rung. "Seriously, you're going to fall," I holler out, squinting as I turn the heel so it catches the dim light coming up from the open attic door. It's broken in one clean line, and the edge is coated in what seems to be a thin layer of dried glue.

Suddenly the attic walls seem to tighten around me, the insulation like glass splinters sticking a fever into my damp skin.

Because the way this shoe broke—it doesn't look like it happened by accident.

CHAPTER THIRTY

SARAH LYNN

"That seems like a pretty stupid idea, even for you, dumbass," I say.

Hannah, Olivia, and I are working our shift at Smoothie Palace. The place is empty except for Kayden and his idiot friends, who have come up with the brilliant plan to throw a party at The Hollow.

"Before this cold front blows in," Kayden says. "Come on. We need chicks."

He's banking on me bringing all the Lone Star girls along.

"Yeah, I don't know," Olivia says, worrying the dish towel between her fingers. "Isn't that place, like, haunted?"

Silence hangs a beat, and then Kayden grins, milking it. "I can protect you," he says, leaning on the counter toward Olivia. Olivia dips her head, a blush creeping up her face as she wipes around the tubs of fruit.

I shove Kayden's elbow out from under him. "I meant that it's stupid because you just got in trouble for hanging out down there. You want Dad to send you to military school?" Part of me says it so Olivia knows that Kayden is no good, but I see her peek her eyes over at him through her lashes. Of course she's digging the bad boy vibe. The quiet girls always do. That's why those dark romance books are going wild through all the mom book clubs. Those nerdy girls are closet freaks.

"Hannah," I say. "Back me up."

Turned from us, filling the blender, Hannah lifts a shoulder as she drops a banana in. "It could be fun."

"I knew you were cool," Billy says, pushing up the glasses that are always slipping down his slim nose. His floppy curls fall down his forehead and into his eyes.

Hannah turns on the blender, like she doesn't care either way. But I know the truth. She has a massive crush on Billy, and she doesn't mind the idea of swimming under the stars with him. Fair enough. He's not my type, but he does have that quirky, slightly too pretty, Timothée Chalamet-kind-of-thing going on.

"Fine," I say.

"I don't want to get in trouble though," Olivia says, but even as the worry scrunches her forehead, I can hear the excitement in her voice.

And, to be honest, I think we all kind of feel it, the electric tingle running through the group. We've all heard the stories of the parties our parents used to throw at The Hollow. They talk about them in that glitter-soaked memory way, that God-we-got-up-to-some-trouble-in-our-day way, voices tipping into laughter, without ever giving us the concrete details we want. But for us, it's always been off-limits, making it all the more tantalizing.

The boys grab their smoothies and leave, the bell jingling as the door swings shut. Through the window, I see Kayden stop on the sidewalk when Mr. Magnuson passes. They do one of those complicated handshakes boys always do, and Mr. M. claps him on the shoulder like they're old friends.

Once, when Kayden was about to get cut from the basketball team for flunking history, Mr. Magnuson spent an afternoon shooting hoops with them, then stayed late to help him rewrite his essay. The guys still talk about it like he's some kind of legend.

That's the thing about Mr. Magnuson. He's impossible not to like. Not just because he's ridiculously hot, but because he actually cares.

I shove a finger into Hannah's side, making her double over with breathless laughter. "Cut it out," she says.

"I think you mean thank you," I say, flashing her my sweetest smile.

She rolls her eyes. "For what?"

"Oh, come on. Olivia?" I turn to her for support.

Olivia is biting down her smile, but the mere idea of doing something she's not supposed to has her all puffed up and reckless. "You are pretty thirsty for Billy," she says, covering her mouth like she can't believe she said it. Hannah grabs the dish towel from Olivia's hand, winds it up, and smacks her in the hip with it. Olivia squeals.

Here in the little bubble of our Smoothie Palace world, things are the same as they've always been. Olivia has no idea the way things have shifted, the way we've ended up on two ends of a chessboard, the stakes, at least for me, higher than she can imagine. But when I look at her, her eyes dancing with mischief, her laugh like an invitation, I just can't see her as the enemy my mother wants me to.

We're all still laughing when the door opens again and Mr. Magnuson steps in.

Hannah leans in close to me. "Speaking of thirsty," she nearly purrs in my ear.

He's wearing basketball shorts and a T-shirt with the sleeves cut off, displaying some serious deltoids. I mean, talk about dark romance material.

"Watch and learn," I whisper back.

Hannah spins away to the back counter again, and Olivia retreats into the corner, leaving me alone at the register when he walks up.

"Hi, Mr. M." I have both hands behind my back as I sway my shoulders, jutting out my breasts in a way that is just shy of obvious.

"Hey, Sarah Lynn." He glances up at the menu. "I'll take a protein power smoothie. Extra boost."

"Sure thing." I start gathering ingredients.

"That was pretty intense today," he says, voice low enough that it feels like something private. "You okay?"

I lift my shoulder in a shrug, keeping it light. "What's a pageant orientation without a little drama?" I say, even though my heart had been pounding through the whole thing.

"Still," he says. "Something like that can shake a person up."

"I'm fine," I say, flipping on the blender. "We're all fine."

Hannah sidles up next to me. Once the blender drowns out the noise, she whispers, "I'm taking notes."

"Just wait," I say, and pour the smoothie into a cup.

I turn back to Magnuson and slide the drink across the counter to him, then I pick up two straws. "Small or big?" I ask.

"Excuse me?"

I hold the straws up beside my face. "I like the big ones. They're easier to suck, especially with a thick smoothie, like yours."

"Oh," he says, after a beat too long. "Sure. I mean, that's fine." Then his eyes drop down as he fumbles with his wallet.

Olivia positively squeaks in shock behind me, and Hannah pulls her into the back, shutting the door behind them.

I don't even flinch, my smile locked and loaded, as I set the straw down on his drink lid.

As he pays, Mr. Magnuson's eyes flick to the back room, where we can hear Hannah and Olivia's muffled giggles.

When he's halfway to the door, I say, sweetly, "See you soon, Mr. M."

He turns and looks me right in the eyes now. One corner of his mouth lifts in the most delicious smile I've ever seen. "Looking forward to it, Sarah Lynn. And, hey, if you ever need to talk, just let me know." All my bravado drains in an instant. I swear my knees nearly buckle, as though someone has ripped the floor out from under me.

He strolls out the door, and the girls come tumbling back into the room, cackling.

"I can-fucking-not," Hannah says between wheezing breaths.

"You're a menace," Olivia laughs.

But I can barely hear them over the humming of my skin.

CHAPTER THIRTY-ONE

CAT

The Silverado followed me for three right turns until I finally shook it, pulling into the entryway of a private pasture. Then it was forced to pass me by. I never got a good look at the driver.

I parked the car and called Mark. I couldn't tell him about the truck—he'd only worry. So I made my voice light, asked for the keys to our old storage unit, said I wanted to grab some of my clothes. What I really wanted were his old trail cams from when he and Sheriff Ryan shared a deer lease years back.

Back at Sherman Ranch, I crouched in the trees to set one camera pointed at The Hollow, with the wind clawing at my hair, the dark pressing close. I tucked another into the bushes across the street, so it faced the model home. The cameras are out-of-date, their footage stored on SD cards instead of the cloud, so I'll have to check them physically.

But if that Silverado comes back, I'll catch it. I'll prove to everyone I'm not going crazy.

Now I can't stop peeking between the blinds. Every time I hear a car pass. Or think I do, only to find the street dark and empty. The temperature has dropped and the wind is howling through the trees, moonlight shimmering on the leaves so they look like silver coins shaking from the sky. I keep hearing snatches of voices on that wind. The ice falling in the freezer makes me jump. The heater clicking on sends irritating goose bumps across my flesh. There is too much noise. All around me. Inside my head. I keep pausing the TV, sure I heard something new beneath the dialogue.

I get up to make tea, hoping the warmth will settle me, and that's when I see them in the pantry: seven bottles of champagne.

Is that going to be too much of a temptation for you? Kennedy Claire had asked today at orientation.

Mark had alluded to the same thing. JCW Heritage Homes offers champagne during every house showing, and a free bottle of the good stuff if you sign a contract. Happy couples sip mimosas on all their billboards.

We don't have to do that, Mark had said. *It's dumb.*

I'll be fine, I assured him, and when he paused a beat, I added, *You can count them, if you like.* If he does, he does it discreetly.

It is the quiet I miss. Standing in the open pantry, I close my eyes and press my hands over my ears, suction my palms to them, and listen to my own heartbeat, like when my mother pressed a shell to my ear on a trip to Galveston, and an invisible ocean surged and swayed through my mind.

I pull my phone from my pajama pocket to reread the last text Olivia sent me:

Tomorrow at noon, right?

And my response: I'll be there.

The little heart Olivia added as confirmation.

I missed so many of her birthdays. I'd send her a card, a generic HAPPY BIRTHDAY, DAUGHTER scrolled over a cartoon image of a pink cake. The word *daughter* ringing hollow. I was no mother. I picked out gifts I thought an eight-year-old girl might like without having any idea of her unique interests, her favorite cartoon characters, the kinds of games she liked to play. Mothers are supposed to know these things. They are supposed to be finely tuned in to the day by day, moment by moment whims of their children. At the time, I'd use shame as another excuse to drink and to use, until I couldn't feel, until I couldn't remember the guilt. And when I finally woke up from the haze of it all, it was just me, alone. It was always about me and what I wanted.

I slam the pantry door shut.

As I make my way up the stairs, I hear the sound of tires slowly moving over gravel-scattered concrete, but I don't check the window. Instead, I put my earbuds in, play a relaxing meditation track, and climb into bed. I turn my body away from the window and pull the covers over my head, so I won't see headlights stretching across the wall.

CHAPTER THIRTY-TWO

EMILY BLAKE

2017

Emily Blake sits on her stepdaughter's bed. Olivia's hair is damp from her shower, her head bent as she scribbles her wish on a square of pale pink paper. Emily writes hers too, the way they always do. Every night, they fold the slips into origami stars and drop them into the mason jar on the dresser, a galaxy of paper promises collecting in the glass.

You aren't supposed to peek. If you do, the wish won't come true. But she does, and as expected, her heart sinks, because Olivia wrote down exactly what Emily thought she would. That her mother would take her to the zoo this weekend, like she promised she would. Olivia has been writing the same wish every night for two weeks. Emily always peeks at Olivia's wishes, because she always tries to make them come true. And usually she can. Wishes for cotton candy or a new headband. But Emily is powerless when it comes to this particular wish.

She kisses the crown of Olivia's head, turns on the star shower night-light, and leaves the door cracked just so. Exactly how Olivia likes. She knows these details, because she's the one who is here. Every night.

Then Emily pads down the hall, looking forward to pouring her single glass of wine and curling up on the sofa.

But she stops at the end of the hall, because she hears Mark's voice drift from the kitchen, low and careful, a tone she knows too well. The tone he only uses with Cat.

Emily doesn't have to hear the words to know what this means. Olivia's wish won't come true. Cat will disappoint her. Again and again.

She leans against the wall and she listens. She hates the way Mark softens for Cat. Hates the way he humors her. Hates, if she's honest, that Cat exists at all.

CHAPTER THIRTY-THREE

INGRID

Three Days Before the Pageant

I brought the shoebox with the broken heel down from the attic and tucked it into the back seat of my car. The invitation still sits in my purse.

But I push all that from my mind now, because Dad and I are at Oak Hills to visit Mom and to meet with Dr. Patel, who thinks she'll be able to come home soon. She started her first round of chemo yesterday, and the doctors want to keep her for twenty-four hours to watch how her body handles it. If all goes well, she'll be discharged tomorrow.

Melanie is walking me through the post-op care, just like she promised. It's actually her day off, which I discovered when her co-worker, Tom, caught the three of us walking together in the hallway toward Mom's room.

Melanie, are you serious? he said, hand on hip. *What are you doing here?*

It was only then I realized Melanie wasn't wearing scrubs, just a plain cotton T-shirt and jeans.

Melanie, I started to admonish, *you didn't have to—*

But she stopped me with a hand to my arm, that reassuring smile on her face. *It's fine.*

You're way too nice, I said.

Tom cocked his head and gave her a disapproving look. *That's what I'm always telling her.*

We appreciate it, Dad said simply.

Melanie started with the easy stuff—paperwork, diet guidelines, when to call the doctor—all the things she could explain with a clipboard in hand. But once she pulled on a pair of gloves to demonstrate Mom's drain care, Dad found a reason to duck out. Ostensibly, he's gone to peruse the gift shop in the lobby, the one with CLIF bars and get well balloons, in search of face wash because Mom mentioned that she was nearly out at home.

In reality, he had understood the subtext: She didn't want him in the room for this. Mom is the kind of woman who clips her toenails with the bathroom door locked.

When you've been married as long as they have, I suppose you really do become one unit. I watched a BBC documentary once about schools of fish. Hundreds, even thousands of individuals swim together as one body, swooping in a mass of shimmering scales, contracting, expanding, changing directions without ever needing words. They understand and are understood, at least in the simplicity of motion.

Joel and I were together for most of my adult life, the last of my twenties, the entirety of my thirties, into my forties. But we never had that kind of unity. We just coexisted in the same space, our minds residing in separate worlds.

The only time I've ever been understood, when I've truly and deeply connected with another person, was when I had Izzy.

The flowers on Mom's bedside table have begun to droop, a few sunflower petals scattered around the bottom of the vase. Melanie invites me up beside her as she folds back the blankets on Mom's bed. From beneath the covers, she reveals a drainage bulb attached to a tube that snakes up Mom's hospital gown. Melanie undoes the safety pin clipping the bulb to Mom's gown.

"It's very simple once you get the hang of it," she assures me. "You'll empty each drain twice a day, measure the fluid, and record it here." She points to a notebook atop the stack of papers and prescriptions and information pamphlets we've received.

"Oh, honey, you don't have to do this part. I can do it myself."

The bulb is half full of a pale pinkish-yellow fluid. Mom's lips are tight, and I feel a flush of secondhand embarrassment, like I've caught my mother on the toilet.

Melanie tsks softly. "Now you remember the Bible tells us to 'Carry each other's burdens.' That's what Iggy's trying to do here. Help carry your burden. Don't you dare go stealing her blessing." She says this last part as a teasing admonishment that gets a smile out of Mom. Mom touches the gold cross at her neck and gazes over at the window.

Melanie hands me a small, clear measuring cup and motions toward the bulb. I lift it, release the stopper, and let the fluid drip into the cup.

"See this tissue?" Melanie says, pointing to a string of bloody matter floating within the liquid. "That's perfectly normal. But if you do notice bright red blood or white discharge with a foul smell, give us a call."

"Good heavens," Mom says. "It's all so gross. I hate it."

Melanie shows me how to record the numbers, how to flatten the bulb and replace the stopper, so the suction can keep doing its work. She watches me record the numbers, shows me how to wash the cup. "You're a quick learner," she says.

The kindness in her voice makes the shame come heavy, pulling me back to who I used to be.

I remember once, standing outside with Kennedy Claire in the after-school pickup line. The girl beside us adjusted her My Little Pony backpack.

Oh my God, Kennedy Claire said, loud enough to draw attention. *Do you still watch cartoons?*

The girl flushed, and I jumped in to ease the sting. *I think it's cute*, I said.

She gave me a tiny, grateful smile.

But Kennedy Claire didn't. She turned away, slid into the conversation with the girls on her other side, closing the circle so neatly that I was left standing alone on the curb.

I understood the rules then: you either met Kennedy Claire's expectations, or she iced you out. And I didn't want to be left out in the cold. So the next time she nudged me with her elbow and smirked at someone else's expense, I forced a laugh. After a while, I didn't have to force it. I was a part of it. A joke here, a whispered comment there, little cruelties that became second nature.

And by high school, there was no easier target than Melon-ball Melanie.

That day we skinny-dipped with her at The Hollow, Melanie dove beneath the water. Kennedy Claire looked at her pile of clothes, then looked at me, and I knew what she wanted me to do. So I did it. I grabbed her clothes, and we left her there.

I didn't sleep well that night, wondering if or how Melanie even got home. But she was at school the next day. I ran into her at the lockers, and she smiled sweetly at me. The way she always did. Aside from the blush that stained her neck, she acted like it had never happened at all. And I had just moved on.

But now, the thought of it makes me physically ill, especially as I watch her care for my mother so gently. As she shows me a grace I don't deserve. I want to apologize, but the words feel weak and out of place. Too little, too late.

"Thanks," I say instead.

"Do you mind if I show Iggy your drainage site?" Melanie asks Mom.

Mom sits up so that Melanie can untie the hospital gown, which she then pulls forward to show me where the tube enters Mom's body. Just under her armpit is a hole, the skin puckered around the emerging tube. I can't remember the last time I saw my mother's armpit, if ever. Now I see it, see the naked side of her torso, watch the fluid from inside her body pump slowly along with bubbles and bits of tissue. This moment is so intimate I want to look away, but I don't.

I touch my mother gently with two fingertips like Melanie shows me, to test if the skin is hot. I feel Mom flinch. I think of when Izzy and I had chicken pox when we were seven, how Mom drew us an oatmeal bath, pressed the paste to our itchy skin with her bare hands, how it felt natural, that closeness, that total lack of boundaries between the three of us, that oneness.

Now all I feel is loss. The loss of Izzy. The distance from everyone I've loved. The way the girl who once ran through the Sherman woods feels like a stranger to me now. It overwhelms me.

Beside me, Melanie pulls off her gloves with a snap and tosses them in the trash behind the bed. The sound breaks the moment.

I jerk my hand back fast, knocking my purse from the bedside table. The contents spill.

And there, beneath the harsh hospital fluorescence, lies the invitation, back side up. The scrawled words plainly visible for everyone to see.

CHAPTER THIRTY-FOUR

MELANIE

I drop to the floor before Iggy does to pick up her belongings, but I freeze when I see the note. The jarring words—BEN DIDN'T KILL IZZY. I KNOW WHAT REALLY HAPPENED TO YOUR SISTER.—scribbled in such ugly, frantic lettering. I scoop it up quickly with the rest of Iggy's things and shove it all back into her bag. When I look up, she is standing stock-still, face so white, she looks like a ghost.

Poor Iggy. She's already dealt with enough.

She was already so clearly uncomfortable, out of her depth, caring for her mother like this. Which is normal. I see it all the time. People shy away from the intimacy that comes with caretaking, the rawness of the human body with its wounds and fluids and frailty.

But from the time I was very young, I helped Mama look after Oma Greta. I combed her hair and clipped her toenails when she couldn't reach any longer. I held her elbow as she walked to the toilet, and I rubbed lotion into her arthritic feet.

I set the purse back on the bedside table, and return to the task at hand, walking Iggy through the care routine. And after Mr. Whitmore has come back into the room, has settled in a seat beside his wife, I pull Iggy out into the hallway.

"Are you all right?" I ask, as gently as I can.

"What you saw . . ." she says.

I put my hands up. "You don't have to tell me anything."

But she looks like she wants to tell me, needs to tell someone, like she doesn't have an ear to listen, a shoulder to lean on. Her eyes flick to the open doorway of her mother's hospital room. No sooner than I pull it closed, does she say, "I don't know who sent it to me."

So I sit down on the bench in the hallway, and I pat the seat beside me. She crumples down onto the seat, knees angled toward me. Her eyes scan nervously up and down the hall before she pulls the note from her purse and hands it to me. "Someone sent it to my parents' house. And then nothing."

I run my finger over the jagged cuts of the words, then turn it over. It's written on the back of a Miss Lone Star Princess invitation, just like the one I have hanging on my fridge at home.

"It's really fucking with me, Mel." She rubs the fingertips of one hand into her forehead hard. I wonder if she's been sleeping. "Everything I've thought. All these years . . ."

I put a hand over hers, as if I can take all her jumbled thoughts and straighten them back into the neat orderly rows I know she likes. "Don't make yourself sick over this. You don't know anything yet. You don't know who sent it or why. You don't even know if it's true. Maybe it's a prank."

She scoffs. "That would be a pretty sick joke."

"Maybe it was Ben," I say, because, honestly, it's the most obvious conclusion someone could come to.

Iggy's brows twitch together. She shakes her head.

"Does he know you're back in town?"

She runs her fingernail over her bottom teeth, nibbling at the corner, looking down at the note, studying the words on the paper like she's looking at them anew.

I turn it over again to the raised golden font. "Maybe someone just really wants to get you to come to the pageant."

Behind us a door opens, and Iggy's eyes fly up to her mother's door. But it's only Tom coming out of the room next door. I tuck the note beneath my hands.

Iggy's back is perfectly straight, her eyes and ears trained on that door. She doesn't want her father to come out and see this note. I lean in to her, sliding the note back out and holding it between us. "Look, why don't we take this to my dad?"

"No," she says quickly, ripping the invitation from my hand. Then softer. "No. It'll be too upsetting for Mom. Thank God she didn't see this." She peers down at the message. "Kennedy Claire has been nagging me to come to the pageant for months." She lifts her eyes to mine.

"Oh, honey, I don't know. That would be a really cruel thing to do."

Iggy chews the inside of her cheek, and the way she's looking at me is like a dog that's been caught digging in the trash, like she's got a guilty conscience. I suspect we're both thinking, from opposite sides of the same coin, that we know exactly what kind of cruelty Kennedy Claire is capable of.

CHAPTER THIRTY-FIVE

INGRID

Can we get together tonight? I'll bring wine.

I'm in the passenger seat of Dad's car, phone in my lap, watching Anhalt roll past my window. The skating rink where Izzy and I had our eleventh birthday party is now a laser tag place. The car wash, where Kennedy Claire and I hosed down cars in bikinis to raise funds for Miss Lone Star is miraculously still there, though with a fresh coat of paint and a shiny new sign. I feel Izzy's breath on my neck, her voice in my ear: *Do you see it, Iggy? Do you see?*

Dad has the heat up too high, and he's playing Jim Croce too loud. "Time in a Bottle," which I always thought was the saddest song ever written because he wrote it after finding out that he was going to be a father, wrote it about how happy he was, how he wished he could save up all his time and spend it with his son. By the time the song hit number one in the charts, Croce had already died in a plane crash.

"Have you been able to talk to Joel?" Dad asks.

I reach over to turn the music down, to lower the heat. "Yeah," I say. "Joel's fine."

Dad looks over at me for a second, then back to the road. He doesn't say anything else.

My phone chimes with a response from Kennedy Claire:

I wish! Can't tonight. Rain check?

I darken the screen.

Kennedy Claire and I have been friends for almost thirty years, not call-each-other-every-day friends, but "show up for the big things" friends. I think of her doing my makeup for my wedding, her fingertip on my cheek. I think of when I flew down when Sarah Lynn was born, how I held her when she was impossibly small, Kennedy Claire in the hospital bed, her face bare and her eyes tired, and how I thought she looked her most beautiful.

Dad pulls onto our street, where the trees are old, their branches twisted, intertwined with the ones beside them. I think of the afternoon stretching into evening, Dad and I circling around each other in the house, making small talk, ignoring the photos of Izzy on the wall, ignoring the new medical supplies for Mom, and I feel like there is a vise around my chest, squeezing the air from my lungs.

My phone dings again. Another text, but this time it's from a number I don't know. I swipe it open.

Dinner tonight?

Followed by an address in Wimberley, a town about twenty minutes away.

And then: So we don't run into anyone we know.

I stare at the message, my heart halfway to my throat. I've been half waiting for a follow-up to the invitation, wondering if whoever sent it will reach out again. Then a final text comes in.

This is Travis, by the way. With a wink.

Dad puts the car in park. "What do you think about Dad's best mac and cheese?" he says.

"Don't worry about dinner." My hand is already on the handle. "I'm going out with Kennedy Claire tonight."

CHAPTER THIRTY-SIX

CAT

There is no better feeling in the world than waking up sober, my mind rested, my stomach not tangled up in knots. This is what they mean by one day at a time. In the morning light, it seems so obvious that I was mistaken. That the Silverado behind me was just a coincidence. The sounds I heard were only the wind.

Mark dropped off Olivia and Hannah after my showing this morning, and then Melanie swung by to collect us. She was a hair late after getting stuck at the hospital.

Did you talk to Iggy at the orientation? she'd asked once we were on the road, her eyes flicking up to the rearview mirror to check on the girls. They sat in the way back of the minivan, heads bent together, whispering and giggling over their phones.

No, why?

She shook her head, eyes back on the road. *I just feel bad for her. She's going through a lot.* Melanie is good at keeping her cards close, stuffing down her emotions, but I know she isn't thrilled about today—the four of us shopping for pageant dresses in Austin. She's trying to put on a brave face for Hannah's sake.

I turned toward the window just as we came around a bend that opened up to the heart of the Hill Country. The green bluffs, usually gorgeous domes curving toward the open blue sky, were shrouded today. A cold fog, like the heavy fumes of dry ice, had settled into the deep crevices that scar the terrain between the hills.

Now I'm sitting on a white tufted settee in the back of Z Couture, a boutique in The Domain filled from wall to wall with dresses for every occasion imaginable, rainbow of glitter and tulle. The curtain of the dressing room pulls back and Olivia steps out. Tears spring to my eyes before I can stop them. The dress is gorgeous on her, like she's been dipped in silver, the figurine on top of a trophy. But it's her face that undoes me, the sparkle of her eyes, the simple fact that I'm here to see it. My throat tightens.

She pulls at the tag and gives me a look. "It's really expensive." I know exactly how much it costs. Almost everything I've saved, a deposit and at least a month's rent in a new place of my own. "It's perfect," I tell her. Because I know Mark will be okay letting me stay a little while longer in the model home. I'm lucky we're on the same page, the page he's always been on, honestly: We put Olivia first.

Her smile glows a hundred watts as she smooths her hands down her hips, turning toward the mirror. I'm grateful she is still young enough that something so simple can make her so happy.

The curtain of the dressing room down the way slides open, metal rings scraping along the rod, and Kennedy Claire steps out, Sarah Lynn trailing behind her. "I thought that was your voice," she says to me. Her eyes sweep over Olivia before she tucks an opaque garment bag into the crook of her arm. "Isn't that pretty?"

Olivia looks down at her dress, the smile lingering faintly. Hannah bounds over to Sarah Lynn, tugs her arm, and whispers something that makes Sarah Lynn smirk.

"You're lucky," Kennedy Claire says. "Finding something off the rack. We've been through three rounds of alterations with Sarah Lynn. But you hardly need any tailoring." She tips me a closed-lipped smile. "See you at rehearsal, ladies."

I watch my daughter glance back at the mirror, doubt clouding her face where joy was only a moment ago. And as the shop bell chimes, an unreasonable anger wells up inside me—that primal, mama bear instinct to claw back what Kennedy Claire just stole.

CHAPTER THIRTY-SEVEN

MELANIE

I'm in a bad mood, though I try not to let it show. I'd suggested we just hit the San Marcos outlets—good prices, easy parking—but instead we made the hour-long trek through Austin's stop-and-go circus so they could play dress-up at some fancy boutique. Hannah blew nearly all the money she's been saving for a car on one silly dress. Cat spent hers too. And now the girls are craving Moon Milk Lattes, so I'm navigating this madhouse of a parking lot at the Summer Moon on Burnet.

Last night on the local news, they warned the town of a severe winter storm and cold front. A blast of Arctic air freezing everything in its path coming down south all the way from Canada. They say it might actually push its way into Texas. Probably just another cold snap that'll melt by noon. But everyone is out today anyway, driving aggressively, picking up essentials and stocking up on things that will just dust over in the back of their cupboards anyhow. Texans pride themselves on being self-reliant, and they are, in many ways, but at the same time, they love to get into a tizzy every time the weather drops below thirty-five degrees, going so far as shutting down schools for fear of a little ice.

We enter through the heavy doors and are greeted by a wave of oppressive, manufactured heat. It hits so hard I'm already unwinding my scarf, itching to shed the jacket and sweater layered over my

T-shirt. The place is packed—everyone trying to escape the cold—and the air feels close, smothering.

"I'll get us a table," I tell Cat. "Just get me whatever."

A couple near the window starts gathering their things, so I squeeze through bodies, hugging my purse tight, apologizing as I go, aware of the space my body takes up, aware of every shoulder I bump, every chair I knock.

I slide into a seat the second they stand. They've left a mess of crumbs, so I brush them into a crumpled napkin, fold it up, and shove it in my pocket, so I won't lose the table by getting up.

I couldn't sleep last night, spending hours doomscrolling my phone, researching that plastic surgery boutique listed in the Miss Lone Star Princess prize package, and falling down rabbit holes.

I stumbled upon a story from back in 2015. Catherine Cando, a nineteen-year-old Ecuadorian beauty queen and a burgeoning medical student with a bright future, won a very similar prize when she was crowned the Queen of Durán. She refused the free liposuction procedure at first, bright girl that she was, but was pressured into claiming it. Only, when she went to collect her winnings, the operation went sideways, and Catherine died right there on the table. Murdered, if you ask me. She'd already been crowned the prettiest of all. Just when is enough enough?

A group of Lululemon moms hover, coffees in hand, eyeing my empty table for four. I feel a bead of sweat forming under my boobs before it rolls down my belly. Why is it so darn hot in here?

I wonder what it would be like to not constantly worry what others might be thinking. To be comfortable in my own skin, instead of falling over myself to make sure everyone else is comfortable in theirs. I wonder what I actually am underneath, without this skin—if there's still the soft heart Oma Greta knew, or only the hard, bitter, rotten parts I keep buried.

Cat's name is called, and the girls grab their iced coffees topped with whipped cream and caramel drizzle, but when they walk over, they pass right by me, lost in conversation. As they head out the door, Hannah laughs at something Olivia says, but it rattles me. It's not her laugh. It's borrowed, practiced, the kind of laugh that's meant to be noticed. My daughter is trying it on like a new dress, seeing how it fits.

Cat brings our two coffees to the table.

"Where are the girls off to?"

She hands me my drink and takes a seat across from me. "The salon two doors down. Apparently, they need new hair products for the pageant." She's looking out the window, her eyebrows pinched tight. "Has that truck been there this whole time?" she asks.

I turn to look over my shoulder. The parking lot is packed with countless trucks.

"The Silverado," she says.

And I see the one she means, a white pickup parked right out front, facing right into the café's windows. A man sits behind the wheel. "I don't know," I say, turning back to her, but she's already standing.

She storms out the side door, letting in another gust of chilly air, and I watch her march to the truck, wrapping the sweater tight around herself. She knocks on the glass. The driver rolls down his window. Cat is talking fast, heated. I see the man's face, mid-thirties and so plain and approachable he could be cast in a prescription drug commercial. He looks confused and a little wary of Cat. After a brief exchange, he's rolling up his window, and Cat walks back inside and sits down.

"Honey," I say, "what on earth was that?"

"I showed that man and his pregnant wife the model home a few days ago. John. That was his name, and his wife was Faith."

"Okay," I say.

Her hand goes to her throat, and she begins to scratch. "I've seen him, driving by the model home."

"I'm sure he was just checking out the neighborhood," I reassure her. "Buying a house is a big decision."

She nods, but her fingers haven't left her neck, haven't stopped their scratching, and her eyes haven't left the window. Then she leans in quickly and says, "He was following me, Mel. Yesterday. In my rearview. Every turn I made."

I turn back around to look out the window. The Silverado is backing out of the spot.

"I couldn't see the driver, but it was that truck. I know it was," she says.

The truck pulls away, and not two cars behind it, is another white Chevy Silverado. That make and model has to be one of the most popular in Texas. Cat has had wild suspicions before, paranoid delusions. She used to call me at 2 AM, not knowing or caring that I'd worked a twelve-hour shift and would work another the following day. *Someone is after me*, she'd say, babbling on about a car parked on her street or a man who looked at her too long at the 7-Eleven. Always, I stayed up. Always, I talked her down from the ledge.

She is still scratching.

"Stop that," I snap, harsher than I mean to.

She jerks her hand down immediately and I can see her bare neck, see that she's picked up her old habit of scratching again. The skin is red and raw.

And I feel panic rising up inside me. Because I can't keep doing this. I can't keep holding Cat together.

CHAPTER THIRTY-EIGHT

INGRID

"Two Strangers in Pear-a-dise" the waitress says and places the cocktails in front of us. I take a sip, pick out the promised flavors on my tongue: pear, rosemary, and lemon.

Travis and I are at The Leaning Pear, a cool, family-owned spot perched above Cypress Creek, all warm cedar walls and sleek floor-to-ceiling windows overlooking the water. We're tucked into a corner table, half-hidden from the rest of the room, and, if I'm being honest, it's fun playing incognito with this good-looking man. It gives me a silly high, knowing that he's willing to jump through some hoops to see me. We're not being particularly bad, but the feeling of doing something I'm not supposed to makes me squirm in my seat in the best way. It's just the distraction I need.

The waitress returns with our appetizers, fried brussels sprouts and hummus with sautéed mushrooms. I've already learned that Travis is from Indiana and has three older brothers. One's a surgeon, one's a criminal court judge, and the oldest runs a tech company in Chicago.

"Quite the impressive lineup," I say.

He laughs under his breath, part pride, part long-suffering sigh. "Yeah. They set the bar pretty damn high. Then there was me—baby of the family, professional troublemaker. I got away with everything. A certified mama's boy."

He tells me that when his brothers were rough on him, his mom would come to his rescue, swatting at the older boys and scooping little Travis into her arms. And when the brothers were nice to him, Travis would make things up, cry crocodile tears, just to get that same reaction from her. "I was addicted to attention," he says without an ounce of shame.

"Was?" I ask.

He smirks sheepishly.

"So how'd you end up in Texas?"

He shrugs. "Preston High had an open teaching position." He scoops hummus onto a triangle of pita. "So what does the mysterious Ingrid do?"

I take another sip of my drink. "I'm a client relations manager. Which is just a fancy way of saying I answer emails all day."

"How'd you get into that?"

When I was young, I thought I'd be a photographer. Izzy and I imagined traveling the world, her soaking up experiences and discovering her path along the way, while I documented, capturing reality. The world seemed so big and full of possibility then.

I stir the ice in my glass. "I just needed a job. What about you? How did you end up in teaching?" Travis teaches speech and journalism. He also advises for the yearbook and helps with UIL competitions. He says he loves teaching kids how to ask the right questions. "I bet you wanted to be a news anchor." It isn't hard to imagine him on a television screen. And maybe everyone had a dream when they were young, when their own hunger felt bigger than the world, bigger than common sense and practicality. "All that attention-seeking behavior," I tease.

He sits up, adjusts a pretend tie. He has to know how devilishly handsome he is. He picks up his fork and holds it like a microphone. His voice drops half an octave—smooth, practiced. "I'm here today with the enigmatic Ingrid Whitmore. Perhaps she'll tell us some more of the secrets she's been hiding." He holds out the fork to me across the table, that dimple showing when he smiles.

I look down to my drink again.

"Actually," he sits back, rests his arms on the back of the booth. "I just always wanted to teach."

"Oh?" I say, surprised by his answer.

"Yeah, I had this great theater teacher in high school, Mrs. Calloway. When you walked into her class, whoever you were out in the hallways, whoever you were at home, none of that mattered. There was this guy, Tony Fritz. Big varsity lineman, right? Imagine it, imagine the biggest guy you knew in school, the toughest guy that no one would ever jack with." He's acting it out, sitting up in his seat, puffing up his shoulders, arms out as if they rested on giant lats to display the breadth of Tony Fritz. "Tony takes the class because he figures it's an easy A, but Mrs. Calloway cast him as Lennie. *Of Mice and Men.*"

He pauses, maybe to gauge my interest or maybe to confirm I know what he's talking about. I crunch my brow together and smirk. "I'm familiar."

"Okay, good. By the time we were polishing our lines in rehearsals a week before opening night, Mrs. Calloway had Big Fritz totally in character, bawling his eyes out up onstage in front of everyone in class like he really was Lennie. Her love for teaching was infectious. After that, Tony was all in. He still does local theater back home."

I laugh. He's been leaning in while he talks, words getting faster, and my own heart quickens along with his passion.

"There's just something about kids at that age, you know? It's intoxicating. It's like they're right on the edge of everything. Ready to be molded."

He looks at me. I feel the heat in my cheeks.

"What would you want to do?" he asks. Really asks. As if I'm one of his students, as if he wants to know something about me beyond what I present to the world, wants to know a deeper part of me. "If you didn't have to answer all those emails?"

"Take pictures," I say, swept up in the moment.

He cocks an eyebrow.

I tell him about the time Izzy and I found a box in the bottom drawer of the china cabinet. Pictures of Mom when she was nineteen, on a trip to the beach in Galveston with friends, boys with '70s shorty-short swim trunks and girls in skimpy bathing suits and terry cloth rompers, all the photos slightly out of focus and yellow with age, a sunburnt dream. In my favorite picture, Mom, in her lime-green bikini, is shin deep in the ocean, eyes squinted from smiling. She looks absolutely stunning.

The young woman on the beach—she was my mother, but she also wasn't. It filled me with wonder while also making my heart ache, seeing a version of her that no longer existed. A young woman I'd never be able to meet. Photography was magic. It could cheat time. It could capture a person as she existed within a single point. It made me realize we aren't a single self. We are a series of selves, layered atop each other like a stack of negatives.

Somehow Travis, with his dimpled smile, with his enthusiasm, his disarming honesty, pulls these words from me like a magician pulling scarves from my mouth.

And soon I'm talking about Mom and Dad. And Izzy. Her disappearance but also her dreams of traveling the world. I'm fessing up to being an overthinker, an overplanner, that he was my one and only one-night stand.

"A YOLO alarm? Well, I'm flattered I'm the lucky guy who got to get you out of your shell."

I take a sip of my cocktail and lower my head with a sly smile, peering up at him. "You mean my panties?"

That dimple again. "Were you wearing those?"

Over drinks and food, we get closer. I Ubered here—no small feat this far out—but Travis insists on driving me back to town. I hesitate at first. It's a little reckless, I know, but the night's gone soft and blurry around the edges, and he swears he'll drop me a few doors down from my parents' place so no one will see. It's late anyway. The roads are empty.

In the truck, I watch the last of Wimberley's lights disappear behind us, replaced by the dark stretch of country road. We don't talk much, but he's holding my hand, thumb tracing slow circles over my fingers.

I point out my parents' house when we turn onto their street. He pulls up to drop me off a few houses down, as promised. There are so many feelings inside me, jostling for attention—worry for Mom, disappointment in Joel, confusion over the invitation and the broken high heel and Kennedy Claire's laugh in my ear, memories of Ben Sherman swimming in The Hollow, of Izzy nuzzling her chin into my back, her body the same temperature as mine, and anger. So much anger. It all coils tightly, like kindling packed, like something ready to ignite.

Travis lifts the center console divider, and I scoot into him. He kisses me, one hand on my waist, grip firm as he pulls me tight against him. I inhale as I kiss him, feel that drown of desire dropping over me, feel his hand smooth down to my hip, my thigh, and he tugs my leg over his lap. I take his cue, climbing on top of him.

The sound he makes, half moan, half growl, as I slide my hips forward and back sends a shiver up my spine. The steering wheel jams my back, but I don't care. I lean back so he can kiss my neck. His hand cups my face, and he slides his thumb across my lips and under my chin. Pinching my jaw hard, he kisses me rougher.

Then his grip shifts again, thumb and finger pressing into my pulse points. His fingers tighten around my throat. "You good?" he whispers gruffly into my ear.

A moan escapes me, which he takes as the yes it's meant to be. I'm lost in the moment, and then, as his fingers close tighter, there is the flashbulb pop of a memory, of a dream.

The day before the pageant, the day Izzy went missing, I fell asleep in the bath while soaking my injured ankle. And I dreamt of hands wrapping around my neck, dreamt of being strangled. I woke up gasping for air, clutching at my throat, clawing at the fingers I was sure were there. I couldn't breathe, could feel the crush of my windpipe closing as I thrashed in the water.

Eventually, I took in a mouthful of air, calmed myself down, slowed my breath. At the time, I thought it was just a nightmare. Or a panic attack, maybe, nerves about the pageant.

"Harder," I tell Travis, the word barely escaping from my throat.

I've thought a lot in my life about what it would feel like to die choking.

People say that twins can feel each other's pain. There is no scientific evidence to back up this theory, but Mom swears we did as toddlers. I'd bump my head on the coffee table, and Izzy would cry. Izzy would fall on the sidewalk, and I'd clutch my knee where hers was bleeding.

I still sometimes wake up gasping. I still dream of hands wrapped around my throat.

My lungs begin to burn. A high, thin ringing blooms in my ears and my vision tunnels into darkness. Then bright spots like stars.

"Stop!" I claw Travis's hand off my neck, sucking in desperate breaths the way I always do when I wake from that dream.

Travis pulls both hands from me immediately, raising them like he's surrendering. "Sorry," he says. "Sorry. I"—he tips his palms up—"I asked if you were good. You were saying harder."

"I know." I run my fingers over my throat and sigh, climbing back into the passenger seat. I smooth my hair with shaky fingers.

He looks a little shaken up as well. I grab my purse and reach for the handle. "Sorry," I tell him.

When I open the door, the shock of cold air startles me. The temperature has dropped lower even since the start of our date. I look up at the dark house, at my old bedroom window. I can almost see her standing there, her shadowed silhouette in the frame, as if she's waiting up for me.

I touch my neck, still feeling the ghosts of a hand around my throat.

CHAPTER THIRTY-NINE

SARAH LYNN

The Hollow glows in the light of the full moon, the reflected stars smudging along the ripples of the water, making it look like that Van Gogh painting. The famous one.

All the local Lone Star girls made it tonight, along with a bunch of Kayden's friends, and everyone has agreed to keep this quiet.

On the news, they're warning of freezing rain, slick roads, power lines icing over. It sounds serious, but under the moonlight it feels almost magical, like the night is holding its breath. The air makes my skin goose up, makes my lungs sting and my senses clear. Two of the girls are dancing up on top of the highest boulder. The shapes of them intertwine, as ribbons of moonlight kiss off their skin. The speaker volume is almost silent, but I can hear Chappell Roan sing about someone going down on her in a truck.

Hannah, Olivia, and I are perched on the edge of a limestone shelf below them, our legs dangling out in the chilly air fifteen feet above the water.

After Mom's strategic run-in with Olivia today at Z Couture, she's been in full espionage mode. Olivia's dress was perfection—no tailoring needed—and Mom has already discovered that one of the judges, Mrs. Ramirez, has a granddaughter at Encore Dance Studio, mentored by Olivia herself. Of course that means, in Mom's mind, a built-in bias.

I can picture Mom now, sitting at her desk in the pageant room, pen tapping, plotting our next move.

Hannah is turned from me, hunched over as she types into her phone.

It takes me a second to recognize the flash of hot pink in Hannah's grip. *My* phone.

I reach for it, but Hannah flops back onto her elbows, holding it out of reach, grinning wickedly. Olivia shifts to block me, cheeks pink, trying to swallow her laughter but failing.

"What the hell are y'all doing?" I demand, standing now, arms crossed.

"Now *you* can thank *me*," Hannah says, handing the phone off like a relay baton. That's when I notice Mr. Magnuson's crumpled flyer tucked beneath Olivia's thigh.

I snatch my phone back. My stomach flips as I scroll through the damage.

Hey Handsome, followed by a purple eggplant emoji.

Mr. Magnuson has already responded—Who is this?—and my mouth goes dry at the flirtatious winky face.

Come meet me at The Hollow and find out, signed with a smiling kitty cat.

"You've lost your damn minds," I say, but the words don't land half as sharp as I want. My stomach is a washing machine of butterflies spinning. I watch the three little dots appear, then vanish. Reappear, then vanish again.

"What if he actually shows?" Olivia whispers, half horrified, half delighted.

I slip the phone into my back pocket, shrugging like it doesn't matter. But my body remembers that look he gave me, the one they didn't see. He might not have flirted back, but he didn't exactly shut it down either, did he?

I never do this—catch feelings for a boy. But Mr. Magnuson isn't a boy, is he?

Between pageant prep and workout regimens, honors classes, and volunteer hours, I've never had time to worry about dating. And, always, my mother's voice is in my ear: *They aren't worth your time, Sarah Lynn. A boy will only distract you. Or worse.* And I know she's right, because the boys at school are immature, all loud bravado and Axe body spray.

But Mr. Magnuson is different. Older. Calmer. And he actually listens. Actually looks at me like I'm a person with something worth saying.

I know it's crazy. I know he's my teacher. But not for much longer. Graduation's just a few months away.

When the girls aren't looking, I pull my phone out just to check, but he still hasn't texted.

We see Billy making his way up the cliff toward us, clumsily, as he finds his footing on the rocks in the dark. He grasps a cypress root right below us to heave himself up the last big step onto the limestone outcropping. I nudge Hannah with an elbow. She rolls her eyes, snatching my can of Truly from me, and tips it back to take the last swallow. Billy runs his fingers through his curls, pushes up his glasses, then shoves his hand down into the pocket of his baggy swim trunks. He pulls out a wet five-dollar bill, a stubby pocketknife, and a plastic baggie with a joint and lighter in it. By the look on his face, we're supposed to be impressed.

Hannah takes the joint. Billy lights it, cupping his hand around the flame, his dainty fingers just an inch from Hannah's face. I bet she's feeling the heat in more places than one right now. She inhales deeply, then parts her full lips slightly to release a steady stream of smoke.

"Damn, Hannah, sexy mama," I say, hoping Billy will get the hint. And he does kind of give her the once-over.

We pass the joint around, each taking a puff until it reaches Olivia. She pauses for a moment, just looking at the little rolled-up paper, ash hanging off the end. She glances over, across the river, toward the street, in the direction of the model home. And I know she's thinking about her mom.

“You don’t have to,” I say.

But Olivia does a little shrug of her slender shoulders, puts the joint to her lips, and breathes in, immediately coughing her head off.

The boys didn’t bring enough alcohol, so Kayden’s off on a beer run out to the 7-Eleven on FM 32. The absent-minded cashier who works there always “forgets” that he’s rung everything up twice, and then conveniently “forgets” to ask for an ID, as long as you pay cash.

The other boys are mostly down by the bank, a few in the water, dunking each other and generally acting like morons. Some of the girls are down there with them. The guys are getting louder with each dive and cannonball. The girls above us on the boulder have turned up the music as well. They’re grinding together atop that rock now, riling the guys up even more.

“Jump,” one of the guys yells out.

Sabrina takes off running, pauses just a second at the edge, then leaps. For a breath she’s untethered, and then she twists midair, slapping the water with a brutal thump before disappearing into the blackness of the water.

The Hollow goes deep. We’ve all heard the stories—caverns under the limestone, divers who never came back up, skeletons lost somewhere in the dark. By the time worry starts to set in, Sabrina resurfaces with a spluttering cough, and everyone exhales with her.

Then Teddy hauls his big belly out of the water and lumbers toward the trees. He drops his shorts just before the shadows swallow him, flashing his bare ass in the moonlight. The boys start whistling and catcalling.

Teddy calls back to them. “If Sabrina is willing to go through a near-death experience for our entertainment, the least I can do is show my ass!”

Laughter ripples through the crowd as a few more boys trail after him.

“Are you girls scared?” Teddy says.

"Just of seeing your white ass again," Hannah calls back.

Someone's rigged a length of rope to a big cypress that leans out over the water. Out of the shadowy part of The Hollow they swing, Tarzan-style, only they squeeze their legs shut, or turn their bodies away, before they escape into the cover of water. Billy's wiry frame flies last. He twists while airborne to face the girls, but he's covering his junk.

"Don't judge the shrinkage!" he shouts, just barely getting out the words before being swallowed in water. It has all the girls laughing.

When he resurfaces, he swims straight for Sabrina, who's hugging her knees at the water's edge, vying for attention in a whole new way.

"What a bunch of idiots," I say. "Do they actually think that'll convince us to take our clothes off?"

But Hannah is watching Billy, not me.

"Then again . . ." I say, and Hannah and Olivia both turn toward me. "It *was* tradition."

"No way," Olivia says, tugging her T-shirt down and scrunching up her knees.

I stand up. I hear my mom's voice in my head, telling me to sit pretty, smile sweet. Screw that. "Never hide, right?" I say to Hannah, and I walk back toward the trees, tugging down my leggings as I go.

Behind me, I hear Hannah stand. She meets me in the shadow of branches, and slips out of her pants too, following my lead.

"Are we seriously doing this?" Olivia says, trying to catch up, unbuttoning her jeans as she jogs toward us.

We all lift our shirts, toss them to the ground, so we stand in our bikini tops and bottoms. Then we slip out of those. I take my girls' hands, and we walk out into the moonlight. To the edge of our limestone stage.

The boys below us are dead silent, like I imagine Adam was the first time he laid eyes on Eve.

Yes, pageants build poise and confidence. And whatever the hell else you need to tell yourself to feel better about objectifying the female form.

But let's be honest. Pageant girls?

We're fucking hot.

Together, we leap.

CHAPTER FORTY

INGRID

After Travis dropped me off, I came into the house quietly, easing the door shut and slipping my shoes off. Dad was asleep in the recliner with the television still on. I'd found him like this every night, and I wondered if he'd been sleeping in the living room ever since Mom was admitted to the hospital, avoiding the empty bed upstairs. It's been forty-five years since he's slept alone. I turned off the TV and covered him with a blanket.

Now I'm sitting on my old bed, flipping through the stack of photos I brought down from the attic. In one, Izzy and I are helping Dad paint the garden shed, both of us with our hair tied up in messy buns, wearing paint-splattered Preston High T-shirts. I squint at the picture, trying to figure out which one is me. *No one will know it's you*, I'd told Izzy when I had tried to convince her to do my gymnastics routine. Because even Ben, who had known us both a lifetime, with his face close enough that I could feel his breath hot on my ear, hadn't been able to tell us apart.

The truth is, the last time I saw my sister, I was angry at her. For emailing that college guy, for stringing Ben along. Every time Ben kissed her, every time he reached for her hand in that easy, familiar way, it boiled me up. It wasn't fair to him. She'd always had him, and so she didn't appreciate him. And what was she going to do? Wait until the day we left for college to pull the rug out from under him? Let him play out this charade all summer?

Don't even go to dinner, I told her. I knew exactly how that would play out: Ben would kiss her as soon as she arrived, and she'd lose her nerve. She'd end up staying over with him, telling Mom and Dad in the morning that she'd fallen asleep on the Shermans' sofa, or she'd sneak back home late in the night. Either way, she'd tell me that she hadn't gone through with it. That she'd break up with him next time. We'd been playing this game for months. *Just go straight to his house now. Rip the Band-Aid off. Tell him it's over. You owe that to him, Izzy.*

I don't know, she'd said, flustered. She was packing her date-night purse, a little black clutch that barely fit her wallet and ChapStick, fiddling with the zipper to avoid eye contact with me. *I have to go to the library first and study.*

There were only a handful of people at the library that day. Sheriff Ryan interviewed them all, and no one had seen Izzy. I always thought that meant she'd taken my advice. That instead of waiting to meet Ben up at the square, instead of breaking up with him in a crowded restaurant in the middle of town, she had gone straight to the Sherman house. That I was the reason she had been alone with him that day in the middle of the woods.

That I had practically marched my sister to her death.

What if that wasn't true? What if, when she pulled away from the house that day, she hadn't gone to the library or to the Sherman house?

But then where did she go? And who had been waiting for her there?

CHAPTER FORTY-ONE

SARAH LYNN

Kayden came back with the liquor and everyone is a few steps past tipsy. We have our bathing suits back on, but our exhibition show worked, because Billy and Hannah are making out on the rocks near the mouth of the cave. Sabrina is off somewhere pouting about it, I'm sure. I'm floating on my back on the surface of the water, hand interlaced with Olivia's, and we're both feeling the effects of a few more puffs of pot. When I first waded back into the water, she asked me where I'd been.

Nowhere, I told her, sliding my hand into hers.

I was looking for you, she said.

Our bodies have adjusted to the freezing cold spring-fed water, and now it's the air we're breathing that stings.

"Do you ever think the stars are, like, talking to you?" she asks.

I laugh, because that's the highest question I've ever heard. But the stars do look beautiful. The night, inky black and pinpricked with light. My body feels numb, but the numbness feels nice, like I'm just a beam of moonlight. I turn my head to check on Hannah just as she's pulling Billy into the cave. Good for her.

The stars do kind of talk to us, though. Don't they? Destiny, and all that. Mom would say nothing's written in the sky. *If you want something in this life, you make it happen, Sarah Lynn.*

Olivia squeezes my hand. "Thanks for being here with me," she says.

I close my eyes and feel the bobbing sensation of floating, the night sky and the black water melding, so that I am suspended in nothing. I hear the laughter and the conversations and the music, the wind through leaves and the water lapping against stone.

And then, so sharp it splits the night:

A scream.

My heart rockets to my throat.

It's coming from the cave. It's Hannah.

CHAPTER FORTY-TWO

CAT

I'm sleeping with earbuds again, the sound of the ocean overlapping my dreams. My mother picking seashells from the sand in Galveston.

Dad skipped out on us when I was three, and Mom worked two jobs most of the time. I hardly ever saw her. I was a latchkey kid, making ramen or microwave nachos for dinner, falling asleep in front of the TV. Looking back, she was trying her best, but at the time I was angry—angry she couldn't make it to the play, or the awards ceremony, or anything that felt important to me. So I acted out. I snuck cigarettes and alcohol. I got into fights at school. I think I just wanted her to notice.

But the summer I was twelve, we rented a house within walking distance of the beach, and for three days I had all her attention.

In my dream, a wave rolls in, then out, the sand slipping from beneath our bare feet. Mom bends down, scoops a handful of wet sand, holds it out to me. A tiny clam wriggles down, burrowing into hiding in her palm. She smiles at me.

But when her mouth opens, it's a black hole.

And from that darkness, a scream emerges.

It sounds far away. Then another. The third rips me awake, and I realize it isn't a dream. It's cutting through the tranquil ocean in my earbuds.

I slide on my slippers. I race down the stairs, out the door, toward the screaming. It's coming from The Hollow. My blood is fire. My feet barely touch the ground.

And I run.

CHAPTER FORTY-THREE

SARAH LYNN

Everyone is scrambling, knocking into one another as we claw our way out of the well. We run along the bank, up the rocks, toward the sound that keeps coming.

The cave looms ahead. Jagged stalactites hang like teeth. Its entrance is a locked jaw, forever opened. The scream is its own.

Our feet slip on wet stone as we slosh forward into pitch-blackness. Hannah's sobs echo from deep within, bouncing off the walls, pulling us farther in.

Finally, our phone lights catch them. Hannah is curled against the rock, knees to her chest, shaking. Billy stands a few feet away, arm stretched, pointing deeper into the dark.

We swing our lights that way, and at first, there is just water. Then a face breaks the surface. Green moss climbs her cheekbones. The rest of her skull is yellow with age. Her jaw is missing.

All this time. She's been right here.

Isabelle Whitmore.

CHAPTER FORTY-FOUR

INGRID WHITMORE

2000

The high school auditorium is dim except for the spotlight illuminating the glamour of beautiful young contestants. Ingrid Whitmore stands amid the finalists, pain radiating up her leg. Her talent portion was a last-minute change of plans, a gymnastics routine she'd previously scrapped after suffering an ankle injury three days prior. Still, she smiles.

Squinting past the lights, she can make out the table of judges, and the first few rows of the audience. Her parents, who sit front and center. The empty chair beside them. Something begins crawling its way through the folds of Ingrid's brain.

She was meant to do a magic trick tonight, a vanishing act with her sister. One twin disappears from one end of the stage—a bit of theater, a puff of smoke, the ripple of silky fabric—and the other "reappears" on the far side, as if she had teleported.

But Isabelle never showed. And behind Ingrid's bright eyes, a worm folds and wedges its way through her skull. Earthworms breathe through their skin, through the cuticle, a thin, moist layer that protects the worm's body while allowing for gas exchange. It must be worming its way through her hypothalamus now, or maybe curling itself around her brain stem, because the dark thoughts she's been trying to keep at bay now pulse through her nervous system, and begin to overtake her.

There is a chill in the air. Ingrid can see her mother clutch at the front edges of her cardigan. In the wing, she notices a few of the tech theater kids, who designed and painted the grand backdrop behind the contestants. They pull a blanket tight around their shoulders and watch. Goose bumps rise on her own bare arms. A cold hand reaches out and grips hers tight, and she can feel the eager energy of her fellow contestants, an electric pulse of anticipation. But the connection is severed. She feels none of this excitement herself. Feels only the dark, wriggling thoughts.

Still, she smiles.

Her sister has, in fact, disappeared. And when she finally reappears so many years later, there will be no applause. There will be only worms.

CHAPTER FORTY-FIVE

INGRID

Two Days Before the Pageant

Mom's in the passenger seat, Dad is driving, and I'm in the back of the Subaru, just like when Izzy and I were little. Only now, the seat beside me is empty.

We arrived at the hospital first thing this morning to bring Mom home. It should have been a happy day, one bright moment in a cloud of darkness. Instead, while we waited for the final paperwork to be signed, Sheriff Ryan knocked on the door to Mom's hospital room. As soon as I saw him, saw the look on his face, I knew. I just knew.

They had finally found Izzy.

I wanted you to hear it from me first, Jim, he'd said, and Dad reached out and shook the sheriff's hand.

Mom burst into tears. I stood frozen, unable to even look at them. It wasn't until that moment that I realized I'd still been holding on to hope.

Early on, I'd comfort myself with daydreams of Izzy's return. They burned within me, hot and full of light. How when I saw her, I'd have already forgiven her for whatever stupid reason had made her run away, some embarrassing mistake she thought she had to hide from, some naive adventure she'd skipped off to without me. All that would matter was that she was back. That I would hear her laugh again, that I could pick up the phone and she would answer, that we could share jeans and secrets and dreams of things that would happen in a faraway future. That I would have my sister again, be whole again.

But as the weeks turned to months, turned to years, those daydreams faded. Time killed each and every one, made them all the more improbable with each passing day, until only one possible ending remained.

So, when Sheriff Ryan told us that they found human remains in The Hollow last night, I was surprised to feel that last ember fade. Surprised that it had been there at all.

We haven't talked about it. We remained quiet as we grabbed the last of Mom's personal belongings to bring her home, loading up a few stuffed bears, her suitcase, and some knit blankets into the back of the car. She left her jigsaw puzzles behind for other patients. *Oh, I don't need this thing*, she fussed as Dad pushed her wheelchair through the hospital hallways.

Already our phones have been ringing off the hook—calls from well-meaning neighbors offering condolences and quietly fishing for gossip, but also from the news stations and the true crime podcasts angling for interviews. I've silenced Mom's phone. She doesn't need to deal with any of that. Not today, at least.

Now, she puts a hand over Dad's on the center console. I watch the way her wedding ring glints in the sunlight. He interlaces his fingers through hers. "We can finally have a service," Mom says. "Lay her down beside her grandmother."

"I'll call the funeral home," Dad says, and I want to hurl myself at him, jerk the wheel and flip the car. I want him to bellow, to break things, to be anything but practical. I want him to be the kind of dad that would have marched onto the Sherman property on day one and found out what happened to his little girl. Then maybe I wouldn't have wasted so much of my life daydreaming.

Because she had been there all along. Right where we'd thought she'd been. Right where we had known. Cold and alone. *Do you see it, Iggy? Do you see?* But I hadn't wanted to see. A sob claws up my chest and lodges there, burning, because I know if I let it out, I won't be able to stop. I hadn't wanted to believe that Ben had killed her. Not back then. And not now. But of course he had. And I was the fool who let myself think otherwise.

Sitting in the back of my parents' car, only the nightmare of our reality remains. And, more than anything, I want that last ember back.

But Izzy is gone. And without that last bit of hope, I am consumed by so much anger.

I reach into my purse and crumple the invitation tight in my fist.

CHAPTER FORTY-SIX

CAT

I keep replaying it. The way my hand shook as I called Sheriff Ryan, trying to sound calm, trying to sound like the adult in charge. Within minutes, The Hollow was lit with headlights and flashlights, yellow tape strung across the cave. Deputies kept the kids back while we waited for the coroner. Cans of alcohol littered the bank. Marijuana smoke lingered on the air. The girls clumped together, mascara smudged from crying, their bare shoulders trembling in the cold. I kept Olivia close, her head pressed against me.

The sheriff asked a few quick questions, jotting in his little notebook—who found it, what they saw, whether anyone touched anything. There would be more follow-up later. For now, he just needed names and parents' numbers.

By two in the morning, cars were pulling up fast, headlights slicing through the dark. Parents climbing out in slippers, half dressed, faces pale with fear.

And then Emily, storming from her silver SUV, marching down the bank. *Where the hell were you, Cat? There was a whole party going on, and you didn't hear a thing?*

The other parents turned, some whispering. Emily didn't have to say the rest out loud: *You were drunk. You were passed out. Same old Cat.*

I wanted to scream that I hadn't touched a drop, that I'd been home with my earbuds in, drowning out my thoughts with ocean waves. But the words wouldn't come. Not when every set of eyes there knew my history, knew the stories, knew all the times I hadn't been reliable. The shame clamped me down, silent.

I just stood there, heat burning my face, while Emily took my daughter away, back to her home, where she is safe and looked after. The truth was, I had no explanation to give. Emily is right in the way that counts. As they left, Olivia looked back over her shoulder, and the faintest flicker passed between us—enough to keep me standing, enough to remind me I hadn't lost her completely.

Now, I see Isabelle Whitmore's face. I watch it decay in a rapid time-lapse, unable to turn away. Her skin white and waterlogged sloughs off in strips that float in the stagnant, iron-colored water, flies and beetles lay eggs in the creases of her closed eyelids, larvae worm out to consume soft tissue, rats take chunks, a grotesque frenzy of movement, of degradation until she is nothing but bone.

I wake in a puddle of sweat, the sheets and pillowcase damp beneath me, my nightgown twisted up between my legs. I strip the bed, throw the laundry in the wash, and put on clean sheets.

The model home is so quiet I can hear the toilet filling, the hum of the central heat, the buzz of my own thoughts like hornets.

I think of the champagne bottles.

It's only champagne. People give their kids sips of champagne on New Year's Eve. There's more alcohol in most people's mouthwash. It hardly qualifies.

I can hear the cork pop so clearly. The release of tension. Cold bubbles that promise a warm honey oblivion.

I haven't poured out yesterday's half-empty bottle yet. If Mark is secretly keeping count, he'd never know if that bit went down the drain or not. And how much could a glass or two hurt, really?

I get up casually, open the fridge like I'm grabbing a snack. Because if Mark is counting bottles, who's to say he hasn't installed a nanny cam to keep an eye on me as well? I make a face at the champagne, act like I'd forgotten it was there. I bring it to the sink and unhook the airtight stopper. The pop is subtle, but the smell makes my heart flutter. I tip it over the drain, but move my thumb to cover the opening, to trap the champagne inside. I feel a little thrill. And then Emily's voice slices in, that cut-glass edge: *Same old Cat.*

I grip the bottle harder, ashamed of how quickly I'm proving her point.

I set the still half-full bottle in the recycling bin, upright so that it doesn't spill, pull the strings of the trash bag tight and tie it, lift the bag from the bin. I'll set it out by the trash, and no one has to know it's there. No one has to know anything at all.

When I open the door, I'm jolted back to my senses. Melanie is standing on the porch. Relief washes over me when I see her. What the hell was I thinking?

"Honey, I wanted to check on you, with everything that's going on. We can't have you spiraling again."

I place the bag down and throw my arms around her.

"Oh, Cat," she says, rubbing circles on my back. "Everything will be fine."

I hear the bag slump and shift, then feel the chill of the champagne on my bare feet as I squeeze her tight.

CHAPTER FORTY-SEVEN

SARAH LYNN

I sit on the love seat in Mom's pageant room, whitening strips on my teeth, staring at the giant portrait of her in her crown and sash, the gleam of her teeth, the perfect slope of her nose, her high cheekbones. But all I can picture is the skull beneath, the bones that give her face its shape.

Mom is at her desk, phone to her ear. She's been fielding calls all morning. By now, everyone in town knows that The Hollow is taped off. They want to know if the pageant will be postponed, if maybe it will be cancelled altogether. They're also concerned about the weather. Warnings crawl across the bottom of every local channel: temperatures dropping into the twenties, windchill in the teens, a chance of sleet. A handful of counties have already called off school, and the power company is urging people to "prepare for disruptions." And still, Mom keeps assuring callers that the show will go on.

"The Amenity Center is not considered part of the crime scene," she says crisply, as she clicks her pen against a legal pad. "We're still planning to meet tonight to set up the venue, and I expect all contestants and volunteers to show up as committed."

People don't understand how much work she's put into this, how every vendor has been wrangled, how the deposits have all been paid, funds raised because she's been buttering up sponsors for months with favors and fancy lunches and a thousand phone calls. But I do. I have seen every single thing she's done.

When she finally hangs up, she exhales sharply, then turns to her corkboard. The headshots are pinned in neat rows, contestants lined up like soldiers. Olivia's face sits at the very top, skewered with a red pushpin.

Last night, when Mom picked us up from The Hollow, she didn't yell. She didn't ground us or threaten to take away our cell phones or tell Dad. She just drove home in silence, her hands tight at ten and two. In the garage, she got out, walked straight into the house without a word.

Kayden smiled slyly, like we'd gotten away with something, and he slipped away to his room.

But I found her in the dark kitchen, pouring a glass of wine with her back to me.

Mom?

Go to bed, Sarah Lynn, she'd said, her voice flat and calm, like a door clicking shut. This is what she does when I disappoint her. She locks me out in the cold.

Now, she crosses the room and sits beside me. She takes my hand.

"I'm proud of you," she says. "You know that, right? You've worked hard for this. You deserve it."

And the tension in my chest loosens enough for me to breathe.

Once, when I was little, Mom caught me chewing on my nails. I hadn't even realized I was doing it until she popped my hand with the back of hers, quick, like the strike of a snake. Her ring caught my lip and I tasted blood. Tears stung my eyes.

But then she pulled me close, wrapped her arms around me and held me against her perfume and her warmth. I could feel her heartbeat against my ear, and I felt safe. *I just want what's best for you*, she said.

And, still, I know that it's true.

Because Mom does want what's best for me. She found a way

to break away from the shitty life she was supposed to have. She forged her own, exactly the way she wanted it to be. And now she wants the same for me—wants it so badly she'll bend the world until it breaks.

"You're going to win this," she says now. "We'll make sure of it. Do you understand?"

I want to tell her that Olivia is my friend, but she wouldn't care. After all, Iggy was her friend. "Yes, ma'am," I say instead.

Her phone rings again and she goes back to her desk, straightening the stack of extra Miss Lone Star Princess invitations as she answers.

"Yes," she says. "Venue setup will proceed this evening as planned. Yes, of course, I heard. . . ."

The whitening strips burn on my teeth. I peel them off and toss them into the trash. My tongue runs across the fresh enamel, tingling. I try not to think of Isabelle Whitmore's teeth still locked into her skull. The missing jaw beneath.

Mom has always been determined. I know what she's capable of when she wants something badly enough.

CHAPTER FORTY-EIGHT

MELANIE

Waylon is asleep in the back bedroom. Unfolded laundry is heaped across the kitchen table, the TV blares to an empty room, and the boys' bickering echoes from the playroom like a pair of feral cats. The timer dings, and I rush to pull out the muffins. I made two batches, as I have a couple of stops with patients today. And I move them to a wire rack to cool before heading down the hall to check in on the girls.

I pause outside the door, the sound slipping through before I even touch the knob. A man's voice. And for a moment, there's something familiar about it. But maybe it's just that he's speaking in that Keith Morrison *Dateline* voice, the one that makes every sentence sound like a eulogy: ". . . the bones discovered deep in The Hollow raise more questions than they answer . . ."

I frown, opening the door quickly. "What on earth are you listening to?"

Hannah and Olivia, sitting on the bed, huddled over a phone, jolt up.

"One local teen described the gruesome discovery . . ." the voice continues.

Olivia scrambles for the pause button. "It's just a podcast. Everyone at school's been passing it around."

My stomach knots. "Turn that off. Right now."

They both blink at me, startled.

"That man doesn't know what he's talking about. None of them do. It's not entertainment, it's people's lives." It comes out harsher than I mean it to, but I can't stand the thought of some stranger making a spectacle out of what happened to Izzy. "He's making it out like Izzy's bones are props from a horror movie. She was someone's daughter."

The girls look down, chastened.

I draw a breath, lower my voice. "Actually, why don't you girls come with me? I'm bringing muffins to Mrs. Whitmore. She's back home now, and it'll mean something to her to see you girls there."

Hannah hops right to it. She's been sweet to me this morning, trying to make up for sneaking out last night and scaring the life out of me.

When I brought her home, she was braced for a lecture. *I'm sorry, Mom*, she'd whispered. I pulled her into a hug and told her just to get some sleep. Her hair was still damp, carrying the smell of The Hollow, of that damp, dark, mineral cave.

It's strange how certain scents are like direct lines to memories. How some memories tattoo themselves on your mind, become a permanent part of who you are.

After Kennedy Claire and Iggy left me swimming naked in the well, I climbed into that cave for cover, tucked myself deep into a fissure in the very back, just large enough for me to sit inside. I wrapped my bare arms around myself and waited. For hours. Listening to the wind in the trees, to water dripping from the limestone, to my breath echoing. I didn't know what to do. I couldn't walk home. And I couldn't bear the thought of someone finding me like that, boys from school floating down the river. I'd rather die.

Then, eventually, I heard footsteps, sloshing through the water. I prayed it was the girls, coming back to laugh at me and return my clothes. The best I could hope for.

But the steps were heavy. And then I saw him, filling the mouth of the cave, blocking the light. My whole body went cold.

I try not to think of the rest. But some things stay with you, whether you want them to or not.

CHAPTER FORTY-NINE

INGRID

I march across the road that leads into the trailer park just outside Anhalt, the loose gravel shifting under my feet. Late-afternoon sun slants behind me, but it carries no warmth. The air bites, and I can see my breath in faint puffs. I tug the collar of my jacket higher, but the wind cuts through. It rattles a loose sheet of tin on one of the trailers. Bare branches clatter together above, like dry bones clicking in the rising gusts. My shadow stretches ahead on the rocks, as if I am led by a darker side of myself.

I think about the time Izzy and I stood face-to-face with Ben and dared him to tell us apart, a fifty-fifty chance of creating his own doom. About all the dinners Ben had at our house, how he and Izzy would lay around on the sofa, legs tangled up together beneath a blanket on lazy Saturdays. About the time Dad helped Ben fix the transmission on his truck, Dad standing on the bumper with a dowel, muscling the serpentine belt back into place. The time I third-wheeled it to the movie theater with Ben and Izzy to watch *The Sixth Sense*, how we got dipped cones at Dairy Queen afterward and teased Ben that he needed a haircut. How he plucked an eyelash off Izzy's cheek and held it out to her on his fingertip, asked her to make a wish.

How I never heard one single word from him after she disappeared.

I spot Ben's rusty old truck, parked in front of a trailer with a set of rotted-out wooden steps and a dirty screen door.

This wasn't planned. After I'd helped Mom to bed so she could take a nap, I went out to find her a body pillow, something more comfortable for when she's lying on her side and the nausea returns. But before I made it to the Target in San Marcos, that trilling of the bells radiated from my purse, my ridiculous spontaneity alarm. *What do you want, Ingrid?* It gave me permission to be reckless. So I jerked the wheel hard, U-turning in the middle of traffic, and slammed the accelerator. Oncoming drivers laid on their horns, but they parted all the same. What I've really been wanting for my entire adult life is to confront Ben Sherman. To get answers.

I see an empty Wonder Bread bag in the high grass and weeds along the edge of the trailer. I notice a white five-gallon bucket at the bottom of the stairs, filled with empty beer cans. One step wobbles, like it's holding on by a single nail, as I make my way up. The screen door screeches as I swing it open. I make a fist and slam it against the front door. It's more solid than I expected. I shift my keys in my other hand, wedge them like claws between my fingers. But there's no answer. I continue to pound.

Then my own shadow is swallowed by another. One much larger than mine. The air shifts, cold against my skin. I turn. And there he is. Ben Sherman, close enough to touch.

CHAPTER FIFTY

INGRID

When I see Ben, everything I meant to say dissolves in my throat like sand, because strapped to his chest, in a soft-sided carrier printed with moons and stars, is a sleeping baby. Downy haired and cute as a button.

"Iggy," he says.

Just my name. It's the first word I've heard him say in twenty-five years, and the sound of his voice hits me harder than the sight of him. When we were little, no more than six or seven, Izzy told Mom that *Ben doesn't talk much, but when he does, he has a voice like he's standing up for someone*. His voice is even deeper now, worn down at the edges. But beneath the gravel, I hear the shape of the boy I'd known. And for a dizzying second, I can hear him calling my name across the riverbank.

But then the weight of all the years between us drops back into place, heavy as a stone. Ben's eyes flick to my keys, still wedged between my fingers like claws. He reaches past my shoulder to the door of the trailer, holding it open and gesturing for me to enter.

"Come on in," he says. "You only waited twenty-five years for this."

I step inside. I expected a mess. I expected the sour tang of unwashed clothes, the stagnant air of neglect. But the house is warm. Tidy. A blue quilt drapes along the back of an armchair, the end table holds only a neat stack of dog-eared paperbacks and a coaster, pale blue curtains soften the light at the windows. In the corner, there's a rainbow-patterned baby swing. The whole space hums with domesticity, so at odds with what I'd imagined that it leaves me disoriented.

Ben unbuckles the baby, slides her free, and settles her on his hip as he hangs the carrier on a hook by the door. Then, without ceremony, he hands her to me.

I take her awkwardly, caught off guard by the gesture. By everything.

While I'm still finding my balance with her in my arms, he disappears into the kitchen.

I peek down at the baby. She blinks up at me with big brown eyes—Ben's eyes—and inspects me curiously before her face scrunches and she squirms, making small, discontented grunts.

"Oh, no, no. There, there," I whisper, swaying without thinking. The rhythm soothes her, her tense little body relaxing into mine.

"You stop moving, she starts crying," Ben calls, pulling a prepared bottle from the fridge. I watch as he fumbles with a bottle warmer.

On the kitchen table, I notice a rolled-up set of survey maps. "What are those?"

"Work," he says with a shrug. "Got a job with a land use firm out of San Marcos. Did my degree online while I was working the rigs. Want a beer?"

"No."

Everything feels wrong. I came ready for a fight, but here I am swaying his baby in a tidy living room, staring at maps and paperbacks, and nothing about it matches the image I've carried all these years of Ben as some half-feral recluse, holed up with his old man, drowning himself in guilt.

Beside the maps, there's a notepad with the baby's schedule, written in neat, girly, slanted handwriting. I picture him moving through the day, measuring formula, coaxing tiny spoons of mush into this baby's mouth, giving her lavender-scented baths in one of those plastic baby tubs. His hands, slick with soap, working through feather-soft hair.

For twenty-five years, I've imagined those same hands gripped tight around my sister's throat. *He's, like, totally obsessed with me*, Izzy had once said, and I went back to those words again and again. Because Ben had loved Izzy. He would have done anything for her, and when she broke his heart, I could imagine the dark wave of anger filling him. The feeling of losing something that was supposed to belong to him. I could imagine him not letting her leave, imagine her struggling, his hands finding themselves around her neck. Imagine the squeeze. Strong, firm fingers gripping her windpipe. I have. I have so many times.

It's an image I can't get unstuck from my mind. And yet, standing here, trying to rectify the boy I knew with the man in front of me and the monster I'd conjured in between—everything inside me is starting to feel unstuck.

The warmer gurgles softly as the water heats.

Ben pops open a can of Shiner and leans against the counter. He knocks his cowboy boots off heel to toe, then runs his fingers through his shaggy hair. For the first time, I get a good look at him. He's put on weight—less wiry and more solid than when we were young. Time has carved lines into his face, creases linger around his squinty eyes. But still, there is something familiar about him—the eyes, the mannerisms—I can picture him at some party at The Hollow, leaning back on a boulder in that same way, sipping from a beer.

"Laurie's out of town," he says. "Delayed the honeymoon until after they had Mabel." He tips the beer at the baby. Ben's little sister is eight years younger than us. Back then Laurie wore hand-me-down cargo shorts that hung to her knobby knees and had waist-length hair she let tangle behind her when she ran around the scrubby property of the Sherman Ranch. Ben kept a brush in his back pocket, and I think of how he'd hold her hair by the roots so he could comb out the knots without hurting her. I glance down at Mabel, and I recognize Laurie's upturned nose.

The bottle warmer hisses, snapping me out of this mirage.

It makes me suddenly livid that Ben gets to be an uncle, when I'll never have the chance to be an aunt. That was taken from me. "I thought Laurie and your mom moved away. Figured they didn't want anything to do with you." There's venom in my words, and it shifts the air in the room.

Ben just watches me a moment, the way he always did, careful with his words. "When I got back from Odessa, Mom wanted me to move in with her. I still talk to both of them all the time."

"Then why'd she leave?" The words come out like an accusation, like the proof I'd always thought they'd been. Carol fleeing that house, this town, everything I knew she loved because she couldn't stand looking at her son, knowing that he was a killer.

Ben breathes an unamused laugh through his nose, gestures toward the door. "Everywhere she went, people looked at her like—" A muscle in his jaw tenses. He takes a sip. "She just couldn't stay here."

I think of Mom's story. Running into Carol at the grocery store. The way Carol had left her full grocery cart just sitting in the aisle. I'd always thought it was out of guilt, simple. And maybe guilt was a part of it, but layered between so many more complicated things. I think of how close Carol and Mom were back then. How Carol must have felt, seeing her best friend, and not being able to comfort her, not being able to face her. I think of Mom too, and how the loss of Izzy was like a pebble tossed in the water, the ripples unending.

"So why didn't you?" I ask, shifting the baby in my arms as she starts to fuss. "Move in with your mom when you came back?"

He looks at the beer in his hand, finger fidgeting with the metal tab. "I couldn't leave Dad alone, and he wouldn't leave the ranch." He shrugs, like it just is what it is, like it doesn't matter that his life has been on hold since he was seventeen. That both our lives have been, like a part of us stayed behind with Izzy. "But that's all changed. I'm planning on getting us some land, maybe closer to Laurie and Mom, building us a house."

"Makes sense you'd run away again." I fling the words at him. The bottle warmer starts to spit and fizz. "Now that they've found her." I say it to remind myself too—that's why I came here today.

He fixes me with a look. "Have a seat."

I sit, nestling Mabel into the crook of my arm.

Ben rolls up his sleeve and tests the milk on his wrist before holding the bottle out to me. "Tilt it, so she isn't sucking air. The last thing I need is her screaming through nap time again."

I glare up at him. "You think you can just hand me a baby, and what? I'll melt? I'll believe every word you say?" Mabel starts squirming at the sight of the bottle, and only seconds later begins crying for it.

"No." He sets the bottle on the table. "I just think it's time for her bottle."

I give in. Mabel relaxes as soon as the nipple touches her lips.

For a long while, there's only this moment. The faint hum of the fridge and Mabel's tiny, satisfied gulps.

Ben takes the armchair. "Izzy never showed up that night. That's all I know."

"You left." My voice cracks—because I've never been able to speak that hurt out loud—but I force it down like a pill. I focus on the anger instead. I picture my sister's bones, organized into evidence bags and boxes, labeled neatly. "You left," I say again, my voice steady this time. "And I didn't hear a Goddamn word from you. For twenty-five years, Ben."

"What was I supposed to do? Call your house? Ask your dad to put you on? I was scared, Iggy. I was seventeen. Okay? I'm sorry." He tosses it out roughly, moving on quickly, but I don't miss the words. "I didn't know what the hell was going on, and it all happened so fast. Dad. He just . . . hunkered down. You know how he can be."

I shake my head. "If Abel thought Izzy was alive, he would have been out there looking for her. But he knew she was already dead. Didn't he?" Mabel is beginning to doze off, but her eyes pop open wide at the sound of my rising voice.

He scrubs a hand over his jaw. "I don't know. Okay? I don't know why Dad . . ." He exhales. "But I did try."

I scoff. "You tried what?"

"To talk to you."

I almost laugh at that.

"I told Kennedy Claire."

My head snaps up. "Told her what?" Mabel's eyes are drifting closed again.

He sets the empty beer can on the coffee table with a dull metallic thud. "Before I left town, I ran into Kennedy Claire at the Dollar General, and I told her that I wanted to talk to you. Asked her to tell you to meet me at the park. I wrote it down for her. When you didn't, I figured . . ." His eyes drop. "You believed what everyone else believed. So I left, like Dad wanted."

The room sways, like I'm stepping out onto a rope bridge, the whole of my world suddenly uncertain beneath my feet. I have no way of knowing whether he's lying to me. "They found Izzy on your land," I say, reaching out for the only thing I know to be true. The evidence that proves Ben is guilty.

He leans in. "Every kid in school partied at The Hollow. Anyone could have found her there. Anyone could have put her there." His words come out like he means to stamp them in the air. Like he wants them to be permanent in my mind.

I feel Mabel's hand wrap around my finger. I glance down at her. She's back awake and staring at me, smiling when I meet her gaze, like she's been waiting for me to look down.

"That's the last place I would have put her, Iggy," Ben says. "Sherman Ranch is nearly eight hundred acres, and I'd have had twenty-five years to hide her wherever I wanted."

The air suddenly feels soupy thick in between the narrow walls of the trailer, the heat emanating from the baby agitating.

"If I had buried Izzy, you would have never found her."

CHAPTER FIFTY-ONE

CAT

Thank God for Melanie, showing up just when I needed her, stopping me from doing something so incredibly stupid. She's always been my life preserver, there to keep me afloat just before I sink.

My sponsor says exercise and routine are supposed to help—stress relief, mood regulation, all that. So I take a walk around the neighborhood, avoiding the road that winds along the river, past The Hollow, where the forensic team is still at work. I zip my fleece up to my chin. The sky is low and gray. The trees shiver and sometimes bend. In the distance, the hills are obscured by the mist, so they look like the backdrop of a stage play, somehow both less vivid and more beautiful. It isn't raining, but the air is wet with the threat of it, every gust of wind spritzing my cheeks with cold moisture. And the cold feels nice in the way it brings me fully into my body.

The walk clears my head, and when I spot the food truck that comes around each day to bring lunch to the construction workers, I buy two foil-wrapped tacos, and walk down to the construction trailer, planning to bring Mark the extra and ask if Olivia can stay the night.

It isn't her job to look after her mother, but it will be easier to stay focused on my goal when my reason is right there under my roof.

But when I knock on the door, it's Emily who answers. I step back. "Oh, hi. I was just bringing Mark some lunch."

She leans against the doorframe, arms crossed. "He's meeting with the developers. They aren't too happy about this." She tips her head in the direction of The Hollow.

"Right," I say. Then, after an awkward beat, I remember the tacos in my hand. "Well, here." I hand her one.

She takes it, turns it over. "You and Mark have lunch together a lot?"

"No. I mean—I was going to ask if Olivia can stay the night with me tonight."

"Do you really think that's the best thing for Olivia?"

I feel that same wash of shame from last night, but then the heat in my cheeks meeting the stinging cold of the air only makes me burn hotter. Olivia is my daughter. This is between Mark and me. Not her. I take another step up, so that we're on equal footing. "Sorry," I say. "I meant, Olivia will be staying with me tonight. I just wanted you to know that I'll pick her up from the Amenity Center." The words feel strange in my mouth, but solid too.

Her eyes narrow, but she doesn't respond.

"Enjoy your lunch." Then I spin on my heel and leave her to stew. I hear the door shut behind me, and my steps feel lighter than they should as I head back toward the street.

And this time, I can't help but look over at The Hollow, at the team of people in white coveralls and face masks, taking photographs, bringing bags of evidence to the van parked up on the road. There are onlookers too. People from town who have come to see it for themselves.

And then, farther along the bend, I see Abel Sherman standing on the bank of the river that used to be his. He has his hands in his pockets as he watches the officers. Then he stoops to pick up a stray beer can that must have floated downstream from the kids' party, just like he used to do all those years ago.

The sight of him turns my stomach, dragging me back in time.

We have to tell your dad, I told Melanie once. *He can help.*

But Melanie was so desperate, so frantic. *Please, Cat. I don't want him to know. I'll die. He'll never see me the same. Please.*

But we could have stopped it all.

Abel looks over and spots me, up on the hill above him. And the way he's looking at me, it sends a chill through me.

It's like he knows.

CHAPTER FIFTY-TWO

MELANIE

Hannah, Olivia, and I follow Mrs. Whitmore down the narrow hallway to the kitchen. The green floral wallpaper is covered with pictures of Ingrid and Isabelle, filling almost every inch of wall space. As we pass the stairs, I glance up to see the pictures running backward through time, each step up the stairs another year erased. They must lead up to Isabelle's room, the place she grew up and grew out of, until the day she disappeared. I think of Mrs. Whitmore climbing these stairs over the past twenty-five years, rewinding, watching her daughters grow younger. I wonder if the pictures play like movies in her mind, the sound of their laughter, the smell of the ocean.

Outside, we ran into Mr. Whitmore, all bundled up and covering his flower beds. *Supposed to be something else come this weekend*, he'd said.

My dad used to talk about the blizzard back in eighty-five. Said it took them a week to clear the county roads, I said.

We stood on the porch while he went inside to check on his wife, to make sure she was fit for company. Fifteen minutes later, she answered the door in a quilted housecoat, but she'd put on her makeup and jewelry.

I notice that she's moving slower, and as she walks, she leans on the chair tops to maintain balance as she makes her way around the table.

"I brought cards." I hold them up with a small smile, hoping to coax one from her in return.

"Oho," Mrs. Whitmore chuckles. "I don't know that I'm up for that today, dear." She uses the table for support as she lowers herself down into a chair.

I take the seat beside her and open the Tupperware. "Banana muffins?"

"Any nuts? My mother used to always make banana bread with walnuts. But Iggy's allergic." I watch as she pinches the muffin's top with two fingers, then places the soft, sweet bread into her mouth. Even though she's feeling nauseous, she's put on lipstick and doesn't want to be impolite.

"No nuts," I say. "I use chocolate chips. Is Iggy here?"

Mrs. Whitmore swats the air. "You know Iggy. She always has an errand."

Cat asked me once how I do it, spend my time with sick and dying people every day. *Isn't it depressing?* It's sad sometimes, sure. I meet a lot of people toward the end of their life, spend a lot of days saying goodbye to people I've grown to care about. *They're dying whether I'm there or not*, I told her. *I'd rather be there to help.* I like keeping them company, bringing them little tidbits of happiness, stepping in when their loved ones can't bear it. I'm weak in a lot of areas in my life, but I'm strong enough when facing death.

I was the one who found Oma Greta dead in her bed, after she'd slipped away peacefully in the night, and that is exactly how it had felt the minute I saw her lying there, eyes closed and still. I hadn't, even for an instant, thought she was sleeping. I felt distinctly that she had slipped out of her body, like in the Bible when we are told that our bodies are just jars of clay, just vessels for our souls.

"These are cool," Olivia says, peering into a curio cabinet filled with porcelain figurines, Victorian women in blooming, frilled dresses holding parasols, put together in that high society way of the time.

"Aren't they pretty? Those are my Avon dolls," Mrs. Whitmore says. "I used to collect them. See that one in the yellow jacket with the matching hat? I got her for earning the President's Club Award one year. Oh, that was forever ago. I just loved her little pearls and the roses on her dress." She flutters her fingers over the neckline of her housecoat, where the flowers would be. "You know I had roses like that on my dress when I was in Miss Lone Star."

"You mean when you won Miss Lone Star," I correct.

"Oh," Mrs. Whitmore says, playing at modesty, but I see her little shimmy of pride.

"Mrs. Whitmore," Hannah asks, "do you have any pictures from the pageant?"

"Hanging upstairs in the hallway, over by my bedroom. Go on up, it's all the way in the back. I keep them there, so Jim doesn't forget what a catch I was."

The girls run off. We can hear a flutter of laughter, their voices carrying lightly down the stairs. Mrs. Whitmore tilts her head, eyes drifting closed for a moment as she takes a deep breath and lets out a slow sigh. I wonder if she's remembering a time when it was her two girls giggling up there.

There are some memories that I only allow myself to return to every so often. The time my Oma Greta sewed me an exact replica of Cinderella's silver-blue ball gown, way back when I barely came up to her hip. It took her nearly a month to stitch it together, staying up late, cutting patterns with crackling paper attached. *I'm beautiful*, I'd said, when she slipped it over my head, even though there was no mirror in Oma Greta's room. I didn't need one. I could see my beauty reflected in her eyes.

Memories like that are too perfect, too precious to withstand everyday wear and tear. They are like the good china, only to be brought out on special occasions. And then, when I've given myself permission, I can slip into the memory, feel the satin around my ankles, fill up with the warmth of being cherished. The details are sharp because I haven't worn away their edges. I wonder how often Mrs. Whitmore must think of Isabelle. Of her treasure box of memories with her. I wonder whether she has worn them all out.

Isabelle was only seventeen. Same age as our girls now, Cat said the other day, as if I wasn't already perfectly aware. As if I didn't think about it every time I checked Mrs. Whitmore's temperature or played canasta. What it must be like for her. What it would do to me if I ever lost Hannah. The thought alone scoops me empty.

I look to the Avon dolls, to their pretty painted exteriors. Mrs. Whitmore is like one of her figurines. Behind her pleasantries, the hellos and how-do-you-dos of everyday life, behind the teased hair and makeup, her insides are surely hollow.

While she picks at the muffin and I make her a cup of hot cocoa, she tells me that they're looking forward to finally being able to have a service for Isabelle.

"Are they even sure it's her?" I ask, setting down the cup in front of her, the spoon to the side. "I mean, have they had time to—"

"It's her," Mrs. Whitmore says, firmly. "The items they found in the cave belonged to her."

I sit back down.

"You know those stories you hear?" she says, pausing to sip her cocoa. "The one-in-a-million stories. The girl who's kidnapped and held captive for a decade before escaping and being reunited with her family. Every few years, you hear a new one. Jaycee Dugard, held captive for eighteen years. Or those girls in Ohio, the ones they found in that house . . ." she trails off.

"It's amazing what people can endure," I say.

"I always hated myself for hating those stories. Deep down I knew my Izzy was gone, but those stories wouldn't let her die." Mrs. Whitmore smiles sadly. I expect her to cry, but she doesn't. I put a hand over hers. It's frail and cold.

Looking at Mrs. Whitmore now, a calm relief settles on her face. No more stories to tease her. And I realize that the real cruelty of it all was not knowing.

The girls come back down, peppering Mrs. Whitmore with compliments, with questions about the pageant fifty years ago, what her talent was, if she still remembers the opening dance sequence.

I snap the lid on the Tupperware and tuck the remaining muffins into a corner of the cabinet, refill Mrs. Whitmore's water bottle and get her situated comfortably in a recliner in the living room with a book on her lap. The girls climb into the back seat of the minivan, and we wave goodbye to Mr. Whitmore, who is moving potted plants into the garage now.

It is only then that I let myself feel the full weight of Mrs. Whitmore's prolonged pain. It presses down on me, and it's worse than death, cracking hairline fractures deep into my own happy porcelain veneer.

CHAPTER FIFTY-THREE

SARAH LYNN

Metal grinds against metal like a toothache as Olivia climbs the ladder, my foot planted firmly on the bottom rung to keep her steady. Mom's barking orders, clipboard in hand, as her minions—mothers, volunteers, and pageant girls, myself included—transform the Events Hall into a full-blown gold explosion. Balloon arches, sequined curtains, foil streamers, tinsel, tassels—gold as far as the eye can see. Mom would puff glitter straight into the audience's eyeballs if she could. It's Miss Lone Star Princess's Golden Jubilee this year, and she's never been one to shy away from a theme.

What she *has* shied away from is the actual manual labor. That's where we come in. A group of us girls spent an hour arguing over the instructions for the scaffolding, like it was a group project from hell. Sabrina got so frustrated, she chucked her Allen wrench across the stage and stormed off in a huff. A tantrum like that doesn't go unnoticed. Mom says you're never safe from judging. Not onstage. Not off it.

Eventually, we figured it out and got the whole structure assembled, even bolting down the heavy stage lights ourselves.

Now, Olivia's looping a garland of glittering stars across the top of the scaffolding, stretching on tiptoe to adjust the strand just right.

Mr. Magnuson crouches near the stage lights, untangling wires. I wore my white tennis shoes today, paired with the pleated skirt Mom picked out. Short enough to show off my legs, still "sweet" enough to pass her inspection. Mom says every moment is an audition—orientation, grocery runs, even hanging lights in a drafty Events Hall. There's power in controlling how other people perceive you.

I stretch my calves, arch my back a little, the way Mom taught me. I peek over my shoulder, wondering if he'll notice. He doesn't, not at first. Then when I call, "How does this look, Mr. M.?" his eyes flick upward, catch on the hem of my skirt, the long stretch of my thighs for half a second, before he jerks his gaze back to the cables.

"Maybe a little higher on the left," he says, directing Olivia instead.

She flashes him a smile, all gratitude. "Thanks, Mr. Magnuson."

"Sarah Lynn." Mom's voice, sharp as a snapped bone, cuts across the stage. She's off to the side, arms folded. Her mouth is set in that line that means I've already disappointed her.

I whisper to Olivia as she climbs down, "Total mood killer." Olivia giggles nervously, and we drag the ladder a few feet over. The spreader bar catches wrong; it doesn't lock into place. Olivia doesn't notice. She starts climbing again.

She's near the top, shin braced against the last rung, reaching for the garland. One more step, and the whole ladder could fold beneath her.

I see Mom watching. She doesn't say a word. Her silence says it all. Let it happen. Let Olivia's own poor choices undo her.

For a second, I almost move aside. My body remembering Mom's lessons. It's always been the two of us. Pacing the living room at midnight in my rhinestone heels, practicing my walk for evening wear, the overhead light catching the glittering edge of my gown. Mom correcting, over and over, staying up for hours with me until my stride was fluid, my turn sharp, until the silent laugh that refreshed my smile came effortlessly. Her hands on my wrists, guiding me into each pose—elbow soft, palm angled just so—until it was muscle memory.

But I think of Olivia's hand in mine as we floated in the freezing water.

"Hold on," I tell her, reaching for the lock. I snap it into place with a firm click. The ladder steadies under her weight.

She exhales, smiling down at me. "Thanks."

Behind me, I hear Mom's heels retreating, sharp stabs across the floor. I don't turn to watch her go. The thrill of ignoring her instruction fizzes under my skin like soda bubbles.

When Olivia makes it safely down, I cross the stage to where Mr. Magnuson is kneeling by the rig. I drop to a crouch beside him, close enough that my knee brushes his arm.

"Need help?"

He doesn't look at me, just gestures vaguely at the mess of cords. "Nah. Just trying to keep this from shorting out." His voice is calm, but I catch the tension in his jaw, the stiffness in his shoulders.

I lean in as if studying the wires. And our bodies are so close to touching, but they don't. The inch of space between us feels like the slow pull between magnets. I am aware of the heat radiating off his arm. The smell of dust and stage lights. "You left quick last night," I whisper. Because, this is the part that I haven't told anyone, not even Hannah and Olivia. The secret that belongs to only us.

At The Hollow, after Kayden got back with the beer, while everyone splashed in the water, I saw Mr. Magnuson's truck pull up, the headlights off. I slipped away and met him where he had parked in the cover of thick cypress trees.

He glances up, our faces too close, then quickly looks away.

CHAPTER FIFTY-FOUR

CAT

At five, I'm walking through the doors of the Sherman Ranch Amenity Center to an overwhelming amount of gold décor and a flurry of activity. Teenage girls arrange vases, move folding chairs, carry buckets of paint. They've made good progress. Scaffolding on the stage supports the backdrop, a castle cut-out silhouetted against gold sequined drapes interwoven with twinkle lights, a shimmering garland of stars scalloping the top. Hannah is offstage, stringing more lights along the edge.

Olivia sits center stage, her back to me, while she paints a giant plywood star with gold glitter.

As I slide closer to the stairs that lead up the side of the stage, I notice Sarah Lynn tucked behind the scaffolding, talking to Magnuson, who is adjusting the lights. I can see immediately what she is doing, in the tilt of her head, the feline grace with which she weaves her way around him, finding little excuses to linger too close. He's young enough to make a teenage girl's imagination run wild, and the kind of good-looking that'll have her drawing hearts in the margins of her homework. I picture that scene from *Raiders of the Lost Ark* when the student writes LOVE YOU on her eyelids.

"That must have been . . . a lot," he says, as he tightens a bolt. "Finding something like that in The Hollow."

She looks up at him through her lashes, playing the perfect damsel in distress. "It was really scary." She leans just slightly closer, and for a moment his eyes catch on her like he can't quite look away.

Then he rests a hand on her shoulder. "My door's always open."

On the surface, it sounds innocent enough. Just a concerned teacher, offering a sympathetic ear. But I can see exactly how dangerous it is, how easily it can be read another way. He should be shutting her down right now, drawing a clear line. Then, over her shoulder, he catches sight of me, and the color drains from his face like I just yanked the covers off the two of them.

I open my mouth, ready to cut in, when a sharp crack splinters the air, and we all whip our heads toward the sound. The massive scaffolding structure shudders, then, horrifyingly, begins to lean. The cables running to those heavy canister lights pull taut, then snap. For a terrible heartbeat, the whole structure hangs midair, groaning like a beast. And, in that time-clung moment, I realize my daughter sits directly beneath it.

Then it is falling. Fast. Too fast.

"Olivia!" The name tears from my throat, a strangled, useless shriek.

She leaps, springing toward the edge of the stage, just as the scaffolding comes crashing down, metal screeching as it buckles, aluminum bars collapsing in on each other. Lights burst, popping like firecrackers, exploding fragments of glittering glass across the stage. Girls scream. The impact shakes the floorboards, the vibration running up through my shoes, rattling my bones.

I run to her. Olivia is on her hands and knees, clear of the wreckage by mere inches. She blinks up at me, wide-eyed but upright. I drop to the floor, grabbing her face in both hands. "Oh my God, honey, are you okay? Are you hurt?"

"Mom . . ." She breathes. I'm already running my hands over her shoulders, down her arms, checking her. Patting for injuries, for cuts I can't see. But her bones feel solid. Her skin is warm. She's whole. That simple fact—that my daughter is alive—nearly shatters me. I pull her into a crushing hug.

Over her shoulder, in the space left by the fallen scaffolding, stands Kennedy Claire, hand to her chest, a look of perfect shock painted on her face.

I don't buy it. That bitch did this. And for what? A crown? A title?

White-hot certainty floods my veins, and I'm on my feet before I can think. Anger consumes me, dark and feral. I march to her, so close I can see where the mascara has fallen to dust her cheekbones.

"What is wrong with you?" I spit.

"With me?" Her voice is a flawless mix of confusion and hurt.

"You could have killed her," I say, through gritted teeth. My hands are in fists by my sides.

Kennedy Claire's eyes go wide, feigning innocence. "Catherine, you can't possibly think . . ."

I want to knock that smug look off her face. I want to deck her, like I promised I would so many years ago.

Someone's hand finds my arm. "Cat, it was an accident, sweetie."

I shrug the woman off, my vision tunneled down to Kennedy Claire alone. But before I get the chance to open my mouth again, to tell Kennedy Claire exactly what I think of her, Olivia's voice snaps me back: "Mom, please."

Olivia stands, working the long sleeve of her oversized sweatshirt over her hand nervously. She looks so small, so vulnerable. All I want to do is protect her, but I can see the desperation in her face, the plea she won't make out loud. *Don't embarrass me. Not again.*

And then I notice the room, all the other mothers watching, pity on their faces, the tightness of their lips. Kennedy Claire says nothing to defend herself, just lets the stark relief of her cool composure against my wild panic speak for itself.

I deflate. For Olivia's sake, I won't say any more. Not here. Not now. "Let's go home," I tell her.

But as I walk toward the glass doors, I make myself a silent oath: She touches my daughter again, and I'll put her in the fucking grave.

CHAPTER FIFTY-FIVE

INGRID

The air has that charged stillness that comes before a storm, the kind that makes every breath feel heavy in your chest. I lace my shoes tight and run. The gravel pops beneath each step, the rhythm clean enough to cut through the knot of thoughts in my head.

But Ben's voice follows me: *I was scared, Iggy. I was seventeen.*

I push my legs harder, like I can outrun my own mind. The wind shifts cold against my damp skin, scattering dry leaves across the pavement ahead of me.

The sky glows yellow, light refracting through clouds heavy with ice, shading the world in strange sepia. I think of all those versions of myself, stacked like camera negatives, one on top of the other. And I wonder what happens to those selves you never get a chance to become.

I know I'm doing it again—playing the game of what-if. Sheryl would tell me not to. *What-ifs don't change anything, Ingrid. They only trap you in the past.*

But what if Ben really did ask Kennedy Claire to deliver a message? What if I had met him at the park that night, just the two of us, away from the eyes of our parents, the whispers of the town? What if he had told me, way back then, that he was innocent?

My breath rasps in my throat as I keep the clipped pace. Would I have believed him?

I know the answer before my other foot even hits the ground. My chest tightens, shame and longing rising together. Of course I would have believed him.

By the time I make it back to the house, my legs feel like rubber bands pulled too tight. The run hasn't cleared my head—it's only left me raw and gasping. I bend forward on the porch, hands braced to my knees, dragging air into my lungs. The screen door rattles when I pull it open.

Inside, the heat makes the air heavy. I toe off my shoes and pad to the kitchen, yank a glass from the cabinet, and fill it at the tap. The first swallow is ice cold, painful going down, but it cuts through the dryness in my throat. I press the glass against my forehead, condensation slick against my skin.

The house smells faintly of coffee and the lavender detergent Mom insists on, even now, even sick. That normalcy presses against the storm inside me, almost unbearable.

I lean against the counter, glass sweating in my hand, trying to sort it: Where did Izzy go that day? And if Ben didn't kill her, then who would have wanted her dead?

The screen door rattles again, followed by the thud of boots across the floorboards. Dad's voice carries from the entry, steady and practical as always. He steps into the kitchen, pulling off a pair of gardening gloves.

"Air's dropping fast," he says. "This storm's got real teeth."

"Dad," I ask, dropping into a seat at the kitchen table. "Do you think it could have been anyone else?"

He takes the seat across from me. "No, honey. They found your letterman jacket with Izzy. It's her, sweetheart."

"No, I mean . . ." I swallow, because I know it will sound crazy when I say it out loud. But I can't stop the sprinting of my mind. "Could anyone have done this other than Ben?"

Dad is quiet. He sighs in light frustration, like he hates that all this pain has been dragged back up. "That's doubtful, given everything we know," he says, measured as always. "But we'll know more soon. Sheriff Ryan called earlier. He said they've got warrants.

They'll be tearing through Ben's and Abel's trailers tomorrow, looking for anything that ties them to Izzy."

He says it like he believes this will all be settled soon enough, like the case will be closed, and we'll have some semblance of justice. But what could they possibly hope to find after all this time?

We have Izzy now, and I guess that's all that really matters. That we don't have to wonder anymore. About that, at least.

My eyes fall on a photo that has hung on the wall for as long as I can remember. Dad, much younger than I am now, holding one of us in each arm, fresh out of a bath. We are wrapped in fluffy towels. Izzy's tiny foot pokes out, her toenails painted green—the only way to tell us apart.

CHAPTER FIFTY-SIX

CAT

It's 3 AM and I've just dumped sweet-and-sour sauce over stale rice from the takeout I ordered more than seven hours ago. I shovel it into my mouth without looking, my eyes locked to the screen, and the plastic fork squeaks against Styrofoam. The kitchen is dark, and the dark is a blanket covering me, the screen of the trail cam illuminating my hands, my face.

After I cracked the bedroom door to make sure Olivia was asleep—her breath slow, her chest rising steadily—I slipped out, crossed the yard like a thief, the air so clammy it stuck to my skin. A fine mist slicked the concrete, making the sidewalk gleam under the porch light. Beyond it, the earth was soft and wet. I picked my way between roots and low brush until I found the trail camera, cold and fogged with condensation where I'd strapped it near The Hollow. When I came back inside, the heater blasted dry warmth into my face, making my skin sting as it thawed.

Now, I'm pressing the hard plastic button on the camera to skim quickly through hours of footage. Forward. Back. Pause. Rewind. Again. Again.

The screen shows trees, shadows, empty water, but in my head the scaffolding falls. The metallic groan. The shriek of lights. Olivia's body caught beneath it. Glass raining down, opening her soft skin before her pearly bones snap like brittle birch tree branches. My stomach lurches and I force my mind back to the footage.

My eyes ache, but I can't stop, not until I find what I'm looking for.

And then I do. My pulse quickens. It's all right here. Clear as day.

"Mom, what are you doing?" Olivia's voice sends my hand slapping across the camera's screen as I fumble for the off switch.

She stands behind me, peering down over my shoulder, wearing pajama bottoms and a big T-shirt, hair pulled back, her face scrubbed clean. In this dim light, she looks young enough to make me cry.

I don't know how long she's been there. I don't know what she saw.

Protecting you, I want to tell her. But she wouldn't understand.

Because if Kennedy Claire wants to play dirty, she has no idea who she's up against.

CHAPTER FIFTY-SEVEN

MELANIE

One Day Before the Pageant

The Amenity Center smells of perfume and fresh flowers. Down the hall, the girls are fussing in the bridal suite they've claimed for a dressing room—a gilded vanity piled with brushes and glitter, racks of gowns and sequined jackets, an Instagram-ready chaise lounge and a full-length mirror catching every sparkle. They're doing run-throughs for tomorrow, nerves buzzing loud enough to fill the whole wing.

The Events Hall is full of mothers wrestling with bows and balloons, straightening chair rows, stacking programs on the welcome table, and Kennedy Claire is everywhere at once, barking orders.

Across the room, Mark has pulled in a few men from the construction crew to deal with the mess from last night's collapse. They're clearing debris into wheelbarrows, sweeping up broken glass and twisted metal. A half-built skeleton of replacement scaffolding rises on the stage, sturdier this time. Magnuson is still crouched at the edge of the platform, elbow-deep in cables, testing a light fixture and muttering to himself. He swears he'll have the rigging finished in time for the pageant tomorrow.

"Those tablecloths go on the rectangles, Melanie. Not the rounds." She doesn't even look up from her clipboard when she says it.

"Oh, sorry." I tug the cloth free, moving to the judges' table at the foot of the stage.

Outside, the sky hangs low and bruised. On the news, officials are warning that temperatures will plummet tonight, urging people to fill bathtubs in case of overnight outages and to avoid travel tomorrow unless absolutely necessary. A light drizzle has been falling all morning, and I worry that it will flash-freeze by nightfall.

I would ask Kennedy Claire if we should postpone the pageant, but she's already been biting off the heads of anyone who suggests such a thing, like she's the queen from *Alice in Wonderland*, so I keep my mouth shut.

I'm just getting the tablecloth straight when the glass doors swing open with a knife-edge gust of cold air. Cat strides in, hair damp from the mist, eyes blazing.

"Honey, are you all—" I start, but she blows past me and goes directly for Kennedy Claire.

"I need to talk to you," she says, voice low and dangerous.

Magnuson, crouched at the edge of the stage with a light fixture, glances over, but then returns his attention to the wires.

She folds the clipboard to her chest and smiles tightly. "How can I help you, Cat?" Her tone is falsely honeyed.

"I have security footage from that party the kids threw in The Hollow," she says.

At the words, Magnuson's head lifts, his hands stilling on the rigging.

"I have videos of your underage daughter drinking, doing drugs, skinny-dipping. Videos that I know you wouldn't want getting out, posted online, emailed to pageant judges and college admissions boards."

Kennedy Claire's eyes flare, but the rest of her face freezes into marble.

I drop the stack of folded tablecloths and hurry forward, slipping between them. "All right, okay, let's . . . let's all take a breath here."

My nerves prickle, remembering Cat's late-night call about the scaffolding collapse. She's convinced herself that Kennedy Claire was behind it, but I'm not so sure. That seems a step too far, even for her, and Cat's been in one of those moods, seeing shadows everywhere.

"Are you threatening me?" Kennedy Claire asks at last, her calm so steady it lifts goose bumps along my arm.

Cat doesn't blink. "I'm warning you. Stay away from Olivia."

CHAPTER FIFTY-EIGHT

SARAH LYNN

Hannah, Olivia, and I are in the dressing room. Tomorrow is the big day, so today's about staking out territory. Olivia hangs her garment bag on the rack with the others. Hannah riffles through her makeup bag, and I clear space on the long vanity for my case, which I'll keep locked until morning.

"I think I'm going to puke," Hannah says, looking into the mirror and arranging her curls. She's been looking a little pale this morning, and maybe the reality of stepping onto a stage in front of a crowd is catching up to her.

Olivia is still fiddling with her dress, but her eyes keep flicking to the open door, watching moms and contestants drift past.

"Hannah, you walked out naked in front of half the school," I say. "I think you can walk in a dress in front of some old church ladies."

She smirks.

I line up my curling iron and comb on the table. Out of the corner of my eye, I notice Olivia, still acting cagey. She hasn't met my eyes once today.

Maybe she's still thinking about what Cat said—about Mom and the scaffolding. I've tried not to think about it myself, but every time I replay the crash, the way the metal buckled and the lights swung, a chill crawls up my spine.

In the car ride home, Mom let out a long breath through her nose. *What a mess*, she said.

I'm just glad Olivia's okay, I told her.

We'll figure something out, she said.

And I wasn't sure whether she'd heard me. Whether she meant she would figure out how to get the scaffolding back up in time for the pageant. Or if she'd meant that as a response. That she would figure out another solution to our Olivia problem.

And I didn't want to know. Didn't want to think about what my mother was willing to do. What she might have done before.

So I turned my face to the window, watched the Sherman land slip away, the bulldozers, the mountains of overturned earth, and the crime scene tape that wound its way around The Hollow.

"Hey, Liv," I say now. "You okay?"

She turns to me and blurts, "My mom has videos of us at The Hollow."

I freeze. "What do you mean, videos?"

"Like, from a security camera or something. She was watching them last night." Olivia's voice drops lower with each word. "Videos of us."

Hannah's lip gloss pauses mid-swipe. "Are you serious?"

My pulse spikes. "Those cannot exist."

Olivia flinches. "I know—"

"I mean, whatever," Hannah says, sliding the gloss again. "Our parents already know."

"No, you don't get it." Mom's warnings echo in my head: *Don't send boys racy pictures unless you want them printed out and taped to every locker. Don't post anything online unless you're okay with the entire pageant board watching it together in a room.* I fumble for my phone like I can somehow erase it all myself. "If anything ever ends up on the internet, it's there forever. Forever. That's like . . . rule number one."

"Shit," Hannah says, chewing her bottom lip.

"This is how celebrity careers die." I'm up now, pacing a circle between the chairs. "One leaked picture. One stupid video. Next thing you know, your face is a meme." I picture Mom in the dark kitchen, her back to me, her silence like a pillow pressed over my face.

I replay the tequila shots, the joint to my lips, the three of us stepping naked from the woods. Mr. Magnuson leaning against his truck, parked in the shadow of trees.

The girls are looking at me, worry clear on their faces. Hannah winds one curl tightly around her finger. Olivia hides her face in her knuckles. I meet my own eyes in the mirror, lift my chin the way I've been trained.

"We're getting rid of those videos," I say, rolling my shoulders back, letting the worry fall away. If my mother taught me anything, it's how to follow through with a plan.

CHAPTER FIFTY-NINE

CAT

The wind howls against the siding, rattling the model home like it might shake loose from its foundation. Grains of ice scatter against the windows. Night presses in from every side. I pace from the front window to the back, back again, peering through the blinds, wearing a path through the staging company's rug. My pulse won't settle.

Last night, after Chinese takeout, Olivia and I watched *The Princess Bride* on the sofa, a bowl of popcorn between us. Within the first ten minutes, she was laughing. When the popcorn ran out, Olivia moved the empty bowl to the side table. She scooted over to fill the space, lifted the edge of the blanket so we could share. The warmth of her beside me pinched my heart like a set of surgical tweezers. I want, more than anything, to be the kind of mother she deserved.

Another gust slams the windows. I twitch open the blinds. The street outside is drowned in mist, thick as smoke, shifting in sheets across the half-paved road. Through it, a car glides into view, headlights cutting a pale tunnel before blinking off.

My breath sticks.

Rain lashes sideways behind the fogged glass. For a second, I think I see the driver's side door swing open, but the haze closes over it again. When there is another break in the rain, the door is closed, and no one is in the road.

I retreat to the kitchen, pacing in front of the island, checking my phone. Every muscle in my body feels braced, and I'm so tired, like all my life I've been waiting for the inevitable.

Then I hear the sound of wet boots on the porch.

CHAPTER SIXTY

INGRID

The Day of the Pageant

The sky is a low ceiling of pewter, and last night's sleety rain has crusted into slick patches across the parking lot of the Sherman Ranch Amenity Center. Dad and I guide Mom in, one of us steadying each of her arms.

"For heaven's sake, I can still walk," she says, though I don't miss the faint wince when her boot slips on the icy curb.

Inside, the room is a flurry of mothers adjusting hair and sashes, fathers clutching bouquets, little brothers and sisters weaving between rows of chairs. The heat from so many bodies fogs the glass doors behind us, and for a moment all I can think about are the germs, the coughs, the sneezes. Mom's first round of chemo has stripped her defenses thinner than she'll admit.

But she was determined to come. *It's my big day*, she said with a girlish giggle. And who was I to try to steal that from her?

Just inside the entrance, Magnuson appears, flashing that easy smile. "Mrs. Whitmore," he says, warmly. "You look absolutely radiant. No wonder they crowned you Miss Lone Star."

Mom actually blushes, placing a hand lightly to her chest. "Oh my," she murmurs, then leans toward me as Travis offers her his arm. "He's a real charmer, isn't he?" she whispers.

I laugh under my breath. "That's one word for him."

Travis escorts her toward the front row, fussing over her in all the right ways—steadying her elbow, clearing the way as if she's royalty. Dad trails behind them with a thermos of cocoa, smiling and shaking his head. He unscrews the lid once they reach her seat of honor and passes it to her, steam curling between them as she cups the hot drink in both hands.

I slip my camera strap around my neck, tucking the bag beneath the welcome table, the familiar weight grounding me.

Through my lens, I spot Kennedy Claire, sweeping through the crowd in her heels, hugging, smiling, sprinkling *sweetie* and *honey* like confetti. When she spots me, she hurries over and enfolds me in a perfume-scented hug.

"Sweetheart, I've been trying to call you." Her voice is pitched low, meant for just the two of us. "How have you been holding up?"

I've been ignoring her since Izzy's body was found, unsure how to untangle our shared grief from the things I've found out, the broken high heel still tucked away in my back seat, the message she maybe didn't deliver from Ben.

"The decorations look great," I say instead.

She gives my arm a squeeze, sadness flickering in her eyes before she masks it with another smile. "Isn't it perfect? Make sure you get pictures of all the little details." She taps my camera with a painted nail. "I have a million things I need to be doing, but we'll catch up, okay? I promise."

She drifts away, and I let the camera become my shield as I weave through the room. Girls squeal and compliment, air-kissing like they're not in direct competition. I focus my lens, waiting for the cracks in the veneer—the palms wiped on a skirt, the pleading glance toward a mother. I know the game. I remember it well, the petty rivalries. They laughed at the newbies for not knowing better, sneered at the veterans for knowing too much. Like so much of girlhood, you're damned if you do and damned if you don't.

And, of course, the sabotage. Costume props gone missing. Makeup kits tampered with. The day of Miss Lone Star Princess,

I came to my station in the dressing room to find my favorite red lipstick missing, and I knew without a doubt another contestant had swiped it just to throw me off.

I should have known when my shoe broke that it had been Kennedy Claire. She wanted so badly to win. Miss Lone Star meant more than just a crown to her. But it hadn't even crossed my mind. Because she'd been my friend. Because when it happened, she'd shrieked and dropped to her knees beside me, acting shocked.

Acting.

I end up at the refreshments table and fill a plate with cucumber sandwiches and cheese cubes. Two mothers hover nearby.

"I'm amazed they got it back up," the short brunette says, glancing toward the stage. "It looks great."

"I was terrified," the blond says.

"What happened?" I ask, taking a bite of the sandwich.

"Oh gosh, didn't you hear?" The blond puts a manicured hand to her chest. "When we were setting up the venue the other night. The whole backdrop collapsed. Nearly landed right on top of poor Olivia. I mean, she jumped out of the way just in time."

The brunette leans in, eyes bright and whispering conspiratorially. "You know, Cat came in yesterday, mad as all get-out, accusing Kennedy Claire of having something to do with it."

The blond gasps.

But the brunette cocks an eyebrow at her. "I wouldn't trust anything Cat says. I mean, you know her." She sticks out her thumb and pinky, miming a bottle, which she tips into her mouth.

I keep my face neutral, but a cool trickle slides down my spine. I look to the glittering backdrop, to the lattice of steel pipes holding it up, the heavy stage lights. That isn't lipstick gone missing. The weight of that scaffolding would kill a girl.

Yet one more mother-daughter pair forces the doors open, and a gust of icy wind barrels through the room like it's hunting something, rattling the balloon display and flipping tablecloths.

I scan the crowd and spot Kennedy Claire across the room, embracing another mother, her hug a performance, her smile polished to a blinding gleam, her laugh dropping on cue like she's hitting her mark. I raise my camera and fix her in my lens, but the longer I stare, the less I see my old friend. Instead, I see a woman who knows exactly what she wants you to see. And nothing else.

She has always been in control of the script, always onstage, never breaking character. The crown, the spotlight, the audience—she lives for it. She's built her whole life around it.

And my mind begins to flip through the years like photographs developing in a darkroom, each image surfacing in stark relief: her pout the night of the pageant when I wouldn't celebrate, oblivious that Izzy was missing. Her tears in my bed the next morning, after the news spread. All those years of listening, of knowing exactly what to say, as if she were memorizing lines from a script.

Has she been acting all along? Has she known, this whole time, exactly where Izzy was—and how she got there?

I steady my finger on the button, lining up the shot. The overhead lights stutter once, a sharp blink. Heads turn. Someone gasps. Then the power cuts completely—the music, the voices, the hum of the vents—and we are all swallowed in darkness.

CHAPTER SIXTY-ONE

MELANIE

The girls' dressing room is windowless. So when the power goes out, we are plunged into a black so absolute, it feels heavy on the eyes. Girls shriek. Compacts clatter to the floor. Hannah's "Mom?" finds me in the dark, a thin plea that tugs on a cord tied directly around my heart. I grope for her hand, but find nothing.

Then the lights blink back on, hum above the mirror like nothing happened. I feel the collective exhale in the room before the girls scramble twice as fast, laying out makeup kits and plugging in curling irons, as if hurrying can hold the power steady.

I don't say it out loud, but I know better. Lights don't just flicker once. Not in weather like this.

I check my phone to find another text from Waylon, checking on us, making sure we made it safely. He says the drizzle out there has started freezing on the roads, and even sent a picture of a car that slid right through the intersection by the H-E-B. He's already been called out—downed lines somewhere south of town. *You and the kids just stay up there until this blows over,* he wrote. *Or I'll come get you in the truck. The van can't handle this kind of ice.*

Olivia is getting wound up, in that way she does sometimes, not mean or snappy. She just sort of nudges the panic up in notches like she's slowly turning up the burners on a stove.

"I can get your hair started, sweetheart, until she gets here," Emily says, picking up a brush.

"No, she has all my stuff," Olivia whines. "Mom's supposed to do it. We practiced. She knows how I like it now."

Emily turns, setting the brush back down, but I can see the hurt in her face. She's been mother to that girl since she was eight years old. Every ballet recital, every competition, every rehearsal—it's been Emily with the brush and bobby pins, buns tight enough to hold through hours onstage. It's been Emily in the school pickup lines and at parent-teacher conferences, Emily packing lunches and cheering from the audience.

Now she's expected to step aside, to let Cat swoop back in and claim the spotlight. And I can't help but feel for her—how hard it must be to love a child like your own, only to be reminded she isn't.

Silence hangs a beat between us, and I clear my throat to break it. "I'll go get Cat," I say.

Dad wants to come with me. Today was supposed to be his day off, but he's been sheriff of Anhalt for thirty-one years, elected eight times because this town trusts him. It isn't a switch he flips on and off. He's been on the radio all morning with his deputies, watching the weather, people's safety always his first concern. And right now, he's not too happy with Kennedy Claire. Pushing this pageant forward goes against his code of being responsible and doing the right thing even when it's hard. Forcing families to brave icy roads? Putting people in jeopardy like this? He doesn't like it one bit.

When we open the Amenity Center doors, we're both misted with a freezing sleet. It's already colder than when we arrived, the kind of cold that cuts to the bone, and sunset is just a few hours away. As we walk down to the model home, Dad rubs his toe against the concrete, frowning at the slick shine.

We don't get ice or snow often, but Dad knows these roads, knows how they can go from safe to sheet glass in minutes. He's seen families trapped in their homes when rescue vehicles had to turn back. "This ain't good," he mutters, and I zip my jacket tighter.

We march ahead to the model home. I see the flags outside whipping wild in the wind, hear the ropes clanking their warnings.

Then we hear Emily's voice behind us in the distance. "I told you not to come out here. It's freezing."

We turn to see Olivia rushing to catch up with us. She's wearing nothing but a tank top and leggings. "Come back inside, young lady. I don't want you out there."

"I want to see Mom," Olivia yells without looking back or heeding her warnings of the cold.

Just as Emily catches up, snow begins to fall. "Just what has gotten into you?" She throws an oversized zip-up hoodie over Olivia's shoulders, masking her bare arms from the cold.

At first it's just a few flakes floating down, but by the time we make it to the yard, large clumps of snow land on my eyelashes and blur my vision.

Through the white, I see lights are on inside the model home, glowing warm behind the blinds, but when Dad knocks on the door, there's no response. He tries again. Nothing. The four of us shiver in sweaters and jackets too thin for this weather.

He tries the handle, but the door is locked.

"Have you heard from Cat?" he asks me.

I shake my head.

"Put the code in, honey." He steps aside, clearing space for me at the door. I punch in the numbers, my fingers clumsy from the cold. Beep-beep-beep, and then a long trill, the keypad glowing red.

"Mom changed the code," Olivia says, shifting around me to press the numbers, and the door unlocks. I watch her hand, watch her thumb depress the lever on the oil-rubbed bronze handle, and push the door open.

There is a sound, like a billiard ball rolling across a pool table. I see one of the artificial green apples from Cat's dining room centerpiece, which was nudged by the opening door. It trails slowly down the entryway, getting caught in the groove between two stones. Across the floor, more apples are scattered. Discordant in their chaos, out of order and unsettling against the backdrop of this magazine spread of a home.

Outside, ice pelts the windows like pebbles. The eaves groan from the force of the wind, a low moan that sounds almost human.

I shoot out an arm to stop Olivia, like when I brake hard at a red light and one of the kids is in the front seat. I push past her so I can be the first in the house.

As I make my way slowly through the entryway, Dad calls out from behind, "Catherine?" his voice a blend of frustration and worry, but it's met with an eerie silence, broken only by the whistling of the wind. I glance back to see one of his hands on his radio, the other hovering above the holster at his belt.

Aside from the apples, the house is staged for a showing. A lamp and a potted plant arranged just so on the console table. A plush blanket folded neatly over the back of the sofa. My throat tightens as I force myself forward.

And then—Cat's feet, one bare, the sole facing me, and on the other, twisted at an odd angle, a house slipper.

When Cat was drinking, she'd pass out. She always drank until she couldn't feel anything, until she'd drowned her guilt, until her body shut itself down. I was always worried about her. Always. Every second of every day. What she would do when she drank. What she would say.

Once, the Austin cops arrested her because they'd found her passed out in Zilker Park. I'd had to travel back and forth to the Travis County Jail, bringing her socks and shampoo, getting together money we didn't have to post bail, to hire a lawyer. The truth was, I was impossibly tethered to her addiction, having to ride the turbulent waves of her ups and downs, always working to get her back to solid ground. To start again.

I want to stop, to turn back, but my body drags me on. One step. Another. Until I see the rest of her.

Cat lies face down. The heavy marble bowl that used to hold the apples sits beside her, broken into two large pieces. Blood pools around her head, matted in her blond curls, staining them red. The blood is clotted around the wound, which is a canyon, deep and long. The back of her skull is cracked open, so deep I can see past the bone, so deep I can see her brain. I turn away, sickness bubbling up inside me quickly and violently.

I turn and watch Emily, already with her arms around Olivia, pulling up the large hoodie that she threw over her shoulders to shield her. "Mama," Olivia says with such desperation that I break inside, that I have to steady myself on the counter.

Cat is dead, and a piece of me is dead with her.

Dad steps forward, his hand brushing the grip of his gun before lifting his radio. "This is Sheriff Ryan at the Sherman Ranch model home. I need units and the medical examiner on scene. Possible homicide."

The words hang in the air, and I feel them settle in my chest, heavier than the storm outside.

This wasn't an accident. Cat was murdered.

CHAPTER SIXTY-TWO

OLIVIA BLAKE

2015

Olivia Blake is only seven years old, but she's been going to Encore Dance Studio for four years. She's the only girl in her grade chosen for a solo at the annual recital, held in the auditorium of Preston High. The high school feels as big as a theme park. She peeks around the curtain to see the audience packing in—moms and dads, aunts and uncles—and all their chatter feels like the hum of bees that gather at the mountain laurel her dad planted at the end of the driveway, the one that always smells like grape candy when it blooms.

The older girls stretch backstage, their limbs long, their smiles pretty, like princesses in movies. They coo over Olivia, clap at her pliés and sautés. They smooth gel into her slicked-up hair until it shines. They paint up her face like theirs, overly garish, so it shows under the harsh stage lights. Red-red lips, thick layers of mascara, round stamps of blush like you would draw onto a doll's face.

In her platter tutu, Olivia poses in the mirror, fifth position, arms arched above her head. She is excited, excited about everything, most of all excited because her mother will be here today. Her mother will see her dance.

The thought of it fills her up with warm sunshine. She can feel it shooting like beams of light from the tips of her fingers, from the points of her toes, as she takes the stage, as the crowd cheers, awestruck at her grand fouetté into arabesque, balanced, spinning on one foot and then sweeping her straight back leg forward into quick, sharp leaps. The move takes both strength and grace, impressive for a girl so young, and when she is done, she knows she has done it well.

She is proud. Her heart hammers. Her breath is quick.

She searches the audience, searches with applause in her ears, searches as that sunbeam in her heart dims, searches for a mother who isn't there.

CHAPTER SIXTY-THREE

MELANIE

Dad sweeps his flashlight along the threshold of the back door, shoulders taut, checking the lock, inspecting the slushy ground outside.

Emily led Olivia back toward the Amenity Center on Dad's orders. She didn't need to be in this house one minute longer than necessary. *Don't say anything yet. Not until we know more*, Dad had told her, and Emily only nodded, face ashen and expression numb with shock.

On the coffee table, a plastic camo-painted trail cam sits. The side panel is unlatched, hanging half open. I work my jacket over my finger and open it fully.

I bend closer, my stomach crawling. The slot on the side of the camera is empty. I think of Cat's words to Kennedy Claire yesterday morning: *I have security footage.*

"Dad," I say hesitantly.

He turns from where he has moved on to check the windowsills, where the wooden dowels are still in place, the ones he cut and fitted himself weeks ago. To keep Cat safe. "Don't touch anything, Mel," he snaps.

"Sorry, yeah, I know. Cat said she had some videos from that party the kids threw at The Hollow. But I think the SD card is missing."

His face tightens, and he joins me around the coffee table, leaning down over the trail cam. "Is that one of mine?"

"She must have gotten it from Mark," I say.

He shines his flashlight down into the empty SD slot.

"Do you think someone took it?" I ask, hugging my arms around myself, nails biting crescents into my arms.

His head turns back toward where Cat's body still lies on the kitchen floor. But I can't bear to look again, to see her that way, the dusky blue of her hands, the dark, tacky stain of her blood.

"Could have," Dad says slowly. "Could be that you found the motive, kid."

We lock eyes, the storm rattling the windows around us. Anyone who would want that footage, anyone who would steal that card, is already back at the Amenity Center. Waiting for us.

CHAPTER SIXTY-FOUR

INGRID

The Amenity Center buzzes like a disturbed beehive. Whispers are spreading fast. It started with Olivia, stumbling in with Emily's arm clamped around her shoulders, her face blotched with tears. Mark pulling them into a side room, and then the sounds of muffled sobs.

The mothers still move through the motions—fussing with flowers, smoothing tablecloths—but there is a hum to the air. The collective instinct of a small town that knows trouble when they see it.

The flurry of snow outside has thickened to wool batting, the shift happening faster than anyone anticipated. A few parents press close to the doors, peering out into the blur. Someone murmurs, "We'll never get home if it keeps up like this."

Dad hovers, fussing over Mom, who keeps insisting she's fine. I lean my shoulder into hers.

Then the doors open and Sheriff Ryan strides in, eddies of snow swirling after him, his white hair damp with sleet. Melanie is behind him, and forces the doors shut against the wind.

The hum of the room falters as the sheriff climbs the stage, looking every bit the lawman he's been for forty years. His radio is clipped to his chest, static crackling faintly from it. "All right, folks. I'm going to need everyone to take a seat."

Chairs scrape, and chatter dwindles to a hush. The room stills.

Sheriff Ryan clears his throat, scanning the rows like he's studying faces. "There's no easy way to say this, so I'm just going to lay it out straight. Cat Dennis was found dead today in the model home."

A ripple breaks through the room—gasps, sharp cries, hands pressed to mouths. A girl sobs out loud. Mark steps from the side room, pale and stricken, closing the door softly behind him.

Dead? The word is so small and solid, so final. I feel it like a punch to the chest. It seems impossible—Cat dead—when we all just saw her alive. But, of course, I should know better than anyone how easy it is for someone to be here one day and gone the next. Pressed against my shoulder, I feel Mom trembling. I reach over and pull her shawl more tightly around her.

From the crowd come overlapping questions:

"What do you mean, dead?"

"What happened?"

"How?"

The sheriff puts up a hand. "It's too early for me to say, but I do have to ask that everyone keep clear of the model home. It's a crime scene now."

"A crime scene?" one mother says, grabbing a little girl who looks about seven and holding her close. "So she was murdered?"

Every phone in the room erupts at once, that awful government-issued screech cutting through the air. I dig mine from my back pocket: WINTER WEATHER EMERGENCY.

Chairs squeak as people start to stand, grab coats, grab children's hands. "We're going home," one man says.

"Folks, folks," Sheriff Ryan booms, both hands up. "I need you to listen to me." He doesn't wait for them to sit back down. "I've heard back from dispatch. An ambulance was on the way, but the bridge on 20 iced over. The unit went sideways and had to turn back. No vehicles are getting through. Not anytime soon."

The silence that follows is thick. Only the sounds of a toddler whimpering, his mother shushing comforting words, the hiss of the heating system struggling against the storm.

Sheriff Ryan lets the words settle before he adds, firm but steady:

"The roads are closed. No one is coming in, which means no one is going out. You understand? We stay put. We stay safe. That's the best thing we can do right now."

For a heartbeat, no one moves. Then the voices rise again, layered and frantic:

"How long?"

"What if it gets worse?"

The pageant banners ripple as another gust rattles the glass doors. Outside, through the veil of snow, only the faint shapes of trees and half-built houses are visible. The sinking sun stains the clouds a sea-sick shade of yellow. Soon it will be dark. Soon it will be colder.

I can't shake the chill in my spine, the image of Cat's body in the model home, the creeping suspicion that her killer might be in this very room, with the storm closing in, and every one of us sealed inside.

CHAPTER SIXTY-FIVE

MELANIE

The Amenity Center kitchen isn't stocked for a blizzard, but I was able to find a stash of Styrofoam cups and some coffee. Now I'm making slow laps through the room, carafe in one hand, a stack of cups in the other. It keeps me from sitting on my hands, keeps my mind from replaying the crack of Cat's skull. People take the cups with grateful murmurs, and I smile, telling them I hope it'll help them warm up.

But while I pour, I watch every face closely. I eavesdrop on every whispered conversation.

Some of the teenage boys—Kennedy Claire's son and his curly-headed friend and that big linebacker—are huddled up around a phone, watching YouTube or whatever nonsense. I whistle and their heads snap up at me. "Turn that off," I say. "We might need the battery in case the power goes out again." They grumble something under their breaths, but I don't pay it any mind. "Go on and help your daddies." The men have been raiding the cars in the parking lot, bringing in all they can find—blankets and flashlights and cases of bottled water.

There's a cluster of women in the corner, and I break up their group with the offer of coffee, which they gladly accept, and while I pour, I listen.

"I'm not one to gossip," Beverly Jean says, though we all know she'd tell secrets to a fence post if it had ears. Beverly Jean works reception up at Preston High, and there isn't a person in town who doesn't know which kids slip in late after Sonic runs and which mama pitched a fit over the homecoming court ballots. She leans in close now. "But we all saw that fight between Cat and Kennedy Claire."

"Those two have been sniping at each other since orientation," Maria piles on, sipping her coffee and looking down her nose. "Things were reaching a boiling point, if you ask me."

"Oh come on," Lindsey says. "I don't think we need to be spreading bear tales." Lindsey is the youth pastor's wife over at First Baptist, so she needs to at least put on a show that she really is above gossip. "There's a pretty long mile between pageant bickering and . . . what happened to Cat." She looks at me, rubs a hand on my shoulder. "You holding up okay, hon?"

"Managing," I say with a weak smile, then I drift off to hand out more coffee.

Kennedy Claire is across the room, tucking a strand of hair behind Sarah Lynn's ear. She'd be fuming mad if she knew the kinds of things her friends were whispering behind her back. And Lindsey is right. Pageant bickering is a far cry from murder.

But they don't know about the missing SD card, about Cat's threat to upend Sarah Lynn's life with the push of a button. I watch her, slicking her daughter into perfection even now, and I know if there's one thing that would drive any of these women to kill, it would be to protect their kids.

I set a cup of coffee in front of Mrs. Mackey, who's wearing a blanket around her shoulders like a shawl, I point out where she can find some sugar if she needs it, and when I straighten, my eyes catch on Magnuson. He's sitting at a table with one of the girls, his hand on her shoulder, like he's saying something comforting. She peers up at him, and I see the blush rising in her cheeks. I bet Magnuson doesn't even know what a blush is, because he's never seen a girl's or a woman's face without one. He smiles, and his hand slides down her arm just an inch.

It's nothing, and yet I feel that motherly instinct raising a warning flag. And suddenly I'm thinking again of Cat's threat to Kennedy Claire. *I have security footage from that party the kids threw in The Hollow.* And Magnuson, tinkering with the lights onstage, his head lifting at Cat's words, his hands stilling on the rigging.

He'd heard her words, her threat. And for some reason, they'd meant something to him.

He looks up and catches me watching. He leans back in his chair, taking his hand off the girl to raise his hand in a wave, that slick charm of a smile slipping its way onto his face.

The wind roars with a sudden force that sends a tremor through the walls, a hollow thud echoing from the roof. Then, with a pop, the lights go out. The dark is thicker this time, settled and certain, like it's here to stay.

CHAPTER SIXTY-SIX

SARAH LYNN

This time the lights don't come back on. Neither does the heat.

My hands are buried in my jacket pockets, but my legs are bare under the tailored minidress Mom insisted on, flimsy against the cold that's already seeping through the glass doors.

Olivia's still locked away in that room with Emily. The awful sounds of her crying have gone quiet, and I tell myself she must have fallen asleep. But the truth is, I don't know how to face someone laid bare like that. The only funeral I've ever been to was my Great-Aunt Birdie's, and she was almost ninety, so it wasn't exactly a big surprise to anyone.

If I were a better friend, I'd knock on the door, curl up beside her, just sit with her in the silence, I guess, or whatever you're supposed to do. Instead, Hannah and I keep our distance. And the longer I wait, the heavier it settles in me, a knot of sickness that feels too close to guilt.

Through the windows, I watch Olivia's dad and a couple of the other men lean into the storm, shoulders hunched, hauling a generator off the back of a truck. There's still some gray to the sky, but it'll be dark soon. We'll have to stay the whole night.

Snow whips sideways across the lot, stinging the guys' faces, catching in their beards and wool caps. They wrestle the heavy machine just outside the doors, boots thudding, voices raised above the gale. Someone drags in a coil of orange extension cord, while other men set down tall construction lamps and a few electric space heaters. The whole place smells of cold air and gasoline now. A sharp pivot from pageant prep to survival camp.

We are trapped here, and my heart feels like a bird beating its wings against a cage.

Mom is beside me. Always. Always right there even when she isn't. "Don't worry, sweetheart." She brushes a hair near my face with her fingertips, then pulls a bobby pin out, holding it between her lips while she resets my curl.

She starts to slide the pin back into place when I reach up, swatting her hand away. "Mom, stop."

She pulls back, looks at me sharply.

"Sorry," I say, dropping my hands to my sides.

She purses her lips and re-spirals the lock of hair around her finger, then secures it back in place. "I know this is stressful," she says, smoothing her hands down my arms. "But everything will be fine. We'll reschedule Miss Lone Star for a few weeks from now."

As if that's what I'm worried about.

Image is everything. That's what Mom has always taught me. If you control how you're perceived, then you control the narrative.

Every time I leave the house, I feel her eyes on me, evaluating my outfit, my makeup, my hair. She watches my plates of food, watches my grades. She approves every post I make to social media, rehearses my answers to pageant interviews. She chooses the shows I watch and the books I read and the color I paint my nails.

"I promise," she says. "Pretty soon, it will be like none of this even happened."

I smile like I mean it. But inside that guilt is swelling, coiling, and writhing, like one of those giant pythons, swallowing me from the inside out.

CHAPTER SIXTY-SEVEN

INGRID

I settle Mom into one of the side rooms off the hallway, and Dad plugs a space heater in, the glow of the coils illuminating the room like candlelight. I'm tucking a blanket around her lap when someone knocks on the door, and in steps Melanie, a steaming Styrofoam cup in her hand.

"Chamomile," she says softly.

She sets it on the table, then crouches a little so she's eye level with Mom.

"You keeping warm enough? Any chills?"

Mom shakes her head, giving a tired smile.

Melanie nods, tugging the blanket a little higher on her shoulders. "Good. Chemo can make you more sensitive to the cold. So keep sipping fluids—it helps more than you think." She rests her hand briefly on Mom's wrist, as though checking her pulse without making a fuss. "If you start shivering or feel lightheaded, you call for me, all right?"

"Thank you," Dad says, sitting down next to Mom and taking her hand.

"Of course," Melanie says with a light chuckle, "I'll keep the chamomile coming."

When she slips back out the door, I follow her, shutting it behind us. The hallway is dark except for the eerie red glow of the emergency exit sign at the end of the corridor.

"Is there anything else you need?" she asks.

"No. I just—" I look at her sweet, smiling face, waiting patiently for me to continue. "Melanie, I'm so sorry about Cat. I know y'all were close."

"Oh," she says, dropping her eyes down to her hands. With a thumb she pulls at the skin around one nail. And when she looks back up, there's a sheen to her eyes. "I've been worrying about Cat most of my life. I don't know who I am without her."

"Does your dad know anything? I mean, does he think it was a break-in or . . ." I trail off. *Or was it someone who knew her?* I mean to ask, but can't make the words come out.

"No signs of a break-in necessarily. The back door was open though."

"Was anything taken?"

Melanie looks over her shoulder, down the shadowed hallway. She takes a step closer, talks in a fast, faint rush. "Well, don't tell anyone, but Cat had this security footage of the kids partying at The Hollow. She had it on this SD card, and she threatened Kennedy Claire with it. You know, saying she had these pictures of Sarah Lynn drinking and doing drugs. Cat just wanted Kennedy Claire to back off Olivia, you know? I don't think she would have actually done anything with that footage."

A cold pulse ripples through me, like the draft in the hallway has slipped straight beneath my skin. "What are you saying? You think Kennedy Claire—"

"I don't think anything," Melanie says, quick, shaking her head. "All I know is that Kennedy Claire loves her daughter, and that the SD card is missing."

Melanie's eyes bore into mine. I'm thinking of that scaffolding falling down, of the broken heel, and the message I never got, of how Kennedy Claire would do anything to protect her reputation, her image.

But before either of us can say another word, a teenage girl's high-pitched scream of terror slices through the building.

CHAPTER SIXTY-EIGHT

MELANIE

I run down the dark hallway, toward the sound of the screaming girl, hoping it isn't Hannah. *Please, don't be Hannah.*

There is a crush of bodies pressing toward the sliding doors that lead out to the pool, and I shoulder my way between people until I'm at the front.

It isn't Hannah. It's Sabrina, who's white as a sheet and pointing toward the glass. "He was right there. I swear."

"I didn't see anyone," another girl says.

"I saw him," Sabrina insists. "There was a man outside."

Then Dad's voice, calm and authoritative. "Let's stay calm," he says, and people step aside for him. "Maybe someone was going to their car. Who's missing?"

People shift, craning their necks to scan the room.

"It might have just been someone's reflection, sweetie," Sabrina's mother says. "Or shadows in the snow."

Sabrina shakes her head. "No. He had his hands cupped around the glass—like this." She mimes the shape, fingers pressed to her face. "He was staring right at me."

I look out. The storm has smeared the world to charcoal and white. The pool is frozen over, ice glazed across the water in uneven patches. Drifts of snow pile in the corners, cabana curtains whipping like frantic flags, sharp icicles dangling from the swim-up bar. The whole deck looks eerie, like a carnival left to rot in winter.

Sabrina's voice wavers. "I think it was that man. The one who came to orientation."

A hush drops. The name passes through the crowd like a shiver.

Abel Sherman.

"Oh, honey," Sabrina's mom says, folding her into her arms, but then over Sabrina's head, in a kind of stage whisper to the room, she says, "Sabrina's been having nightmares about Abel since orientation."

"Mom," Sabrina whines, drawing out the word while she shoves her mother away. "I saw someone." She crosses her arms, and this time when she says it, she sounds a little petulant. "I swear."

Behind my shoulder, Beverly Jean leans in to gossip. "Sabrina's always had a flair for the dramatic."

"How could Abel be out there?" a man says. "The ambulance couldn't even get through."

"Unless he's been here since before the storm started," Lindsey offers.

Outside, the snow moves in ragged curtains. Things blink into view, then vanish again: a roofline, a dark frame, an empty porch. For a moment a vacant home, nearly completed, shows itself, then the wind erases it.

"All right, that's enough," Dad says. "Keep your heads, folks."

There's a murmur of agreement, a course of whispers, as people disperse back out into the room, but more than a few eyes flick once more to the glass, as if expecting to catch sight of a phantom in the snow.

CHAPTER SIXTY-NINE

INGRID

Snow clutches at my ankles, soaking through my shoes, my pants heavy and wet halfway up my calves. The wind cuts sharply across my face, burning my skin raw. I hunch forward and push through it, teeth gritted, as I cross the parking lot.

I look up to search for my car and for a moment, I'm disoriented, blind in the cloud of swirling snow all around me. Panic claws at my chest. I know I'm only a few feet from the Amenity Center, but I suddenly feel I could get lost out here. The veil parts. At the tree line, a dark shape stands, then it's gone.

I shake the thought from my mind. Abel isn't out here. He couldn't be. And, besides, I've never been afraid of Abel.

Finally, I spot my car, and hurry to it. Inside, I slam the door, a flurry of snow following me in, and I punch the ignition. The engine coughs, then catches, the promise of heat sputtering from the vents. I cup my hands in front of them, my skin stinging as the air slowly begins to warm. Outside, the storm buffets the car, snow sliding across the windshield like wind trails over a jet wing.

The battery icon flashes 10 percent when I plug my phone into the charger.

I reach into the back seat and pull the shoebox onto my lap. The cardboard has that papery crackle from years in the attic, and it smells faintly of mildew. Inside, the broken heel rattles—the only piece of evidence I have, the only thing left after twenty-five years.

But proof of what, exactly? I think of Kennedy Claire's perfumed hug today. I think of her fingertip spreading cream blush onto the apples of my cheeks on my wedding day.

The storm groans around me, rocking the car. I check my phone again: 12%. For a second, I wish I had Ben's phone number. Ridiculous. But I can't help picturing him and Mabel in that trailer, the thin metal walls the only barrier between them and this storm.

The governor of Texas has declared a state of disaster in all 254 counties. That's what they've been saying, whenever anyone is able to pull up a bit of news. The entire state's power grid has gone down—ice on machinery, disruptions to natural gas supplies, an unprecedented increase in demand—our state's own little isolated power grid, disconnected from the national grids. A landlocked island. I peer up through the windshield and try to imagine it. More than a quarter million square miles, from El Paso to Beaumont. From space, we'd look like a big black hole.

A knock on the passenger window makes me jump. A man, bundled up in a jacket and scarf, stands outside my car, pulls once on the locked handle, then again, harder. That panic from before slams back into me. My hand flies to the gear shift, my foot bracing over the gas. Then a gloved hand wipes away the snow, and Travis Magnuson's face appears, blurred behind the glass.

I exhale, hand to my chest, and I feel my heart racing beneath my fingertips. I reach across and pop the lock. He climbs in, clapping his hands together, shaking off snow. "Hell of a storm," he says, breath clouding in the cold air. "Saw you come out here. Wanted to check on you." He takes off his gloves and rubs his palms near the vents. "Mind if I—" He picks up my extra cord, plugs in his own phone, and sets it on the dash. The screen glows, but it's tilted away from me.

I wait for my pulse to steady, watch the wipers in their futile sweep across the windshield.

"I heard they found your sister in The Hollow," he says gently. "Are you okay?"

His tone is kind. Earnest. And, to be honest, I kind of appreciate the candor. Everyone keeps hedging around the point. *How have you been holding up?* Kennedy Claire asked, without actually saying what we both knew was wrong.

"No," I admit.

Travis nods, turning his body toward me. "When my granddad died, we spread his ashes in Cataract Lake. That's where he always took us fishing. It was his favorite place in the world." He says it with a happy fondness, then his brow furrows. "I don't even know if it was legal for us to do that," he says, like it's just now occurring to him.

I'm surprised to find myself breathing out a laugh along with him.

"You told me Izzy always wanted to travel, right? Maybe now, you could take her with you. Leave a piece of her in every place she wanted to see."

I swallow, caught off guard. I hardly even remember telling him that. But he remembered. The thought touches something tender in me.

He nods at the box in my lap. "What's in there?"

I should say nothing. I should lie. But Travis has a way of lowering my guard. He's the only one who knows about Joel, about my marriage falling apart. The only one I've trusted with pieces I've told no one else. Maybe it's because he's so open himself, so genuine when he talks. Maybe it's because he's a stranger, really, someone I know won't be around forever. Because when you're honest with the people you love, you could hurt them, and they could hurt you.

So what the hell.

I open the lid, show him the broken heel, and I tell him—about the betrayal I feel, my doubts about Kennedy Claire, how I don't know what to believe anymore. He listens without interrupting, his face open, patient. When I finish, he says quietly, "You should talk to her."

And I know he's right.

"Ready to head back in?" he asks.

I hover my hands over the vents one more time, soaking up the warmth, then kill the engine. I'm about to reach for the handle when he pulls his phone from the dash. For a second, the screen tilts my way, and I see the voice memo app that's been recording this whole time.

CHAPTER SEVENTY

SARAH LYNN

All the Lone Star girls are hanging out together in the very center of the Events Hall, sitting in a circle, knees pulled up to our chests, around a space heater like it's a campfire. We've gathered ourselves as far as we can from the windows. Because of the cold that emanates from them, but also because of Sabrina, who insisted she saw Abel Sherman lurking around like some kind of walking dead. We're keeping eyes on each other, going to the bathroom in pairs.

All the girls except Olivia, who is still hidden away in that room. I keep thinking I hear her crying again, like that Poe story we read in American Lit last year, "The Tell-Tale Heart."

Kayden and Billy and Teddy found a deck of cards, but no one knows how to play anything, and it's not like we can look up the rules on our phones. The internet barely loads, and our parents don't want us wasting the batteries anyway. *In case of emergencies.* As if things could get any worse.

So Billy has resorted to performing magic tricks, which has the girls falling all over him in a new way. Hannah should be annoyed, but she's as distracted as I am.

She nudges me, her hand tugging at the drawstring of the hoodie she's thrown over her dress. "We have to tell someone," she whispers.

I nod, but my throat feels tight. My hands are buried in my jacket pockets.

Between my fingers, like a fidget spinner, I turn the SD card over and over in my pocket.

Yesterday, after Olivia told us about the videos her mom had of The Hollow, she gave us the key code to the front door. Olivia stayed behind at the Amenity Center to keep an eye on her mom, while Hannah and I slipped away, hoods pulled tight, the mist beading on our sleeves. Inside, the model home was too quiet and reeked of floral air freshener. We split up, Hannah veering toward the office, while I rummaged through drawers in the kitchen. Then I spotted the trail cam, just sitting right there on the coffee table, out in the open. My heartbeat ratcheted up when I yanked the SD card out and shoved it in my pocket. *Hannah*, I hissed. *Let's go.*

I was almost to the front door when my phone buzzed with a text from Olivia: Hide. She's on her way back.

I bolted up the stairs, into Olivia's staged bedroom, and dove into the play tent in the corner, zipping myself inside. The vinyl walls smelled faintly of plastic and dust, the little mesh windows no protection at all.

The front door chimed open, and I ducked as low as I could, listening to the footsteps rising up the stairs toward me. One by one, the doors opened, each hinge creak a warning shot. My pulse thudded in my throat.

Then the handle twisted and the door yawned open. I tried not to move, tried not to breathe, as I squinted through the thin plastic wall at the blur of her silhouette in the doorway.

I was sure she could see me—my outline, my heartbeat, the heat of me. The SD card burned in my clenched palm, and all I could picture were the worst clips—me with a joint at my lips, me stumbling drunk at the edge of the water, me pulling Mr. Magnuson into the shadows.

Image is everything.

"Sarah Lynn." Hannah's voice yanks me back, like she's pulling me out of that pink vinyl tent by force. And the way she's staring at me—she knows exactly where my mind just went.

CHAPTER SEVENTY-ONE

MELANIE

Night has fallen. Outside the tall glass windows, snow slants down in silver sheets, moonlight bouncing off the drifts so that the night looks strangely bright, like twilight stretched too long. Every time the wind gusts, the flakes swirl and scatter shadows across the glass.

Inside, the room is dim, except for the orange glow of the space heaters, the harsh slice of a construction lamp propped on the floor. Every time someone walks past it, their shadow balloons up the wall, stretching long across the beams of the ceiling. The neat rows of chairs are gone, dragged into circles, blankets spread over the floor where girls have curled themselves into nests. A few moms lean against the wall with their eyes closed, heads tipping forward, while others sip champagne from paper cups, laughter too sharp in the cold.

I count my children—one, two, three—the way I always do when we're out in a crowd, making sure everyone is accounted for. Then I slip down the hallway.

The door is partly open, and I peer in. Olivia lies on the sofa, knees curled up to her chest, and she looks so small it makes my heart ache. Emily perches by her head, stroking her hair, humming, "You Are My Sunshine," as if Olivia were a toddler.

I knock on the frame. Emily looks up, offers a weak smile, then whispers something in Olivia's ear before joining me in the hall and shutting the door behind her.

"How is she?"

Emily shrugs, crossing her arms. There are dark shadows under her eyes.

"What about you?" I touch her elbow. I've always gotten along fine with Emily. Waylon and I have dinner sometimes with her and Mark, whenever the girls are getting together for one thing or another. Sometimes in the beginning, Cat would lash out at me about it, when she was drunk or high, throwing punches at the world. She'd say I betrayed her, that I replaced her with a new best friend. But that wasn't true. No one could replace Cat, not for me. The bond we had went deeper than friendship. Our souls knitted together so tightly sometimes I felt I'd suffocate. Now it's like half my heart's been ripped from my body, the wound raw and open. "You can't pour from an empty cup," I tell Emily. "Why don't I get you some food?" The refreshments table is still laid out, picked over and stale.

Emily tips her head toward the main room. "Mark's getting us some sandwiches now."

"That's good."

"I hate seeing her hurting." Emily means it. She's been a good mother to that girl. When she and Mark first got married, they tried for kids of their own, but after two miscarriages, Emily didn't want to try anymore. *God already gave me a daughter*, she told me once. Now, Emily grinds the heels of her hands into her eyes. "I'm just so tired, you know? I've done this so many times. Over and over. Sitting on Olivia's bed, rubbing her back while she cries because Cat let her down."

Heat flashes through me. "Cat didn't let her down," I remind her. "She's dead."

"Oh, God, I know. Sorry. I know. I'm just tired."

We both turn to see Mark heading our way, a plastic plate piled with finger sandwiches.

I give Emily's arm one last squeeze. "Take care of yourself, all right?"

Back in the main room, I scan for my children again. The women drinking champagne are talking louder than I think they mean to. "She was the first one here. That's all I'm saying," Beverly Jean says, throwing up her hands.

"Who was the first one here?" Kennedy Claire asks, the sharp click of her heels echoing across the floor as she marches up to the group.

"Oh, hey, honey," Beverly Jean croons, all syrupy sweet, the tops of her ears blushing pink. "Why don't you join us?"

Kennedy Claire looks down on Beverly Jean like she's a piece of gum stuck to her stiletto. "Don't let me interrupt you. Go on."

Lindsey laughs nervously. "We were just saying you were the first one up here, getting things ready for the pageant."

"All by yourself," someone else adds.

The air hums with implication. Early morning, the construction site deserted, the Amenity Center empty, not a single witness. Only Kennedy Claire. And Cat, of course, down at the model home.

"I got here at 8 AM to meet the florist," Kennedy Claire says. "Ask her yourself."

I watch the exchange, uneasy. Suspicion feels like a living thing, something in the air as real as the chill. There's too much time with nothing to do but speculate. One wrong look, one gossipy whisper, and suddenly you're on trial.

I turn away and nearly bump into Iggy. Her dark hair is damp, strands sticking to her cheeks. She's holding a wet shoebox tucked under her arm. "Did you go outside?" I ask.

"Hey," she says, lowering her voice. "How well do you actually know Magnuson?"

Before I can answer, her gaze flicks past me, measuring the room like she's fitting puzzle pieces together.

Then, without warning, the doors swing open, a gust of icy wind rushing inside. Snow whirls in, flurrying across the floor before the door slams shut again. Conversation stalls, every head turning. For a beat, no one breathes.

CHAPTER SEVENTY-TWO

INGRID

When the doors blow open, and the man steps inside, for a moment, I can't tell who he is—just a figure staggering in, shoulders hunched, a bundle pressed to his chest. Someone gasps. A few of the men get to their feet.

The doors thud shut and the snow settles. He pulls back his hood, and the sight jolts me.

It's Ben.

Hair plastered to his skin, ice clinging to his brows, his eyes dark and burning. He's shaved, suddenly younger, heartbreakingly familiar. In his arms, tucked inside his coat, swaddled in blankets, is Mabel.

It's like a switchboard in my brain lights up all at once, every bulb sparking hot with questions and fears. But through the noise, one signal blares the loudest: relief. Ben is alive. Mabel is okay.

Recognition shudders through the room, a ripple of whispers. "What the hell is he doing here?" someone mutters.

Sheriff Ryan moves toward him. "Ben. How'd you get here? I heard the bridge is iced solid."

Snow falls from Ben's boots as he stamps them. "It is. I ditched the truck and came up through the deer trails. Only half a mile—if you know where you're going."

I'm thinking of the ambulance that couldn't get through, of trucks jackknifed along the road, of the snow swallowing the whole world.

How long would it take for hypothermia to set in if you got lost in all that blinding white?

"What were you thinking?" I snap.

"Yeah." A big, burly man steps forward, mistaking my anxiety for anger. "You've got some nerve coming up here." His hands are in fists by his sides.

Ben stares back at him, jaw clenched. Then he unzips his jacket, shifting Mabel higher on his chest. "I couldn't keep her in that trailer overnight. No power, no heat. It was colder inside than out. I had to get her somewhere safe."

Melanie rushes forward, arms outstretched, maternal instinct overriding judgment. "Here, let me get her into something dry and wrap her up warm. You must be half frozen yourself. We've got some hot coffee."

She scoops Mabel into her arms, immediately moving into a gentle sway.

Ben fumbles with the diaper bag on his back, handing it over like a peace offering. "Thanks."

From the corner of my eye, I notice motion in the hallway and turn to see Mom and Dad rejoining the group. Dad has hold of Mom's elbow, his face stormed over as he looks at Ben.

Melanie scurries off somewhere with the baby.

Another man pipes up. "What about your daddy, Ben? You just left him to freeze in that trailer park."

"That's the other reason I'm here," Ben says. "Dad's missing."

The crowd stirs all at once. My eyes go to the glass, to the clots of snow. The man Sabrina swore she saw at the window. The shadow I caught moving at the edge of the woods.

"What do you mean?" Sheriff Ryan steps between Ben and the men, their nerves already strung too tight, itching for a fight.

"He took off somewhere. He was mad as hell about those warrants you served, Sheriff, and drunk enough to make it worse. I don't know what he was planning."

"When did he leave?"

Ben shakes his head. "Not sure. Could've been last night. I only realized he was gone when the snow came in—went to check on him, and the trailer was empty."

Somewhere close, two women bend their heads together, whispering fast. I can't catch much, but one name slices through: "Cat."

Ben looks past the sheriff, his eyes finding mine. "I wanted to make sure you were okay." My knees feel unsteady, a thread pulled loose inside me. Then he adds, "Dad took his shotgun with him."

And the room explodes in panic.

CHAPTER SEVENTY-THREE

SARAH LYNN

The kitchen is cold. There are no space heaters in here. Just a long orange extension cord slithering beneath the door to power the coffee maker. A battery-powered lantern casts a weak halo of light and some moonlight comes in from the high rectangular windows near the ceiling, gleaming silver off the stainless steel counters.

There's some kind of commotion going on in the main room, but I don't care. I'm staring down at the sink drain, the sharp plastic corners of the SD card biting into my palm.

Hannah wants to come clean, but I'm scared.

I hold my fist out over the drain, open my hand, and the card falls straight in with a neat clink. I don't give myself time to second-guess. I reach for the disposal switch and flip.

Nothing.

I flip it back and forth a few times before realizing I'm an idiot. There's no power. Cursing, I yank open the cabinet, and my lantern's light spills across pipes and bottles of cleaner. The disposal is plugged into an outlet inside. So I unplug the coffee maker, drag the extension cord over, and drop down, reaching deep past metal and plastic.

That's how he finds me, on my hands and knees, half buried in the cupboard.

"Sarah Lynn."

The sound of my name in his mouth sends goose bumps across

my skin. I sit back on my heels and turn to him. Mr. Magnuson's face is mostly a shadow, but in the moon's pearly glow, I can see the wink of his smile.

"I thought I saw you come in here," he says, and he closes the door behind him.

CHAPTER SEVENTY-FOUR

INGRID

"We'll need to cover the gym exits, the pool deck doors, and the service entrance by the kitchen," Sheriff Ryan says, already pointing men toward different wings of the building. "Every lock, every bolt—check them all."

The place seems to have a thousand doors and windows. Each one suddenly feels like a hole in the hull of a sinking ship.

The burly man from before crosses his arms. "I'm not leaving him alone," he growls, jerking his chin toward Ben. "Not for a second."

"He's the one who came to warn us," I say.

Dad's hand clamps gently around my arm. "Let the sheriff handle it." His face is drawn tight with worry, and I let him steer me toward the cluster of chairs where Mom is already settled close to a heater, a blanket around her shoulders.

The sheriff orders us to stay put, everyone in this room within sight of everyone else. Then the men scatter through the hallways, rattling handles, sliding bolts home. The echoes carry back, sharp and metallic, while Ben stays planted at the welcome table, the big guy looming over him like a guard.

The whole room feels jittery, the air stretched thin.

That's when Kennedy Claire slips up beside me, her nails digging crescents into my arm. "I can't believe he'd show his face here," she hisses.

My eyes drop to the shoebox I've been carrying, soggy cardboard soft against my fingers. Seeing her, remembering what's inside—it feels like the moment I've been circling all night.

"Can we talk?" I ask.

"Well, sure, honey."

We find a pair of chairs out of earshot of anyone. I set the shoebox in my lap. "I was going through some stuff in my parents' attic, and I found this." I lift the lid and hold up the two pieces of the broken heel.

For a moment, Kennedy Claire's face doesn't move, just her eyes from the shoe to me and back, quick flicks like she's doing calculations in her head. Then her eyebrow raises. "What's that?" she says, her voice perfectly innocent.

"It's the shoe I was wearing when I twisted my ankle," I say, each word slow and measured. I don't take my eyes from her face, needing to see each subconscious twitch of her muscles. "Right before Miss Lone Star. Right before you won."

She laughs. "I can't believe you still have that. I guess your mama really doesn't throw anything away, does she?"

I turn the heel so the sliced end points straight at her. "If it had broken on its own, this whole piece would have torn off from the sole."

Kennedy Claire's acting is good, because she looks genuinely confused. "I'm not sure—"

"Did you sabotage me?"

"Iggy," she says, a horrified reprimand, like I've slapped her.

"I think you did," I say, picking up steam, as the anger and the adrenaline of confronting her swirls my chest into a furnace. "I think you cut this heel, glued it back on, and then just watched me fall. How could you? You were supposed to be my best friend."

"I am your best friend," she snaps. Then she closes her eyes, inhales through her nose, and tips her head up to the ceiling, like she's trying not to cry. She shakes her head slowly so that her hair, still somehow perfectly curled, sways down her back. "All right," she says softly. She looks at me, chews the inside of her cheek. "I wanted to win, okay? I'm sorry, but you didn't care about it. Not like I did. We were kids. It was twenty-five years ago, Iggy. I'm sorry."

I drop the shoe back into the box and close the lid. "What about after Izzy went missing? Did Ben ask you to tell me to meet him?"

Her brows knit together. "Who told you that? Have you been talking to Ben?" She whips her head over her shoulder to look at him across the room, then leans in and grabs my hand. "Are you crazy?"

I pull my hand away from hers. "Did you see Izzy? The day she disappeared?"

Kennedy Claire's face turns to stone, so fast it sends chills down the nape of my neck. She sits back in her seat, her spine a perfect line. "You never could think straight around him." Then she stands, her eyes flicking over me once, head to toe, dismissive. The chatter of the room and the roaring of the storm all hum together into white noise, until all I can hear are the stabbing steps of Kennedy Claire's stilettos across the floor.

CHAPTER SEVENTY-FIVE

MELANIE

When I come back into the room, Mabel is warm and dry but squirming in my arms, her face blotched and red from fussing.

"She's Carol Sherman's granddaughter?" Mrs. Whitmore asks gently. She's curled into a blanket in one of the side chairs, her cheeks pale but her eyes sharp.

I nod, trying to settle Mabel, but she keeps arching her back, rubbing her face angrily into my shoulder. "She won't quit."

"Here." Mrs. Whitmore stretches out her arms. She takes Mabel and flips her around to sit on her lap, facing the room. "She wants to see what's going on. Her mother was the same way when she was her age." And she's right, because Mabel calms, her bright eyes darting around at the scattered clusters of people, the strange orange glow of the space heaters. "Carol and I used to talk about grandkids," Mrs. Whitmore murmurs, stroking the baby's arm. "She's a sweet thing, isn't she?"

That's when I notice the room feels off. Thinner. I glance around—half the men are missing. "Where did everybody go?"

"Your dad sent them to check all the doors. Said Abel might be out there with a gun." Her voice drops low when she says it.

My adrenaline spikes. I scan the room, counting automatically—one, two—the boys are across the way with a group of other kids, folding paper airplanes out of Miss Lone Star programs. But I don't see Hannah. Or Sarah Lynn. And my heart is suddenly in my throat.

“Can you hold her a minute?” I ask, already moving. “I have to find my daughter.”

Mrs. Whitmore adjusts the blanket over Mabel’s legs, but I don’t wait for her answer. I’m already weaving down the hall, swallowed into red-tinged shadows—the exit sign at the end the only thing glowing down this way. Halfway along, Travis Magnuson appears.

“What was all that noise?” he asks, brows lifted.

“Ben Sherman just showed up,” I tell him. “Put everyone in quite the tizzy.”

His eyes flicker, a flash of interest, and then he strides off without another word.

I keep moving, my pulse quickening. Voices drift from the kitchen—low and furious. I push open the door. Sarah Lynn and Hannah stand frozen in the dim light of a lantern, their shoulders jerking up like I’ve caught them stealing. Hannah’s hand darts behind her back. Sarah Lynn’s eyes go wide.

“What’s going on?”

“Nothing,” Hannah says, too quick. She has that look on her face, like when she was a little girl and spilled a box of Lucky Charms all over the kitchen floor, claiming she had no idea what had happened, that maybe it was the dog that knocked it over.

“Hannah Leigh,” I say. “The truth. Now.”

She glances over at Sarah Lynn, but then back to me. Slowly, she pulls her hand forward and opens her fingers. The SD card sits in her palm.

Shock crashes through me, cold and electric. “How did you get this?”

“I’m sorry,” Hannah says.

I feel the world slip out from under me. “Just what in heavens did you girls go and do?”

CHAPTER SEVENTY-SIX

SARAH LYNN

I made sure I watched that camera footage before handing it over to Mrs. Campbell, double-checked that Mr. Magnuson never once appeared in any of the videos. The night of the party at The Hollow, his truck had been parked just out of the camera's range.

And I was glad about that, at least, because then no one would ever see the way he rejected me.

That night, when I spotted his truck parked in the trees, I peeled off from the group. When I stepped from the dark, my body felt lit from within, buzzing on booze and pot and the rush of diving naked while the boys gawked. I'd been so sure Mr. M. would be just as captivated.

But as soon as his eyes caught on me, he stepped back. *Sarah Lynn? Oh God, was this you?* He held up his phone.

I clasped my hands behind my back, swayed innocently, aware of how good I looked in my bikini even though I was literally frostbitten. *Do you want it to be me?* I'd asked.

He rubbed the back of his neck, glancing toward the splashes and laughter by the well, like he was realizing what it was—a kid party.

He put a hand to the door of his truck. *I need to go*, he said. *Be safe, okay?*

And he drove away, leaving me feeling stupid there in the woods.

But later, floating beside Olivia in the well, her fingers twined in mine, and the water so cold that I couldn't tell where my skin ended and hers began—I felt how unimportant his rejection was. What mattered was the three of us—me, Olivia, and Hannah—together.

Now Hannah and I steel ourselves and knock on Olivia's door. Emily answers, voice dialed low like in a hospital. "Come on in, girls." She glances toward the couch where Olivia lies facing the back cushions. "I'll give y'all a little privacy." She slips out, shutting the door without even a click.

And we are left alone in the room with Olivia and the heavy blanket of her grief.

"Liv?" Hannah whispers, creeping closer like she's approaching a wild animal.

Olivia turns her head, and her eyes are raw, lashes clumped with tears. She sniffs, then rolls back to the cushions.

Hannah sits on the couch at Olivia's feet. I curl in behind her, spooning her. I can feel her heartbeat through her back, thudding right up against mine. Hannah leans across, draping an arm over both of us.

"Y'all are going to suffocate me," Olivia mutters, but it's wrapped in a snotty laugh as she pushes herself up to sitting.

"What do you need?" Hannah asks.

"Yeah," I say. "Anything."

"Anything?" Olivia drags the heel of her hand across her nose, and when she looks at us, her voice is steady, blazing. "I want to do the pageant."

CHAPTER SEVENTY-SEVEN

INGRID

I watch Travis chatting with Ben over in the corner. Travis leans back in a chair, one ankle crossed over the other knee, hands animated in a story. And it makes sense, I suppose, that Travis would be the one to talk to Ben when no one else will. He isn't from Anhalt, doesn't harbor years of suspicion against Ben, against the whole Sherman family. But still, I can't shake the thought of that recording on his phone. Can't figure out why he would have it.

The Events Hall has a strange energy, everyone exhausted, nerves frayed raw, but now a kind of manic cheer has been laid on top as they set up the room, absurdly, for the pageant. Men reset the chairs into neat rows. Women pass out programs. Mark is arranging two tripod construction lights, like spotlights pointed at the stage. The girls are off in the dressing room.

When Olivia finally emerged from her room, she had all the pageant girls rallied behind her.

We can't do the pageant now, someone said, reasonably.

Why not? Hannah asked, and she had a point. All the contestants were here, the audience, the dresses, and the judges, and we had nothing but time on our hands.

It was Olivia, though, who convinced everyone. *This last week, prepping for the pageant with Mom*, she'd said, *those are my best memories of her. I want to do it for her.* How could anyone argue?

Even Mom has a little color back in her face. She's refreshed her makeup and tamed her hair, and she's sitting in the front row, ready for her moment to bring the crown up to the stage.

Outside, the night is inky black, the soft flakes swirling. It's like one of Izzy's snow globes in reverse. I think of how the room would look from out there, all of us encapsulated on the inside, lit up and displayed like specimens in a jar.

CHAPTER SEVENTY-EIGHT

MELANIE

Everyone has taken their seats in the audience. Magnuson, off to the side of the stage, pulls the rope to open the sequined curtains, which glint in the beam of the tripod construction lights.

The girls come out, big smiles on their faces, fringed skirts swinging as they strut in silver cowboy boots to Shania Twain's "Man! I Feel Like a Woman!" The music blares from a single speaker in the back, plugged into the same power strip as the lights. The audience whoops, the feeling in the room swelling with the music, everyone hungry for entertainment, for escape.

I've tucked myself into the dark back row with a borrowed laptop, pulling the computer tight onto my lap and angling the screen away from everyone. My fingers fumble the trackpad, scrubbing too fast through files, and I pray that no one notices.

When they handed the SD card over, the girls told me what happened in fits and starts—the key code, slipping over to the model home, searching the place. How Hannah kept lookout while Sarah Lynn pocketed the card. How Olivia warned them Cat was coming back.

But she was alive when we left, Hannah whispered. *I swear, Mom.*

I believe you, baby. I'd pulled her in, kissed her hair. *But this could still be evidence. Someone else could've come after you looking for it.*

Now, here I am, hunched in the corner with the laptop balanced on my knees, heart racing as the first clips flicker to life. I do believe the girls, but I need to know what's in these videos before I hand them over to Dad.

The camera is aimed to capture The Hollow, and up the bank, there's a good bit of road and the construction trailer. There are clips of white-tailed deer picking through the trees in black-and-white moonlight, of Mark going to and from the trailer, of construction vans passing by.

Then I find it: the night of the party.

My breath stops. Girls and boys drinking, smoking, climbing the rocks. Beer cans crushed into the mud. I watch as the girls—my Hannah among them—step naked from the trees, and I slap a hand over the screen, fingers trembling. I can't help thinking, of course, about Kennedy Claire, tricking me into taking all my clothes off, right there in The Hollow. And, of what came after.

I want to throw a blanket over Hannah in that video, want to shield her. But I watch through my fingers as the girls link hands, as they leap together into the dark water.

I look up now to see them all, crisscrossing each other on the stage, shaking their hips, sending their fringe into a flurry, their big red-lipsticked, white-toothed smiles never wavering.

In a small town like Anhalt, with everything the girls have sacrificed, everything they've put into the community and their reputations, all their big hopes and dreams of futures as bright as Fourth of July sparklers—I understand why they wanted to keep this footage secret.

I click forward, skipping past the kids, past the reckless energy of them, all wild motion and smoke drifting like ghosts. I skim the rest of the night, the cop cars and forensics vans. The footage colorizes with the morning light.

My heart aches when I see Cat walking up to the construction trailer, knocking on the door. I watch her have a conversation with Emily that looks tense, Emily's arms folded across her chest, her mouth a tight line. Then Cat walks away, and I freeze the image, just before she disappears from the frame, because it's the last photo that will ever be taken of her. Alive, at least. The heaviness of that slides through me, settles in my gut like something rotten.

I hit play. I scan through hours of white-coated technicians carting evidence bags from The Hollow. I'm just about to jump far ahead when I see a truck pull up. And all the hairs on my body stand up in unison.

Because it is a white Chevy Silverado. Just like Cat described. Just like she pointed out. I watch it park against the curb. A man exits, his back to the camera as he climbs the steps of the construction trailer.

I lean so close, the screen fogs with my breath. The man knocks, the door opens, and Emily greets him. There is no audio, but the video quality is crystal clear. She pulls something from her purse. An envelope. She hands it to him, and he tucks it into his jacket. When the man turns, I feel the bottom drop out of me.

It's him.

The man Cat swore was following her. The one from the coffee shop in Austin. The one who toured the model home with his pregnant wife.

Cat was right. He had been following her.

And it looks like Emily was paying him to do it.

The music ends abruptly, and Kennedy Claire takes the mic. I join the applause, a beat late, because my mind's been spinning somewhere else. Everyone around me is clapping, and the rumbling vibration sets me uneasy, like when you stay too long in a hot tub. I find Emily in the crowd, cheering for Olivia, leaning her shoulder into Mark, smiling like a woman free of her own competition.

CHAPTER SEVENTY-NINE

SARAH LYNN

"Son of a biscuit, it's freezing," Sabrina says, shimmying out of the fringed-skirt getup from the opening number, only to pull on a silver spandex unitard for her talent act.

The whole dressing room is lit by one of those garage lights, the kind with a bulb in a wire cage, dangling from an extension cord looped over the ceiling rafter. It sways whenever someone walks past, making the sequins blink in restless patterns.

Space heaters hum from the corners, but cold still seeps in through the walls. And, yet, despite everything, the space is a swarm of high heels clicking and sequins rustling like wind through foil, chatter layered between laughter and nerves and last-minute touch-ups. Girls borrowing eyelash glue and doing up each other's zippers. It used to be my favorite part of pageants, like a high-octane slumber party. But for years now it's only been war prep—sizing up the enemy, steeling myself for battle.

I'm at my vanity station, reapplying blush. Beside me, Hannah swipes on more lip gloss.

Olivia has changed into a simple black leotard for her dance routine. She stands at the floor-length mirror, gathering the spirals of her blond hair into a bun. Her eyes are hollow as she turns to see her profile.

I set my makeup brush down. "Hey, are you okay?"

"Mom was supposed to do my hair."

My heart sinks. "I can do your hair."

Olivia opens her hand, her hair uncoiling down her back, glinting golden in the yellow light. "It's fine," she says, floating toward her seat at the vanity.

I catch eyes with Hannah in the mirror and sweep blush up my cheekbone again. Out of the corner of my eye, I see Olivia pick up someone's bikini trimmer. She flicks it on, and the buzz cuts through the chatter.

"What do you need that for?" I ask.

In one motion, she presses it to her hairline and rakes a stripe down the middle of her head.

I nearly choke, my hand flying out like I could stop her.

"What the hell, Olivia?" Hannah snaps.

The room goes quiet but for the hornet hum of the clippers. We all watch in stunned, frozen horror, as Olivia keeps cutting, calm and steady. One blond spiral after another slides down her shoulder, catches on the fabric of her leotard, and then piles on the floor.

When she's done, she studies her reflection, the single bulb gleaming off the golden stubble left behind.

She clicks the trimmer off. No one moves. Hannah looks at me with wide, terrified eyes.

But I think I get it, actually. I think I understand. When everything is unfair and chaotic, you just want something, anything, to be in your control. Like if the world is going to strip you bare, you want to be able to decide how.

And sometimes the only thing a girl has left is her own body.

I reach for the trimmer, because my friend might be sad, but she doesn't have to be alone. I meet Olivia's eyes in the mirror and lift my shoulder in a shrug. "It's just hair."

Hannah makes a choking, startled sound. Someone in the room gasps.

The blade kisses my scalp, snags, then glides smoothly. Olivia covers her mouth with her hands, tears swimming in her eyes. She laughs through her fingers, a broken, beautiful sound.

I wink, then I go for it—no hesitation. As the strands fall, it feels like more than hair dropping away. Like I'm sawing off years of someone else's voice in my ear. Like I'm cutting myself free.

CHAPTER EIGHTY

MELANIE

Sabrina skips offstage in her silver unitard, ponytail swinging, grinning like she just nailed the Olympics. The curtains close with a swish, and Mr. Magnuson's voice carries out over the crowd: "Next, Hannah Campbell."

I set the laptop in the empty seat beside me and knot my hands in my lap. I'll have to decide what to do about that later. For now, the curtains part, and there she is. My daughter.

For a heartbeat, I don't understand what I'm seeing. Hannah stands center stage, the construction lights gleaming on the curve of her bare scalp. Completely bald. The shimmer of her dress only makes the starkness sharper, her head glowing under the harsh yellow beams.

Rage fills me so fast I feel dizzy. This has to be a trick. One of those mean pageant girls with their whisper campaigns and cruel little schemes—did they corner her backstage, did they shave her head just to humiliate her? My throat burns with the scream I want to let out, my body pitched forward in my chair, ready to storm the stage.

The audience ripples with whispers. A cough, a muffled laugh. Heat flashes across my skin, because they're laughing at her, my baby, and she looks so small, so exposed.

And then Hannah opens her mouth.

Her voice rises clear and steady, cutting through the gossip like glass breaking. A hymn she used to hum to herself at night, soft as a prayer, now filling the rafters. The crowd falls silent. I feel the hush like a blanket settling over the room. I can't breathe for how beautiful it is, for how brave she is. My daughter, who never lets anyone hear her sing, standing bald-headed under the lights, singing like there's no one in the room.

As Hannah finishes, the crowd erupts—chairs scraping back, feet stomping, applause rolling through the room like a tide. I realize I'm crying, and I don't care who sees. I've never been prouder in my life.

And then, before the sound has even quieted, the curtains open again. Sarah Lynn walks out. Her head is shaved too, shining under the lights. She takes her place at the center of the stage, chin lifted, as if this were the most natural thing in the world.

And I realize: it wasn't a prank. It wasn't cruelty. It was a choice. Something they did together.

But I feel a dark presence at the corner of the stage. Kennedy Claire stands just out of the ring of light. She isn't clapping, isn't smiling. Her gaze is pinned on Sarah Lynn with a fury so cold it makes me shiver. And then, slowly, her eyes flick toward Hannah.

Like she's already decided who to blame.

CHAPTER EIGHTY-ONE

INGRID

I've brought my camera back out so I can capture this strange beauty pageant in the dark. The silhouette of the audience against the snow-lit windows. Sabrina's clean back handspring in her silver unitard. Hannah, her head shaved bare, her arms outstretched as she hits the high note. Another contestant waiting side stage, exhaling a cloud of breath into the cold.

Near the windows, Travis mans the music. I can just see the shape of him past the blinding beam of the tripod lights.

Ben sits alone in the corner. A man hovers nearby, clearly posted there to keep watch. And I realize—that's been Ben's whole life in Anhalt since he moved back, what, twenty years ago? Hidden in a house that used to be a home, once filled with his mother's cooking and the noise of family, now only his father, drinking himself to death. The woods and the river he loved, haunted by Izzy's ghost. And every time he came into town—just to pick up a package at the post office, to buy a week's worth of groceries—he had to face the same stares. The boys he used to play football with, now grown men who look at him like he's a killer.

I haven't spoken to him since he got here, not really. Just my panicked outburst—*What were you thinking?* And I haven't tried again, not with the weight of the whole town's eyes pressing down. Not with my parents watching.

But, they're all distracted now. So I slip away from the stage, picking my way over the crisscrossing extension cords.

I pass by the boys, Kayden, Billy, and Teddy, hunched against the frosted windows, a phone balanced between them and plugged into a power strip. Some video plays, something they must've downloaded when the internet was stable. But then I catch a phrase—"twenty-five years of secrets"—and freeze.

"Isabelle Whitmore was going places. She dreamt of one day traveling the world." It's the low, deliberate cadence of a man trying to sound more important than he is. But he keeps going, repeating exact details I divulged to Travis over dinner.

My stomach lurches. I turn and snatch the phone from Kayden's hand.

"Hey!" he says.

I jab the pause button before the voice can continue. "Where did you get this?"

Kayden blinks up at me, defensive. "It's just a podcast. Everyone's listening to it."

Heat floods my face. I whirl around. Travis stands beside the speaker, watching Sabrina's acrobatic act, waiting for his cue with the music.

I march straight to him, slam the phone against his chest. "You used me."

For a moment, he has the audacity to look confused, but when he glances down, sees his own podcast clearly on the screen, his face falls. "I didn't use you, Ingrid. I like you."

I scoff, frustration like a vine up the core of me. I don't care if he *likes* me. I think of Izzy lying on the front lawn picking dandelion petals. *He loves me, he loves me not.* I care that he tricked me. That I could be so easily tricked. That I told him things I haven't told anyone else, and why? Because his cheek dimples when he smiles? Because he spun me a story about scattering his granddad's ashes at the lake? I feel stupid and angry, and worst of all, I feel broken. Like

I have no compass for people. I hand out trust and suspicion like I'm throwing darts blindfolded.

"Look, this," he says, pointing to the podcast. "It's important to me, okay? I'm a journalist. I care about what happened to your sister. People care. Lots of people, Ingrid. There are whole subreddits dedicated to this story. People want to know what happened. I emailed you. I called you. I left, like, four voicemails. But you never responded. No one did."

Delete and block. That's what I've always done. I imagine Travis back in Indiana, googling Izzy's name, trolling through internet theories, combing my social media pages. Back in the bar, when he sent me that drink, when he flashed me that smile, he knew exactly who I was. And every word out of his mouth after that has been calculated, tailored to reel me in.

He wanted a story, and he was willing to do anything to get it. Suddenly, a sick thought blindsides me. "Oh my God. Was it you? Did you send me a note? An invitation? Just tell me the truth."

But the confusion on his face is genuine. He has no idea what I'm talking about. He wasn't the one who sent me that invitation. "I sent you emails," he says again. "Messaged you on Instagram. On everything. I just wanted an interview. There is so little information out there about this case, because no one in this town talks. But then I got here, and I realized that they will talk, just not to a reporter, you know? And, man, do they talk." He actually smiles, like he's proud of himself. "I got people to talk. Me. I did that. And then the kids found those bones in The Hollow." A quick, stunned laugh escapes him, like he still can't believe his own luck. "My dad didn't get it. Didn't think a podcast could be a real job." He puts air quotes around the words.

I think of his trio of impressive brothers, of baby Travis, the mama's boy, mediocre in a family where the bar is unattainably high.

"But now I've gone viral," he says, his eyes widening at the word. *I was addicted to attention*, he'd told me. And I had been charmed. That's the word Mom had used for him earlier today. *He's a real charmer, isn't he*? And what is a charmer but someone who casts a spell, who seduces, who deceives?

"Those bones?" I say quietly, repeating his words back to him.

His brow twitches. "You know what I mean." He tries to reach out and put a hand to my arm, but I pull away.

"You don't care about Izzy." She was never a person to him. And neither was I. We were just content.

"I care about the truth," he says. "It's like you with your photography. You said a photo captures a single true moment in time, right? That's all I'm doing. We're the same, really."

He looks so earnest when he says it, like he truly believes he's doing something noble. Like he has fooled even himself. And I almost feel sorry for him.

"No, Travis," I say. "We aren't the same."

I turn from him. Behind me, the boys gape up at us, and I toss Kayden his phone back.

"Dude, is this really your podcast?" Kayden asks, staring up at Travis.

"Wait," Billy says, grabbing the phone, scrolling down through episodes. "This is all . . . our shit. Stuff we told you."

Teddy pushes to his feet. "You've been hanging out with us just to—what—fill your podcast? That's fucked-up, man."

Travis opens his mouth, fumbling for an answer, but the boys are standing now, their voices piling over his, accusations tumbling, overlapping, relentless.

Because I wasn't the only person Travis Magnuson tricked. My heart still hammers, blood rushing hot through my veins, I'm so angry that the cold draft slipping across the back of my neck almost feels good. Almost. Until I realize there shouldn't be a draft. Not with every door and window bolted tight.

I turn. Their voices blur behind me. Travis's excuses are drowning under the boys' outrage, but I'm not listening anymore.

I am being drawn down the dark corridor toward that red exit sign, like a moth who doesn't know better. As the sounds of the pageant—the music and the crowd's applause—fade, the air grows colder, tighter, raising the hair along my arms, every nerve strung tight.

Then I see it: the door cracked open to the storm.

CHAPTER EIGHTY-TWO

SARAH LYNN

I step out into the lights. The air is cold on my bare scalp. I watch the surprise flutter through the crowd like wind through wheat.

Then I see Mom, standing just offstage. Her face is pure rage. Not the tight-lipped disappointment I'm used to. Not even the sharp bursts of anger she usually saves for Kayden. This is different. And for a split second, I regret what I've done.

My whole life, there has never been a better feeling than when my mother is proud of me.

But it was never really me she was proud of. She was proud of her own reflection. Now I can't undo what I've done, and neither can she. I lift my chin, eyes locked with hers. She turns her back to me and walks away into the darkness.

I move through the motions of my routine, limbs lighter, chest buzzing, and when the crowd claps, the applause feels like it belongs to me.

When I finish, I join Hannah in the wings, and we stay to watch Olivia.

Mark rises from his seat and kills all the lights but one, a single spotlight on Olivia in her plain black leotard, her thin frame a silhouette. The opening notes of "The Dying Swan" unfurl, soft and aching, and Olivia begins to dance. I've never heard a crowd go so silent, so still. As if even breathing would shatter the moment. Olivia's body is a sharp blade of elegance, her movements precise, up on tiptoes so long it makes my own calves burn.

Hannah grabs my hand. I'm full up to the top, like a Coke can shaken up. For a fragile second, I feel like the three of us are one body moving together, like nothing could pull us apart.

When the final note fades, Olivia lies on the floor, gracefully collapsed, arms extended above her head. For a breath, the silence holds. Then she rises slowly, her chest heaving, eyes fixed somewhere far beyond the audience. The applause starts low, hesitant, like they are afraid to break whatever spell she's cast. She doesn't smile. She simply bows and turns to go.

That's when I see movement in the audience—Sheriff Ryan rising from his seat, cutting through the rows toward Emily. He leans down to whisper something, and I watch the color drain from her face. The light glints off his badge, off the metal at his hip, as he guides her up the aisle and out of the room.

By the time Olivia steps offstage, we're already reaching for her, pulling her into a hug.

"You were incredible," Hannah whispers.

Olivia exhales, shoulders softening. "I think I'm done," she says quietly. "That's all I wanted. I wanted her to see me dance."

I nod and squeeze her arm.

We walk back to the dressing room together, joining the other girls. The air hums with nervous energy—zippers, perfume, laughter—but it feels muted, like we're underwater. Hannah and I unzip our garment bags, slipping into our evening gowns. Usually, in this moment, my mother would be here, tucking and adjusting, smoothing my hair, retouching my makeup, making sure I am perfect. But she's nowhere to be found.

Olivia just sits there at her vanity, still in her leotard, her bare shoulders trembling.

"You sure you don't want to change?" I ask.

She shakes her head slowly. "No. I'm done."

Before I can say anything, one of the volunteers pokes her head in. "Final lineup, ladies. Time for crowning!"

Hannah and I exchange a look, then back at Olivia. She doesn't move. The volunteer calls again, and Hannah squeezes Olivia's hand before we go.

At the doorway, I glance back. Olivia's still in front of the mirror, motionless, the light from that single, swaying bulb pooling around her like a halo. The reflection staring back at her looks almost like a ghost.

CHAPTER EIGHTY-THREE

MELANIE

After Hannah's performance, I took the trail cam footage to Dad. He watched it in silence, then shut the laptop screen.

What are you thinking? I asked.

He paused a moment, careful with his thoughts, with his words, as always. *Earlier today, when we were heading to the model home, Emily came chasing after Olivia.*

I nodded.

She didn't want her walking over there with us. Because of the cold, maybe. His eyes lifted to mine. *Or maybe because she didn't want Olivia to see what was inside.*

Now, Dad is in full sheriff mode, sitting across a long table from Mark and Emily in one of the conference rooms. The cold tile floor, the bare walls—it feels like an interrogation cell. The laptop glows pale in the dim room, all our eyes on the screen. Dad leans forward, taps the trackpad, and pauses the video on the final image of Emily handing over the envelope.

Mark's voice cuts through first. "What's this all about, Sheriff? Emily helps me out at the trailer all the time. Pays contractors, vendors. That's nothing new."

"I understand that," Dad says, his voice steady but carrying weight. "But Melanie recognizes this man. She says Cat told her that he had been following her all week."

Mark's head jerks back. "What are you saying?" His eyes drop to the screen. And then, slowly, realization begins to settle. Why Emily—who never cared much for Cat—might hand cash to a stranger. His eyes find hers. The blood drains from his face, and I see the thought cross his mind, the same one Dad is wondering: whether Emily had finally had enough of Cat. If she decided to get rid of her for good.

"Mark!" Emily's horrified cry rattles the air. "You can't think—"

But I can see it. The shift. Something fragile breaking between them. Once you imagine the person you love could be capable of murder, you can't unthink it. That knowledge reshapes everything.

"Who is that man?" Mark says finally, each word ground out, measured.

Emily breaks into tears, her shoulders shaking. Mark's eyes widen. His hand drags down his jaw, hard, leaving a red streak. For a moment I see nothing but fury flashing in his face as he stares at his wife. "What about Olivia?" he says.

Because Mark is always thinking about Olivia. After we found Cat's body, he went into triage mode. Focusing only on Olivia, on the hurt she was feeling, on the care she needed. But I know the truth. Mark loved Cat. Always. Still.

Emily lifts her head, eyes glossy, already begging him for forgiveness. "He's a private investigator, Mark. I just wanted to make sure she stayed sober. You hired a PI before."

"To find her," he spits. "To make sure she was okay. And she was okay. She was sober."

"For now," Emily shoots back, her pleas curdling into anger. "But she'd done it before. How many times? Swoop back in, get Olivia's hopes up, and then leave our lives in shambles. I couldn't let her do that again."

Dad clicks the laptop shut, his tone clipped but even. "Emily, do you have this man's contact information?"

"Of course." She digs into her purse, produces a business card, and presses it into his hand.

"I'll follow up," Dad says, standing up and heading for the door to give them privacy. He nods to me, and I follow him out of the room.

He clicks the door shut behind us, but I can still feel the sour air.

"Sorry," I say.

He puts a hand to my shoulder. "No. That had to be done."

I give him a weak smile. But inside, I'm angry at Emily too. Because Cat was doing so well. She'd fought hard for her sobriety, and Emily had no right—no right—to undermine her. To doubt her. To send some man lurking after her until she doubted herself. Until she spiraled.

CHAPTER EIGHTY-FOUR

INGRID

Mom stands onstage, holding the Miss Lone Star Princess crown, with the girls lined up behind her in their evening gowns, hands linked like a single shining chain.

I can't find the sheriff, so I make my way to Ben, and my heart is racing. Outside, the snow keeps coming, piling up against the windows, straining the roof, the wind roaring like an angry thing. And I wonder how long it will go on, how long we will be trapped here and how unprepared we are.

Ben, who's been pacing back and forth to keep Mabel moving, stops and faces me.

"One of the doors was open," I say, the words coming in a tumble.

The man stationed to watch him straightens. "What door?"

"At the end of the hall."

"No way. I checked that one myself." He scans the room, jaw tight. "Where's the sheriff?" Then he stalks off, disappearing into the dark corridor.

The noise of the pageant swells behind us—applause, nervous laughter, the metallic crackle of the mic—but Ben and I are left in a pocket of shadow, only a few feet from everyone else, and yet apart.

A gust of wind slams against the glass. And my mind is a war of questions—what that open door means, and where Abel is, and how I'll keep Mom warm enough through this endless night, and what Kennedy Claire might have done, and her last words to me: *You never could think straight around him*—but when I open my mouth, the one that comes to my lips is, "Why didn't you try harder? All these years. There were a million ways you could have contacted me."

His eyes meet mine. "I hoped you were happy," he says, in that simple, matter-of-fact way Ben says everything.

Ben was always a quiet kid, but when he spoke, you felt like you could believe him. I think of the time I showed him some of the pictures I'd developed myself. *They're good*, Ben said, and though my mom had already gushed over the pictures, going on about how talented I was, and buying a frame to hang one up in the stairwell, I didn't feel it was true until I heard it from Ben.

I believed him then.

And I believe him now.

"I'm sorry," I tell Ben, and I am sorry. Sorry he lost Izzy too. Sorry he lost his own family, sorry that I ever doubted him.

His face relaxes, like I'm the first person to see him in a long time, see him, and not just the things he's been accused of. And in the dark, without the beard, he looks like the boy who gave me my first kiss. And I wonder if he sees me right now. Or if it's Izzy he's looking at. He never got to say goodbye to her either.

I lean in before I can stop myself and press my mouth to his. His lips are cold, but the kiss is warm, familiar. And despite it all, I feel something certain slip into my bones, like remembering the words to a song my heart knew all along.

And then a gunshot cracks the air.

CHAPTER EIGHTY-FIVE

SARAH LYNN

The gunshot rips through the room like lightning. One heartbeat I'm holding Hannah's hand, the next it's pure chaos—girls shrieking, scattering across the stage, the audience surging to their feet. Someone clips the tripod lights and they crash down, bulbs exploding in a white flash before everything plunges into black.

Girls shoulder-check me in their frantic rush off the stage. I lose Hannah's hand, then find it again in the dark.

"Where did that come from?" she gasps.

My throat is tight. "The dressing room?"

"Olivia." Just her name, but it's enough. Enough to send us toward the sound, toward the danger.

I can't see, only feel the crush of bodies, the heat of panic. My eyes strain, useless. We push toward the wings, palms dragging along the wall until the dim red glow of the exit sign finally shapes figures from shadow. Kayden, Billy, Teddy—all three of them bunched outside the dressing room door.

"The door is locked," Teddy says, voice raw.

Beside me, Hannah whimpers.

"Where is Olivia?" I say, each word a silent prayer.

Billy looks wide-eyed. Teddy only shakes his head.

"Fuck it," Kayden mutters, and throws his shoulder into the door. It crashes open, spilling yellow light into the hallway, and Kayden tumbles inside.

I lunge after him, grab his arm to pull him upright.
His sneakers skid. A wet squeak on the floor.
And then I see the blood.

CHAPTER EIGHTY-SIX

MELANIE

I break into a sprint, boots pounding the corridor, breath tearing in my throat. "Girls? Hannah!"

The exit sign glows ahead of me, stretching the shadows long. The dressing room door is open, a rectangle of light spilling out, swinging in a seasick tilt across the hall. A cluster of kids hovers there—Kayden, Billy, Teddy, and, oh thank God, Hannah.

I stop short, clutching my chest.

Sarah Lynn staggers from the doorway. Her face is like white clay, hollowed and stunned, like she's seen something in that room that will forever change her.

I grab Hannah roughly by the arms and pull her to me. "You're okay," I say, more to reassure myself than her.

"Mom," she sobs into my shoulder.

"Honey, what is it?"

But before she can answer, Sarah Lynn gasps. "Where were you?"

I turn to see Olivia walking toward us, still in her black leotard and ballet slippers.

"I wanted to watch y'all," she says softly.

That's when I notice the streaks of blood on the floor, tracking from Kayden's sneakers to the open doorway. I push Hannah back and step toward the light spilling from the room. The smell of iron hits me, metallic and raw, and, at first, all I see is red. The pool of it beneath the chair. The back wall and its racks of gowns, covered in blood. Splatters on the ceiling, on the mirror. Bone and brain tissue scattered.

My hand flies to my mouth as I take it all in.

He shouldn't be recognizable. The top half of his face is gone. I can see the top of his bottom molars, the tongue loose, the exposed shaft of a throat. But the camo jacket, the mud-caked boots give him away. Abel Sherman is dead.

I once had a patient, Mrs. Miller, a real sweet lady who passed away a few days after her ninety-second birthday. She had wanted to donate her eyes to science. The harvester came and I assisted, pulling the thin skin of her eyelid back, watching it fold over the small, polished retractor. Watching as he severed the membrane and the optic nerve with clinical precision, then scooped the eye right out. He filled the hollow pink socket with a prosthetic structure so that when we closed her eyes again, the look was natural. So that, even though that piece of her body was missing, her family could still have an open casket, look at her to say their goodbyes. It was more proof to me that the body didn't matter. I could look at Mrs. Miller and imagine her spirit unbound.

But this, all of this, is just too much. His head flipped back, open unnaturally, the jagged, blown-apart flesh. This isn't an act of healing or preservation. It looks like a demon burst from the very core of him.

I turn away from him, just as Iggy enters the doorframe.

"Oh, God," she says, spinning to shove Ben Sherman back, to stop him from seeing, but still, I see the image printed on his eyes like a scar.

CHAPTER EIGHTY-SEVEN

INGRID

Ben is in the hall, his back to the wall, head between his knees, breathing deeply. Someone took Mabel from him, but I had to go back in. I had to see.

SHERIFF,

I WAS THE ONE WHO KILLED ISABELLE WHITMORE. I'VE CARRIED THAT FOR A LONG TIME, AND I CAN'T CARRY IT ANYMORE. WHAT HAPPENED TO CAT DENNIS, WELL, THAT WAS ME TOO.

I'VE HURT PEOPLE I NEVER MEANT TO HURT. YOUR DAUGHTER CAN TELL YOU ABOUT THE KIND OF MAN I WAS.

I'M SORRY. FOR ALL OF IT.

ABEL SHERMAN

The note lies unfolded in Abel's lap, scrawled haphazardly on ruled yellow legal paper, the words written bold, large, and erratic with no mind for the margins.

It doesn't make any sense. Abel? It couldn't have been Abel that killed Izzy. Time telescopes in on itself, and I am that girl again, her whole world unraveling, rearranging. Because I had known Abel. Or thought I'd known him. Once upon a time, he had been like family.

His shoulders droop, arms hanging at either side, the double-barrel shotgun lying still at his feet. I look to his calloused hands.

They are hard, heavy things weighing down his arms. Even in death, after a lifetime of work and overuse, his fingers curl as if still ready to grip. People warn that a decapitated snake can still bite you, and I take a step back instinctively.

Those were the hands around Izzy's neck. The hands I've dreamt so many times.

Sheriff Ryan barrels his way past us and does his best to get the crowd out of the dressing room, herding us like escaped cattle back behind a barbed wire fence. When we turn, Melanie shrinks in the doorway, twisting her fingers anxiously, eyes flicking to Abel's body.

Out in the hall, voices climb over one another. And after a minute in the dressing room alone, the sheriff enters the hall, closing the door behind him. He makes his way over to Melanie, asking her about the note before any of the town gets the chance to hush and whisper and poke and prod. "What's he talking about, Mel?" He's not a sheriff in this moment. He's a father.

"Oh, Daddy," she says, chewing her bottom lip. "I was so ashamed." Her eyes go to the ceiling, so her tears won't spill down her cheeks. I can see the girl she was back then, always trying to be brave, trying not to let anyone see how much we hurt her, as if, even then, it was her responsibility to put everyone else at ease.

She looks to me, eyes watery. "It was a prank. I know that," she says. "When you took my clothes that day, Iggy, when we skinny-dipped in The Hollow . . ." She pauses to breathe, like she's steeling herself to let something out she's held in far too long. "I know you didn't mean anything by it, not really. But you left me there, and . . ." She trails off again, the center of our collective concern and attention. "Abel found me."

Cold dread trickles down my limbs. I don't want her to keep talking. I don't want to know any more.

"The cold in that cave was miserable, but in the end, it was a blessing. My skin was numb enough to where I could hardly feel his touch. I didn't fight back," she says. "I just—I let him do what he was gonna do."

My insides tilt and lurch—like the floor is sliding out from beneath me. I think again of when I saw her the next day by the lockers at school, how she acted like nothing had happened, nothing but that blush of humiliation creeping up her neck.

She looks to Sheriff Ryan, whose face looks hard as stone. "I couldn't stand the thought of anyone knowing what Abel had done to me. What you or Mom, or, later . . ." She pauses. "What Waylon would think. I just . . . I guess I just wanted to forget. To pretend it never happened. The only person I ever told was Cat. She begged me to tell you, but I couldn't. Cat stayed quiet for me, and she always felt guilty. Because maybe if we had told"—she turns her gaze back to me, pleading for me to understand, words quickening—"Izzy was such a spark plug. She must have fought back. I'd always had that thought. I did." She pauses and looks to her hands, which are folded and holding her belly. "I just wasn't brave enough to say what he'd done."

I hold on to the wall for balance.

Everything I thought I knew reshapes itself.

Izzy over at the Sherman house, lying around in her pajamas, teasing Abel all the time, snatching the hat off his head. How she loved to get a smile out of grumpy old Abel Sherman.

How he liked to watch the teenagers floating the river and hanging out down at The Hollow.

How he brought us warm towels and cold Dr Peppers, kept that Polaroid of us in our swimsuits taped to his fridge, let us ride up in the seat beside him in his pickup.

How he closed up his property after Izzy disappeared and watched the search party with a shotgun on his lap.

It was never Ben he was protecting. He was protecting himself.

And, oh God, I think I might be sick.

Because I had told Izzy to rip off the Band-Aid, to go straight to the Sherman house that day. And she must have. But she hadn't found Ben.

She had found Abel.

"I'm sorry," Melanie says, pleading to everyone now. "I'm so sorry, everyone." She starts to cry. Sheriff Ryan embraces his daughter so gently, it feels wrong to witness. This isn't a moment meant for spectators. He squeezes her shoulders, which are shaking with silent sobs, and shushes her so softly that I know it's the same way he must have soothed her when she was a little girl.

CHAPTER EIGHTY-EIGHT

MELANIE

By the next afternoon, the ground outside is slushy with mud and the remnants of snow as I trudge out to pack our things into the back of the van. Waylon is here now, and he takes my hand so we can walk back to the Amenity Center together.

He'd been worried. He had a front-row seat to the damage—live oaks splintered by the wind, power lines sagging under ice, low water crossings glazed slick as glass. In twenty-four hours the storm had paralyzed the whole state. Highways shut down. Families huddled without heat in stone ranch houses built to trap cool summer air, not keep out the cold. He heard about people sheltering in cars to stay warm, about the pileups on the interstates, about fires sparked when space heaters tipped. He heard about the gunshot too, heard about Abel.

He said he flew over the roads, that he white-knuckled the wheel, as soon as he was able.

That made me swat his arm. *Waylon Campbell, you could have got yourself killed.*

But he didn't care. He burst through those double doors with such force you'd have thought they were made of paper, and he beelined straight for me, Hannah, and the boys, and gathered all of us up in a big bear hug. He didn't even pester Hannah about her hair—though I'm sure he'll have a mouthful to say about it once the shock of all this dies down and regular life settles back into us like sand.

Inside the Amenity Center, only a few of us remain. Most people went home the minute the roads were declared safe to travel. The dressing room and that whole back corridor has been blocked off with crime scene tape, though I guess there wasn't really a crime, just an old man who chose to leave the world.

Mark is up on a ladder, tugging the sequined curtains from the Miss Lone Star stage, and passing them down to Emily. She catches each length and folds it neatly into a box. They work quietly, efficiently, but something's missing. Normally, Mark can't go five minutes without reaching for her—an arm around her shoulder, a brush of his hand at her back, some small sign of affection. Now there's nothing. Just silence, just fabric sliding from his hands to hers.

I hope they can find their way back to each other, because I know that underneath all this ugliness is love. Emily's reasoning for hiring the PI, however misguided, came from her love for Olivia, from wanting to protect her. And Mark will always put Olivia first. If anything can hold those two together, it's her.

I'm glad Olivia has them, two parents who care deeply about her. She has me too. She'll always have me.

And, of course, she has Hannah. I look to the girls now, Hannah, Olivia, and Sarah Lynn, over in the corner, wrapping power cords over their arms. I was all wrong about Sarah Lynn. The three of them now, heads shaved, necks long, and chins held a little higher, look like they're lighter without all that hair weighing them down. It was an act of friendship, of reckless boldness that comes from being together. I think of Cat standing up for me in the cafeteria. I think of the time we jumped from that high boulder into the well of The Hollow. Me, scared to leap. Cat, grabbing my hand. The two of us free-falling and the cool, thrilling reward of the water swallowing us whole.

I was never as brave as those three girls were, stepping onto that stage, heads bare and not a flinch from any of them.

But I do feel braver today than I ever have. It's a scary thing, thinking about the past, dredging it up, speaking any part of it out loud. It still fills me with such an awful shame. Everyone has been so sweet to me, though, fussing over me. I'm not comfortable with all the attention, to be honest.

I find Iggy stacking up chairs in the storage closet.

I grab a pair of chairs and bring them over as well. "Cat was the one who sent you that invitation," I tell her.

She stops and looks at me.

"I'm sorry I didn't tell you. We never knew for sure it was Abel. Just had our suspicions. Cat always felt guilty about it. And, I guess I always felt like she was my responsibility because of it." Guilt is a terrible thing to live with. It's a slow-acting poison, a cancer that spreads to every part of your body.

She looks at me a moment, and then her face falls. "God, Mel, I'm so sorry. For what we did. For everything we did."

I pull her into a hug. I want to tell her that *it's all right* or that she has *nothing to be sorry about*, because that is comfortable to say, because that is a reflex. Instead, I say, "I forgive you," because what I really want is for her to forgive herself.

CHAPTER EIGHTY-NINE

INGRID

Kennedy Claire is bent over a box, tucking tissue paper between glass vases. Her back is to me.

"I think that's the last of it," I say. "I'm going to head out."

She doesn't answer right away. I stand there, watching her shoulders rise and fall. I've known Kennedy Claire long enough to know that she can be selfish and ruthless, manipulative and controlling. But she can also be fiercely loyal. In so many ways, she was a good friend. I think about the time my appendix burst and Kennedy Claire got the first flight out to sit by my hospital bed, reading gossip magazines and making me laugh through the pain. For the big things, she always showed up.

"I'll see you around," I add, and start to turn.

"I thought he killed Izzy."

Her voice halts me cold. I turn back. She's still facing the box, but her hands are motionless now, the tissue paper trembling just slightly between her fingers.

"That's why I didn't give you Ben's message," she says, finally looking at me. Her eyes are glassy, but her chin is high, like she's daring me to hate her for it. "I couldn't send my best friend off to meet a killer in the middle of the night. That would have been completely insane."

I nod my head, afraid that if I speak, my voice will crack. Because it all just makes me so sad, the terrible loss of Izzy, of all of us, for all these years.

She softens. “I didn’t know,” she says. “I’m sorry.”

I step forward and put my arms around her. For a heartbeat she stands stiff, then exhales and leans in, just enough.

“Me too,” I whisper.

CHAPTER NINETY

SARAH LYNN

The house is an icebox. Our breath shows in little clouds as we move from room to room. Mom sent Kayden to the garage to flip the breaker, and we can hear him through the wall, tripping over boxes in the dark.

Mom perches on the edge of the sofa, arms wrapped tight around herself, eyes somewhere far off. I take a seat beside her, the silence between us sharper than the cold.

Finally, I can't take it anymore. "I know you want what's best for me, Mom," I say, and my voice sounds too loud in the frozen quiet, echoing off the tile and the high ceiling. She doesn't move, acts as if I haven't spoken at all.

Suddenly I remember being three, maybe four. Mom had me at some kind of event, adults in suits and dresses, perfume thick in the air. I stared down at my pink cupcake dress and the sparkly shoes with the plastic jewel on the buckle, holding her hand tight.

Say hello to the nice man, Sarah Lynn, Mom said.

But I didn't know the man, so I ducked behind her legs, shaking my head. Her hand slipped from mine. She angled her body away. I tugged at her dress, desperate, but it was like I'd turned invisible.

Then a grandmotherly woman bent down. *Aren't you a little doll? What's your name, sweetheart?*

I told her, smiling my best smile.

That's when Mom's hand found mine again.

Now I look at her, here beside me, and I remember that she was once a little girl too, desperate to be seen. I reach over and take her hand. She looks down at it, startled.

"Thanks for everything you've done to make sure my life is easier than yours was," I say.

Her face turns toward me.

"But you have to let me live it my way."

She scoffs, her eyes flicking to the top of my head. "When you were a baby," she says softly, "I always said you had the most perfectly shaped head."

The corner of her mouth twitches, almost a smile. And I laugh. For the first time in forever, it feels like we're seeing each other.

"Shit," Kayden says, from somewhere in the garage, followed by a crash. Then, with a pop, the house comes alive—the lights blaze on, the heater groans, the security alarm chimes, and every digital clock blinks 12:00 in unison. Like the whole world has started over fresh.

CHAPTER NINETY-ONE

ISABELLE WHITMORE

2000

Isabelle Whitmore drives down Main Street toward the library with the windows rolled down, her long, dark hair whipping around her face. She is thinking of her sister, of how she knows that her sister is right. That she needs to break up with her boyfriend, but the thought of it makes her sick.

She knows exactly how he'll respond, has played it over in her mind for months. He will nod his head. He will not say a word. And it will be done. There won't be tears and pleading conversations. He has none of his father's explosive anger, but he does have his stoicism. Once she does this, there is no undoing it. And that scares her because she knows this will hurt him. She has always hated seeing people hurting.

But she can't stay with him forever just because it's the nice thing to do. It isn't fair to him or her. Not when she feels like a kite about to catch the first gust of wind. She senses the rush of the months, tumbling toward graduation, and then college. And then she will be spinning free-fall in the open sky. She almost gasps sometimes when she thinks of it. All her life has been in this little town, the same parties with the same people. But the world is big, mountains and oceans and foods she has never tried and views she has never seen. She wants to see them all. Wants to experience, wants to taste and smell, wants to make mistakes without being tethered to anyone.

Except, of course, her sister. Not a kite string holding her back. But a wing.

She is lucky to be a twin. That big open world would seem scary if she had to do it alone. But she doesn't, and that thought calms her as the light turns green.

She changes direction on a split-second decision, turning the car without even using her blinker.

CHAPTER NINETY-TWO

INGRID

2026

I move in darkness. Around me hang drying photographs, a series I'm working on of portraits done in mirrors. Henri Cartier-Bresson, the famed street photographer, talked of the fabled "decisive moment," wandering the streets and waiting for time, light, and subjects to arrange themselves. In this moment, the photographer must have a "simultaneous recognition, in a fraction of a second, of the significance of an event as well as of a precise organization of forms which give that event its proper expression." He was capturing his fleeting reality.

That's what I'm trying to do more these days, pay attention to the things that are fleeting.

I time the exposure, then switch off the light on the enlarger, moving the photographic paper into the first bath. As I rock the basin back and forth, fluid sloshing, the image gradually appears. Every time, it feels like magic, even though I know it is science, chemicals reacting with exposed silver halide crystals.

I don't think often of Izzy's last moments anymore, of Abel Sherman's hands around her neck, of how she must have fought, clawed at him, nails tearing, fingers bleeding. I think instead of her spirit, of the photographs that exist in my mind, the fractions of seconds that captured her, the true her. Her long, dark hair tucked behind her ear, the spark in her eyes when she gave someone a present, the sudden tilt of her head and flash of teeth, caught mid-laugh, a blur of motion as if the camera couldn't keep up.

In the dim, ruddy glow of the safelight, I watch the liquid's surface ripple gently forward and back. My faint reflection stares back at me. And it is only me. I feel her breath on my neck, feel her nuzzle the sharp point of her chin into my shoulder. *Maybe you're the real Isabelle*, she whispers. For so long, when I saw my own reflection, I only saw her. I only thought of the future she lost, that we both lost. I didn't think about how I could carry her into mine.

With a pair of tongs, I slide the photograph from one bath to the next, then give it a quick rinse in clean water before hanging it to dry, clipping its corners to the wire strung over my workspace. I put away the unused photographic paper in a light-sealed drawer and turn on the light.

I step out into the hallway. Mom's Miss Lone Star photograph still hangs outside their bedroom. So much of this house is the same as it always was, but we decided to finally clear out the old bedroom, the one Izzy and I shared. Mom, Dad, and I packed her things into storage bins, wrapping each snow globe carefully with butcher paper. There was the cling of pain, of course, like rain on fabric. You could forget it for a moment, until you turned or moved, and caught a whiff of it again.

But there was also joy. I remember Mom sitting on Izzy's old bed, a silk scarf tied around her head, laughing so hard she had to wipe her eyes. Izzy's life wasn't sealed like a shrine anymore. We were touching her things, recalling memories we hadn't revisited in far too long.

Dad turned our old room into a darkroom for me, a place for me to develop my photographs, but also an excuse to get me around the house more often, now that I've moved back into town.

I walk down the stairs past the beginning and end of my sister's life, and, as I reach the bottom floor, I can't help but recognize that I'm stepping into my present. I used to think the camera kept me safely at a distance from life. I was always keeping distance, the miles between Colorado and home, the calculations between what I wanted and what I did, the careful analyzing of pros and cons before I made a decision. But Cartier-Bresson's decisive moment demands that the photographer is acutely present. You must be aware of the feeling, of the significance of the now, and when you press that button, when you choose to act, you only have a fraction of a second to trust your gut.

"Burgers are almost ready," Mom says. I find her at the kitchen table, sipping sweet tea with Carol Sherman, who's come into town to visit for the weekend. Several inches of Mom's hair have grown back, and it frames her head in soft curls. *Chemo curls*, Melanie told us they are called. Her oncologist declared her to be in remission, after her last scans showed no evidence of disease.

I grab a clean plate from the cabinet and bring it outside to the patio, where Ben is tending the grill. When I hand it to him, he slips a hand around my waist and pulls me in so he can kiss me.

After the storm last year, Joel asked me to come back to Colorado, to let him move back into the house, so we could try to work things out. It was a practical request. But I saw the time, light, and subjects arrange themselves, saw the picture of what I really wanted.

Through the open patio door, I take a picture of Mom and Carol laughing at the table. Photography is a way to save and to savor these fleeting moments of happiness. Life isn't something that's meant to be planned, it's meant to be lived. And I feel, more than ever, that it's good to be home.

CHAPTER NINETY-THREE

MELANIE

The weather is absolutely gorgeous, the way it is in Texas in the spring, that itty-bitty sweet spot between the chill of winter and the unrelenting, sweat sop of summer. Just a finger snap of blue sky and sunshine so warm you just have to tip your face to it, a breeze on your neck and wildflowers like paint strokes. The kind of day it seems God makes just for the sake of showing off.

I'm floating the river with Kennedy Claire and the girls. *Keep your chin up*, Mama always says, whenever things are bad, *you never know what trick God has up His sleeve*. And she's right, because there is no dang way I could have ever imagined this right here. This peace on the river, this quiet hum of my mind, the sounds of the water trickling over rocks, Kennedy Claire chattering away about the benefits of Pilates, the girls laughing up ahead, even Olivia. It makes my heart so full to hear her laughter. The girls all room together at the University of Texas now. I'm glad they do, so they can keep an eye on each other. Their hair has all grown out into cute little bobs. Hannah likes to wear it half up these days, two buns on top of her head. The girls staying close means Kennedy Claire and I have been spending more and more time together, another surprise.

They finally closed both Izzy's and Cat's murder cases officially, and, though everyone was already convinced he'd done it, that final bit of paperwork has let the whole town exhale a collective sigh of relief.

"That Abel Sherman," Kennedy Claire says, shaking her head. She slides her sunglasses up to look at me. "I mean what he did to you? I just get sick thinking about it." Then she reaches her hand out across the water and takes mine. "You know, I can't help but feel a little responsible. Though we never could have known, of course."

"Of course," I say, patting the top of her hand. "We were kids."

"Yeah, well that man was grown." Kennedy Claire clucks her tongue. "A true monster."

The fact that she feels only a little responsible scrapes in my belly, but I lay my head back on the tube and breathe in the gentle air all the same. I'm learning to let things go, to give people grace.

***

After I visited with Mrs. Whitmore that day, after I dropped the girls off to help with stage decorations, I made another pit stop. I climbed the rickety wooden steps and knocked on the door, and I could hear a shuffling behind it.

Don't you shoot through this dang door, Abel Sherman. You hear me?

He let me in, making sure to put on a show of fussing and grumbling, but he ate one of my muffins with a cup of black coffee, all the same.

You taking your medicine? I asked, checking the pill bottles in his kitchen cabinet. Nine months before, he'd come into the hospital complaining of muscle twitches and weakness in his right arm, he'd fallen down in his yard and had a mess of a time just trying to get back up to standing. He thought maybe he'd had a stroke.

An ALS diagnosis is a lengthy and complex process, and the last one you'd ever want to get. I made the mistake of popping in on one of his doctor's visits, and he pulled me aside and told me directly—he was dead set on keeping it from his family. And I understood. They sent him home with a whole slew of medications to manage symptoms and slow the progression.

Why in the hell would I do that? So I can live four months longer not even able to chew my own damn food? I'd sooner die where I stand.

Whenever I paid him a visit, I attempted to tidy up, cleaning around the sink and throwing out his empty whiskey bottles, which never seemed to stop piling up. He was always fighting that demon in the bottle, and each time I came around, he was shaking a little worse. I tipped one of the pills into my hand and carried it over to him. *At least take this one then. It won't make you live longer, but it'll slow the functional decline.*

He huffed but took the pill, swallowing it with a glug of coffee.

I sat on his sofa, knees pinned together and hands folded in my lap. *Abel*, I said. *If I had a problem, you'd help me, wouldn't you? I mean, if I had a problem that I needed to go away, you know? You could help with that sort of thing, couldn't you?*

He took a long drink of coffee before he looked at me. He'd once been a handsome man. Now his eyes drooped in the corners, like an old basset hound, making his whole face look sad. Still, in that moment, he was the same man, saying the same thing he'd told me twenty-five years ago. *Your business ain't none of mine, just like my business ain't none of yours.*

Back at The Hollow, back when we were just kids and Kennedy Claire was only "a little responsible" for me ending up in that cave, shivering cold, day turning into night, a shadow fell over the entrance to the cave, and Abel Sherman found me, wearing nothing but what the good God gave me.

Good Lord, he'd said then, taking off his hunting jacket and draping it over me. *Are you hurt?*

I shook my head without looking up at him, clutching the jacket tight around me.

Well, then, let's go. And he turned and walked right back out. I followed him to his truck, and he drove me home. As he idled at the curb of my house, I could see the warm lights in the windows behind the curtains. Could see the shape of my father and mother in the kitchen, and my belly felt so sick with shame. I couldn't stand the thought of anyone knowing what Iggy had done to me, stripping me, humiliating me. *Please don't tell anyone*, I told Abel.

Darling, he said, *your business ain't none of mine, just like my business ain't none of yours.*

Abel didn't want nothing from you. And he didn't owe you nothing in return. That's how he lived his life. A balance of the scales. So when I asked him for help, he didn't want to be involved, and I had to accept that.

He was a good man, after all.

* * *

Kennedy Claire sips from a canned sugar-free chardonnay. "I know Cat and I had our differences, but she deserved better than that. You were a good friend to her. She was lucky to have you in her life. I hope you know that."

As we float below a giant cypress that arches out over the river, its roots stretched out like fingers drinking up the water, I spot a cardinal landing in its branches, red as a valentine heart against the hot blue-white of the sky. Mama always says that cardinals are loved ones paying you a visit from the other side. I hope it's Cat, and I hope she feels light as a bird now. "Well, we had our ups and downs too," I admit, "but I really loved her."

* * *

Before the snowstorm came in, my phone rang, Cat's name lighting the screen, and, just like I'd done so many times before, I answered right away. I was standing at the kitchen sink, scrubbing crusted pasta sauce off my good Dutch oven, but I set the heavy pot down as soon as I heard her voice, felt a cool wire pull my spine tight, despite the steam still rising up from the running water. She was crying on the other end of the line, words indecipherable. I was already stepping into my sneakers, and pulling my purse onto my shoulder, by the time I said, *I'll be right there.*

Cat answered the door as soon as she heard my boots on the porch.

I saw the champagne bottle set out on the island first.

No, I said, my heart a thing stepped on too many times. *What did you go and do?* But the bottle was still corked, and for that moment, I felt such a pulse of relief.

Mel, she said. *I can't do this anymore.*

I know. I laid my palm along her cheek, and she reached up to put her hand over mine. *But you were right to call me. You've been good. You hear me. You've been good. Don't undo all that.* The look in her eyes was so miserable, so helpless, pleading, pleading, always pleading. Always needing more. Here I was, playing nurse for her again, propping her up, talking her down from the ledge, and I'd keep on doing it. I would need to keep on doing it. Forever.

I gave her a hopeful smile, then turned to tackle the kitchen, to make Cat a cup of tea, wash the dishes, take out the trash.

But as soon as I'd stepped away, Cat said, *No, Mel. I mean I can't keep this secret inside anymore. It's eating me alive.*

When I told Cat about Iggy stealing my clothes at the river, about the hours I spent naked in The Hollow, she'd said, *That bitch is gonna pay.*

I'd been afraid to tell her, afraid that if anyone knew, the first thing they'd think would be, *Why the hell were you stupid enough to fall for their trap?* But Cat brushed past that and hadn't blamed me at all, validating the fact that I had done nothing wrong. Only that I had been wronged. Deeply. I thought she was just blustering about making Iggy pay.

But then one day, while we were working on pageant sets, she presented me with a plan: *Iggy's allergic to tree nuts, did you know that?* Together, the afternoon before the pageant, we rubbed almond oil onto the lipstick Iggy kept in her assigned vanity. The one in the dressing area curtained off at the back of the stage. *Her face will get all puffy right when she steps out in front of that audience*, Cat explained. *She'll be humiliated.*

Just like she humiliated me.

But Iggy stopped by the auditorium that day to practice her

gymnastics routine one last time. Cat and I, lying belly down on the catwalk above the stage, watched her from the rafters as she went first to her vanity. I could see her reflection in the mirror, her name spelled out above in glued-on glitter letters, pulling her hair up into that high ponytail she always wore, tying it with a long blue scarf. She riffled through the drawers and pulled out the lipstick. I squeezed Cat's arm. Her eyes were wide. This wasn't the plan. If she did it now, no one would see. No one would be there to make her feel embarrassed, make her feel ugly, make her curl inside herself like a dark and nasty thing.

We watched as Iggy uncapped the lipstick, slid it slowly across her lips, puckered them, then made a kiss. She turned her face in the mirror, this way and that, like she was trying to look at herself from the outside. Then she slipped out of her letterman jacket and draped it over the back of the vanity chair. She took the stage, doing cartwheels and back tucks and roundoffs, her dark, sleek ponytail spinning like a ribbon behind her.

The sounds of her hands and feet paddling the floor echoed in the empty auditorium—thwip, thwip, thud. Replaced by the sounds of her breath when she stopped, when she put her hands to her knees, and took fast, sharp inhales that turned into a wheeze, a narrow whistle as she dragged the air in, the sound of a corpse waking from death, of wind through cracks in stone.

Cat tensed, craning herself forward to get a better look.

Iggy's face was flushed, red creeping up her neck onto her cheeks in angry blotches. Her hands went to her throat, like she was trying to claw off a pair of hands that wouldn't budge.

We have to get down there, Cat said, turning and scrambling to get down from the rafters. I looked back to see Iggy slump forward, tip over the edge of the stage, and fall the four feet, headfirst, off it. She landed with a dull crack. I scurried after Cat, who was already down beside Iggy by the time I made it to the bottom of the ladder.

I looked down at the two of them from the stage. Iggy lay with a gash across her forehead, the skin split, blood dribbling down to the floor. Her face was mottled, her lips swollen, and eyes shut. Her hands were still at her throat, pawing weakly. Then her forearms locked in tight, and she began to convulse, vomit spilling from her mouth, down her neck and onto her chest. I know now, being a nurse, the poor thing was in anaphylactic shock.

What do I do? Cat asked, voice flooded with panic. I was frozen solid, an ice carving. The only thing I could feel was the adrenaline jittering through my veins. This couldn't be real. I couldn't be watching Cat press her hands, one over the other, palms down onto Iggy's vomit-covered chest and pump. *Oh, fuck*, Cat said. *Fuck, fuck.*

That snapped me into action. I ran back to the dressing area, grabbed her tiny black purse and dumped the contents out onto the vanity, spreading her wallet and her ChapStick and her car keys, looking for an EpiPen. There wasn't one. I swept it all back into the purse, grabbed her letterman jacket, and, at the last second, opened the drawer and found the lipstick too, which I shoved into my jeans pocket. I raced back to Cat, who was using her sweatshirt sleeve to wipe Iggy's lips before pressing her own to them.

We gotta get her to the hospital, Cat said, squatting to loop her hands under Iggy's armpits. *Help me*, she said, panicked and out of breath herself. Together, we carried her through the halls, hollering for help. But the school was empty. Not having a car of our own, we dragged her into the back seat of hers. I sat with Iggy's head in my lap while Cat drove, and I watched the blotches on her face darken to a mean purple. I felt the faint tugs for air subside, the blood on her forehead slow, then stop.

It's okay. It's okay, Cat kept saying as she sped down Ranch Road 20.

Cat, she's gone, I said.

No, she's not, Cat said, pressing her foot harder to the pedal, as if the engine revving louder could revive her. I could feel the world slipping away faster, rumbling like it was breaking apart underneath us.

She's dead, I said. *We can't just drop her off at the hospital.*

Cat raised her eyes to the rearview mirror, and we caught each other's terrified looks, held them for a long moment.

Fuck, Cat said, *Fuck*, slamming the meat of her palms against the steering wheel. *What are we gonna do? What are we gonna do, Mel?*

When I spoke, my voice was eerily calm, like it was coming from a me just over my shoulder: *I know where we can put her.*

* * *

"Time to reapply," Kennedy Claire says, pulling the sunblock from the cooler. She sprays the length of her long legs, and I can feel the aerosol mist, cool to my sun-scorched skin, and smell the coconutty sweetness. She hands the can to me, and I spritz myself as we float on past The Hollow. People don't stop here much anymore. They've migrated on to different spots farther down the river, places where the bank slopes gently down or a limestone shelf creates a ledge for picnicking and sunbathing. None of them are as good as The Hollow, but they aren't haunted either.

* * *

We parked the car by the river entrance, right next to the Sherman land, the entrance everyone used. There were always discarded tire inner tubes littering the bank for kids to make use of. They were black and sun-beaten, the kind that got sticky hot in the blistering heat. But that day was dark and damp, and it was getting close to suppertime, so the spot was empty. Not a single car in the gravelly patch of dirt people used as a parking lot. Not a single voice coming from out on the water. We dragged Iggy to the bank. The dead weight of her was heavier than when we'd carried her out of the school. We flopped her down, bottom first, in a tube, hid her face with a sunhat we found in the trunk. Stuffed the jacket in to float down with her. Cat tied all our tubes together, and the three of us floated down the river. I flinched at every sound, every squirrel rustling the leaves, every turtle dipping below the water's surface. Cat kept her head on a swivel too, eyes as wide as my Oma's Blue

Willow saucers as she scanned the banks, sensing things that weren't there from every direction. The river moves slow, but that evening it crawled.

The sunset was unjustly beautiful, the cloud-covered day melting into vibrant striations of pinks and oranges, into purples and midnight blues, so that it was dark by the time we stopped at The Hollow.

It was then that I realized her blue hair tie was missing, that it must have slipped off somewhere along the river, but there was nothing we could do about that.

We pulled her into the cave still in the tube, sloshing over rocks, through the darkness to the back, to the crevice where I had wedged myself to hide not a week prior, where the rough limestone had serrated my bare skin. Iggy's body was less pliable by then, her skin clammy. We shoved her in, our fingertips pruney and waterlogged, forcing her rigid limbs to bend again, to fit into the space. It took the full weight of our bodies, fighting her down like a mannequin into an overstuffed trunk. It wasn't until we saw her pale blue skin tear open that we finally stopped pushing. She fit wholly inside the crack. We filled the extra space, wedging rocks into the folds of her, then on top of her, until she was properly tucked away, and no one would ever see her from the outside looking in. But Cat kept going, reaching down into the water and pulling up handfuls of mud and sticks and pebbles, filling in all the little gaps, sealing her tomb.

We let the tubes float on down the river and walked back home in the cover of night, staying in the trees so no one would catch sight of us from the road. The next day came, and all of Anhalt was frazzled, looking every which way for Isabelle—not Ingrid—Whitmore, and a new type of sickness hit Cat and me, when we realized just what we'd done.

I've spent the rest of my life making up for that mistake, and Cat, well, she spent most of hers tearing herself up about it, a kind of self-flagellation. Always scratching at her neck in welts like the ones that ringed Izzy's throat, checking over her shoulder for eyes watching from every corner, just like we'd done on the river, waiting for the hammer she was sure would eventually fall. Heaven help me, I was always there to bring her back to her senses.

Honey, just calm down, I'd said to her in the model home.

When Cat had told me, all wide-eyed at orientation, about those boys poking around at The Hollow, I had an inkling that she might start spiraling again. Then I saw that note she'd written to Iggy. I saw the scratches on her neck. When the kids found Izzy's bones—twenty-five years of this river rising and falling had finally shaken her loose—well, that when I went to Abel for help.

Cat was always so reactive, so emotional. Every time she had tried AA, she'd get to the step of making amends, and I would need to convince her, over and over, that no good would come from the truth. The program says to make direct amends, "except when to do so would injure them or others." How could she not see the injury it would cause? The way it would ruin our lives, our families, the way it would erase any good thing we'd ever done, so that everyone—Waylon, Hannah, my coworkers, Daddy, Mama, the people I went to church with—would all look at me and see, not sweet Melanie, not oh-you-can-always-count-on-me Melanie, not turtle cheesecakes and home visits, not every time I said yes when I wanted to say no. They would only see me for a single mistake.

I told her that there was no evidence left. There was nothing. But she refused to listen. She picked up her phone, and she was going to call Dad. She was going to tell him.

I didn't expect the bowl to be so heavy when I picked it up. I only meant to stop her when I lifted it above my head. I still can't quite believe it.

But, the fact is, the bowl cracked against the back of Cat's skull, and she dropped fast, like the sandbags we used in theater, and I'm the one who did it. She didn't move after that. There was only the blood, spilling and pooling and spreading. She didn't twitch, didn't make a final sound. She looked almost peaceful, finally at rest, escaped from the memories of that horrible day. Free from the pain and turmoil that had always boiled inside her. And I gasped a lungful of new air, like my insides had been wrapped up tight all this time by the secret we shared, and now I was free too.

* * *

A white-tailed doe, picking her way out of the trees to the water's edge, freezes when our tubes come into view. She watches us with her big dark eyes, through a fringe of lashes. There is something peaceful about wild creatures, who don't worry about the future or punish themselves for the past. They live only in this moment. She dips her head and drinks from the river.

* * *

After I'd left Cat's, I headed straight back to the only place I could think of. Right back to Abel Sherman's trailer.

Only, this time I had a different approach. See, I'd spent so much time with Abel by then, taking out his trash, making him biscuits and muffins, making sure he took some of his pills. And when you take care of a person, especially a person as lonely as Abel, they tend to talk to you. One time when he'd had too many whiskeys, he told me about how he'd found Izzy's bloody headband on the bank of the river. That's how he'd known Ben was guilty, why he suspected she was probably buried somewhere on his land.

So that night, after what happened to Cat, I told him that I'd hate if I had to tell my dad, the sheriff, that story. It would be such a shame if, after all this time, after everything they'd been through, Ben ended up getting charged with Izzy's murder anyway.

Then I told him I had the solution that would solve all his problems, that would make sure his son stayed out of prison and would allow him to rest in peace.

He didn't answer at first, just eyed me more than anything while he considered. Then he twisted the cork out of his whiskey bottle. *I'm listening*, he said, pulling a long drink.

I knew Abel, with his gruff exterior, could handle it. He was a man who liked to hear things straight.

Then I laid out the plan. I didn't tell him to use a gun, but I did give a look over at the double-barreled shotgun he had leaning up by the door, and he looked over at it as well. *Real soon, you won't be able to go out on your own terms, Abel. You won't even have enough strength in your hands to pull the trigger. Do you really want to die a trembling old man who left this world without paying his debts?*

It was my idea for it to happen at the Amenity Center, killing two birds with one stone, screwing over the developers that had stolen his land and ruining the pageant. The rest of the details I don't care for repeating, but when I was done stating my case, he turned his head slowly toward me, mouth agape, with a look of bewilderment that you wouldn't believe, like he was reassessing the whole of me, inside and out. Then he just shook his head and said, *God bless*. He took another draw of his whiskey straight from the bottle.

I wasn't sure what he'd do when I left that trailer. But Abel was reasonable, and, even if he hadn't been, I had taken some precautions. Made sure to exit the model home out the back door, just like Cat said Abel had done when he smashed up all her cookies. Made sure to grab the doorknob with the end of my shirt sleeve. Made sure I didn't leave any prints. His prints on that doorknob in the end were what shut Cat's case solid.

The storm threw me for a loop, but once I knew he was out there, I opened that hallway door for him. Then Abel gave me one last surprise, mentioning me in that letter of his. I've never been quick on my feet, always been more of a roly-poly, tumbling over myself, curling up into a little ball whenever I get put on the spot. I guess the pageant girls were right when they nicknamed me Melon-ball, and that's why it always stung so much to hear it. But I'm proud of myself, because when it mattered most, when everything I've sacrificed for others was put on the line, I was quick on my toes.

I hate that I had to lean into that ugly lie about Abel. I hate that he left this earth believing Ben did that terrible thing to Izzy. I hate that I fibbed about the amount of time Abel had left, even if it was going to end awful for him no matter which way you sliced it. But it's like taking care of my patients. I spend my days changing bedpans, cleaning bedsores, suctioning fluids from drainage wounds. People want life to be pretty, but sometimes it just gets messy.

* * *

We pull our tubes up onto the bank of the river, and Kennedy Claire opens the cooler to hand out lunch.

"Melanie," Kennedy Claire says, a chastising tease to her words as she pulls out my Tupperware of chocolate chip cookies. Cat's mother's recipe, just modified a hair. "Girl, you are bad. You know I'm always watching my figure."

"Baked them with monk fruit sweetener," I tell her, always aware of what people want and what they need.

Kennedy Claire takes a bite of my cookie. "Oh, I take that back. You are good," she says, savoring the bite.

I smile back, because it's just the sweetest thing to hear. And my skin glows in the warm Texas sun.

CHAPTER NINETY-FOUR

SHERIFF RANCH

Sheriff Ryan walks along the paved street of the Sherman Ranch development. He spots a stray nail in the road, picks it up, and tucks it into the front pocket of his jeans. He likes things to be orderly. So much of the world is chaos, but it doesn't need to be, you can make it straight and solid. A place for everything, and everything in its place. That's how he likes to live his life. It isn't so hard, doing the right thing, not if you make it a habit.

There are more houses here now. A handful of families have moved in, their SUVs parked in the driveways, patio furniture on the front porch, welcome mats by the door.

Someone new works in the model home now. They don't live there; they clock out and lock up at 5 PM sharp. Across the street, in the brush between the road and the river, Sheriff Ryan spots a grocery bag on the low-hanging branch of a live oak. Watching it for a moment, it fills and deflates like a lung in the breeze. When he steps off the road to collect it, his boot catches on a plastic box anchored in the brush. He recognizes the camo-painted exterior, now fading. It's one of his and Mark Blake's old trail cams. Cat must have set both the cameras up.

His knees pop when he squats down, and he lets out an involuntary grunt from the effort. He can't help thinking of when he was a young man, how he took for granted the simple glide of a joint, the ease of moving a body that hadn't yet realized it was a dying thing. He unhooks the camera, which runs on solar panels, so the screen powers up when he hits the button. The camera was pointed directly at the model home, catching the street out front and a few dozen feet off to either side.

He rewinds, back and back, flipping quickly through footage of trucks driving by and delivery vans and that new property manager going in and out, back and back, to the night Cat died, to the window of time that the coroner had settled on, the time of Catherine Dennis's death. And there he stops, lets it all play out. The night vision footage is black and white. There is no sound to the video. He only watches it once, double-checking the time stamp to be sure, before ejecting the SD card, and slipping it into his pocket along with the stray nail.

He collects the camera and the stake it was strapped to, and heads back to his truck. The decision on the state of things is made fast and as certain as a reflex, before he even turns over the engine. And it unmakes him then and there. It's as if he'd only ever been sewn together with thread, as if the universe only needed to tug on the right stitch to unravel him.

When he pulls away, he does so knowing full well that the better man he thought he was is being left behind in those woods.

ACKNOWLEDGMENTS

I don't know if you are supposed to start the acknowledgments for one book by talking about another. But how can I not? My debut novel came out this year, and I have felt more love than I thought imaginable.

To my amazing family—all of you—thank you for showing up big. For driving across the state and across the country. For coming to signings. For buying "She's Writing a Bestseller" candles and far too many copies of the same book. For letting me stay at your houses while on tour, for snapping photos of my book on shelves, for sending TikTok reviews, and for celebrating every milestone like it was your own.

To the friends who shared in my joy—friends from high school, from college, from that one book club I attended a decade ago—thank you for cheering me on. I hope you know I am also over here, cheering you on.

To every bookstore and library that took a chance on a debut author, invited me to events and signings, nominated my novel for Indie Next, chose it as a staff pick, or simply put it on the shelf—I am deeply grateful. Special thanks to my local Mammen Family Public Library, for creating such a welcoming and inspiring home for readers and creatives.

And to the readers, my kindred spirits: thank you for the ratings and reviews, the social media posts and DMs, for showing up to events, for annotated copies and hand-drawn gifts. Thank you for sharing your own experiences of motherhood—your messages reminded me why writing vulnerably matters, why connection matters. Thank you to the book clubs who invited me into their living rooms and Zoom calls, who met me at coffee shops and wine bars, shared charcuterie boards and homemade soup, made PowerPoint fan casts, wrote on mirrors with red lipstick, baked birthday cakes, and handed out tiaras. I hope I can keep telling you stories for a very long time.

Second novels are notoriously difficult, and this one would not exist without an extraordinary village.

Thank you to my agent, Stefanie Lieberman. You are fearless, and there is no one I trust more. To Molly Steinblatt and Alysse Rodriguez (and still and always Adam Hobbins), y'all are like my family. And to the entire Janklow & Nesbit team: you are magicians. To my publicist, Brittani Hilles—the fastest email responder in the world and the funnest person in every room—you saved my sanity.

Thank you to my brilliant editors, Alexandra Sehulster, Phoebe Morgan, and Kate Norman. This book is immeasurably better because of your insight, patience, and care. Thank you to the entire team at Minotaur, especially Ashley Quintana, Allison Ziegler, Kayla Janas, and Kelley Ragland. And to my UK family at Hodder & Stoughton and my foreign editors around the world—I am so lucky to have such thoughtful champions for my work.

Thank you to my early readers—my sisters, Mady and Annie; Jessica Leake; Marilyn Boswell; Katie Gutierrez; and Tiffany Crum—for live-texting reactions, for hype and honesty, and for always knowing exactly what to say when I need it most.

This book required research I couldn't have done alone. Thank you to Carrie Pitarra and Savannah Pitarra for letting me tag along to a real-life pageant and sharing behind-the-scenes insight (and drama). Thank you to Nick Enghardt at St. Edward's University for a darkroom tour years ago, when I thought I was researching a completely different book. Your time didn't go to waste! And thank you to the staff at The Leaning Pear in Wimberley for answering my absurd email about winter menu items. Any remaining errors are, of course, my own.

Mom and Dad, this book would not exist without you, quite literally. Thank you for the ridiculous amount of free childcare. You are the reason I am who I am, and you are the reason I can do what I do.

And to my hype husband, Nick: Thank you for pushing me, encouraging me, driving across the country with me, and dancing to Shania Twain in the grocery store. For always wanting to go over one more scene, one more chapter. For listening as I loved this book, hated it, wanted to scrap it, then loved it again. There is no one I'd rather do this with.

Finally, to my girls, Lucy and Edie: You are, quite simply, the best things to exist on this earth.

ABOUT THE AUTHOR

Nick Pitarra

Kelsey Cox received her MFA in fiction from Purdue University and works from home in the Texas Hill Country. You can often find her writing at Mammen Family Public Library, chasing around her two young daughters, or watching British mysteries with her mom and aunts. On nights when bedtime goes as planned, she enjoys curling up on the sofa, glass of wine in hand, and a book with complicated characters and a killer twist in her lap. She is also the author of *Party of Liars*.